W9-AFV-368

"Madame—Sharra?" Ven stammered.

The fortune-teller's eyes seemed to cast around at each of the children. Then she looked back at Ven.

She said nothing.

Ven's skin, already tingling, stung with nervous energy. He tried to look into the dark area behind her, but saw nothing. In the glow that radiated from her he could see the black satin symbols on the tent walls to the left and right of the opening more clearly. The one on the right closest to the door seemed familiar. He concentrated, trying to remember where he had seen it. When he did, his eyes opened wide.

"I know where I've seen that symbol before," he said to Char, who was standing behind him, trembling slightly. "That's the same writing I saw on that thin stone in the Rover's box."

Before Char could answer, the woman's long arm shot out from behind the drape. She seized Ven by the collar of his shirt in a grip stronger than his brother Luther's.

And dragged him into the depths of the tent.

With a soft *whoosh*, all the flaps of the tent slammed shut, plunging the remaining children into darkness where they stood.

FROM STARSCAPE BOOKS:

The Lost Journals of Ven Polypheme
by Elizabeth Haydon

*The Floating Island*
*The Thief Queen's Daughter*
*The Dragon's Lair* (forthcoming)

— The Lost Journals of Ven Polypheme —

# THE
# THIEF QUEEN'S
# DAUGHTER

*Text compiled by*

ELIZABETH HAYDON

*Illustrations restored by*

JASON CHAN

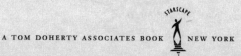

A TOM DOHERTY ASSOCIATES BOOK · NEW YORK

This is a work of fiction. All of the characters, organizations, and events portrayed in this novel are either products of the author's imagination or are used fictitiously.

THE THIEF QUEEN'S DAUGHTER

Copyright © 2007 by Elizabeth Haydon
Illustrations copyright © 2007 by Jason Chan
*The Dragon's Lair* excerpt copyright © 2007 by Elizabeth Haydon
Reader's guide copyright © 2007 by Elizabeth Haydon

*Maps by Ed Gaszi*

A Starscape Book
Published by Tom Doherty Associates, LLC
175 Fifth Avenue
New York, NY 10010

www.tor-forge.com

ISBN-13: 978-0-7653-4773-2
ISBN-10: 0-7653-4773-3

First Edition: July 2007
First Mass Market Edition: June 2008

Printed in the United States of America

0  9  8  7  6  5  4  3  2  1

THIS SECOND WORK OF RESTORATION IS DEDICATED TO

*my father*

Dr. Robert Ungentine Haydon,
Professor Emeritus of Ancient Seren Astronomy,
University of NASSAU,
as well as
Curator of the Paper Airplane Museum of Jierna'sid

and

*my mother*

Dr. Helen Manticore Haydon,
Inventor of the Woolly Mammoth Fever Vaccine,
among other great contributions to medicine

WITH FILIAL FONDNESS

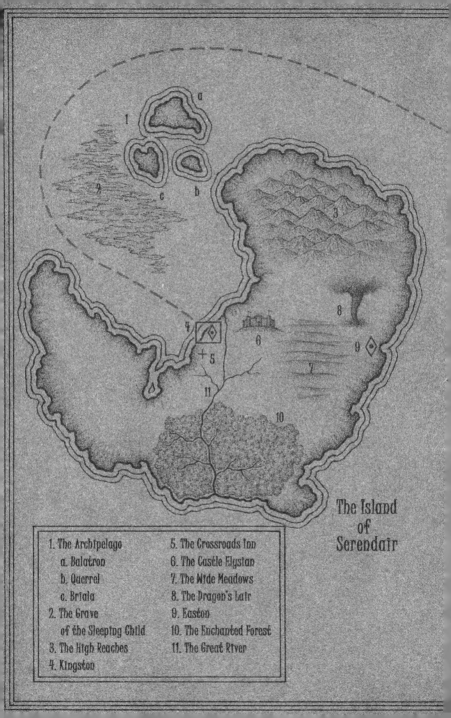

The Island
of
Serendair

1. The Archipelago
   a. Balatron
   b. Qaerrel
   c. Briala
2. The Grave
   of the Sleeping Child
3. The High Reaches
4. Kingston

5. The Crossroads Inn
6. The Castle Elysian
7. The Wide Meadows
8. The Dragon's Lair
9. Easton
10. The Enchanted Forest
11. The Great River

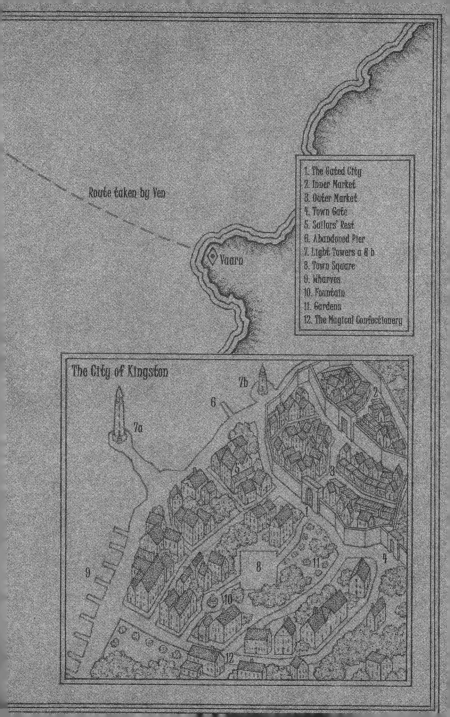

Route taken by Ven

Vaarn

1. The Gated City
2. Inner Market
3. Outer Market
4. Town Gate
5. Sailors' Rest
6. Abandoned Pier
7. Light Towers a & b
8. Town Square
9. Wharves
10. Fountain
11. Gardens
12. The Magical Confectionery

The City of Kingston

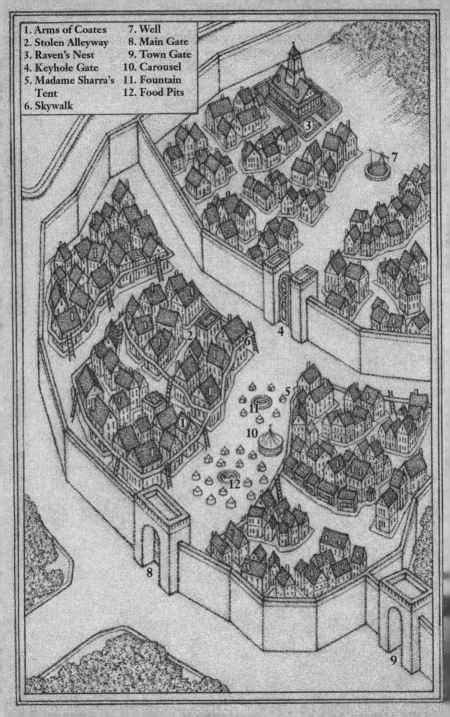

1. Arms of Coates
2. Stolen Alleyway
3. Raven's Nest
4. Keyhole Gate
5. Madame Sharra's Tent
6. Skywalk
7. Well
8. Main Gate
9. Town Gate
10. Carousel
11. Fountain
12. Food Pits

# PREFACE

Long ago, in the Second Age of history, a young Nain explorer by the name of Ven Polypheme traveled much of the known and unknown world, recording his adventures and the marvelous sights he witnessed. His writings eventually formed the basis for *The Book of All Human Knowledge* and *All the World's Magic*. These were two of the most important books of all time, because they captured the secrets of magic and the records of mythical beings and wondrous places that are now all but gone from the world.

The only copies of each of these books were lost at sea centuries ago, but a few fragments of Ven's original journals remain. Recently discovered by archaeologists, some of those diary entries are reproduced in this book, in Ven Polypheme's handwriting, as they were originally written. Some of them are little more than a few words, or a sentence or two. A number of sketches from his notebooks also survived and are reproduced here as well. Great care has been taken to reconstruct the parts of the journal that did not survive, so that a whole story can be told.

A separate notebook containing only sketches of dragons, plus drawings of what appear to be cards made out of dragon scales, is still being restored. It was found, buried with the journals, in a waterproof chest lined in gold. It is as yet unknown what connection these dragons and cards have to the Ven journals, but their importance is clear. In this, the second of the journals, the cards are described for the first time.

These few scraps of text and sketches provide a map back in Time to hidden places, where pockets of magic might still be found.

# Contents

# ∼ 1 ∼

# A Bad Morning

I should have known I would get fired my first day on the job.

All the signs were there. I was just too excited to see them.

This was to be my first official journal entry as Royal Reporter to Vandemere, high king of the Island of Serendair.

That sounds very grand, doesn't it? How does this sound instead—"the former Royal Reporter to King Vandemere"? "Almost the Royal Reporter"?

Oh well.

I guess instead I will just have to be what I am.

My name is Charles Magnus Ven Polypheme, but I am known to almost everyone as Ven. I am the youngest child of the thirteen Polypheme children in a family of famous shipbuilders. I live in the boys' lodge known as Hare Warren behind the Crossroads Inn, on the southern island of Serendair. My home and family are far away on another continent, but that's another story. I am fifty years old, but in my race, the race of the Nain, that's the same as being twelve or thirteen in human years.

*So basically I am a kid on his own, of a different race than most, living in a place I just came to, a million miles away from home.*

*And now I am out of a job.*

MORNING LIGHT WAS SPILLING IN SHINING POOLS ALL OVER THE gardens and walkways of the Crossroads Inn that day, as fine a day as Ven remembered seeing.

He stopped outside the inn's back door and looked all around him.

The sun had been up for a few hours already. The fields across the road were glistening with the last of the morning dew. Songbirds were calling to each other, and the sky was puffed with clouds.

Ven took a deep breath of the morning air. It was sweet, with no lingering bad taste of the haunting that had happened here. Until a few days before, the crossroads had been a sick place, a place where nothing grew and terrible things happened. Now the hollow feeling of fear was gone. No trace of the evil that had been in the ground where the roads crossed could be felt anywhere.

Life was good.

Ven sighed happily and went into the inn.

As he swung open the back door to go inside, he was met with a scurrying flutter of tiny indignant voices. The air around him rustled.

"Oops—sorry," he said quickly to the Spice Folk, the invisible nature spirits who lived in and around the inn. A burst of sharp dust exploded in his face. A moment later his nose wrinkled as he inhaled what smelled like pepper, and he sneezed loudly.

"Bless you, Ven," said a bored voice near the floor. "And bless your beard—even if it is just one whisker so far."

Ven looked down at the large orange tabby cat sprawled under the breakfast table.

"Thank you, Murphy," he said in reply.

*I had still not really gotten used to the concept of a talking cat. Or invisible fairies that throw spice in your face when they are annoyed. Or any number of other weird things in this odd and magical inn where I now live. But I've never had a problem with odd things.*

*I'm odd myself. In fact, my whole family is odd. My official chores around the inn are "odd jobs," which suit me perfectly. Unlike my friends, the other kids who live and work here, I don't have any special skills, like cooking or gardening. But I learned a lot of useful things working in my father's factory where ships are built, so I can fix almost anything. Being Nain, a race of people that normally live deep within the earth, I can dig very easily as well. This means I spend a lot of time digging the holes for bushes and trees around the inn. So even though I am odd, I'm not totally useless.*

*Even if I felt like it by the time the day was over.*

A series of tiny pinpricks pinched him suddenly all over his body.

"*Ow!*" he shouted. He whirled around as his hair got yanked in a dozen different directions. "What's the matter with you Spice Folk today?"

"You spilled their seed harvest when you came bounding in through the door like that," said Murphy, stretching lazily. "They're not happy with you."

"Oh boy," Ven murmured. He looked at the stone floor and saw that it was, in fact, covered with multicolored powder and seeds. "I'm very sorry," he said to the air around him. "Can I help you sweep it up?" He picked up a rumpled napkin from the breakfast table and bent down to gather the spices.

The door swung open again, bumping him on the backside and sending him sprawling face-first on the floor as Clemency came into the inn. She was a tall human girl with bright brown eyes and skin the color of chocolate. She wore the collar of a curate-in-training. Clemency was the steward of Mouse Lodge, the girl's dormitory, and the pastor's assistant in charge of the Spice Folk.

"All right, calm down," she said briskly to the invisible fairies who were now jumping up and down on Ven's back. "Pick up your seeds and meet me in the chapel. We have a lot of cleaning to do and some new songs to learn for the summer festival. Morning, Ven."

"Morning, Clem," Ven said, relieved. He stood up, shook the spice off himself, and headed deeper into the main room of the inn, away from the door. "And thanks." He could hear a tiny chorus of spitting in his direction as he walked away.

In the central part of the inn was an enormous fireplace with a long stone hearth, beyond which stood a bar of polished wood where Otis, the barkeeper, was washing glasses. Ven waved to him, then sat down on the hearth.

Already sitting there was a man with large dark eyes, dark hair, and dark eyebrows, tuning a strange-looking musical instrument.

"Good morning, Ven," the man said without looking up.

"Good morning, McLean," Ven replied.

Though he appears human, like Clemency and Otis and most of the people who live and work in the inn, I know that McLean is more than that. His mother was human, but his father was Lirin, a race as ancient as my own. But while my ancestors lived in mountains, digging coal and gems from the earth, McLean's lived underneath the open sky and sang songs to the rising and setting sun.

McLean, like many of the Lirin race, is a Storysinger. This means he knows a lot of the history and stories and songs of people from all over the world, and can hear things on the wind that other people can't. It also means he has taken an oath never to lie, so it's easy to trust him.

McLean knows a lot of things, a lot of secrets. But I know one about him, something that only a few other people do.

McLean is blind.

But even though his eyes don't work, McLean has ways of seeing things that no one else can see.

"You're in pretty late this morning, aren't you?" the Singer asked, continuing to twist the keys of his instrument.

"Yes, I slept in," Ven admitted. "I was having wonderful dreams."

McLean smiled and began to play a soft, intricate melody. "Really? What were you dreaming about?"

"I don't remember," Ven said. "Strange—the dreams seemed so clear when I was dreaming them, and right after I woke, but I've forgotten them already. I just know that they were full of adventure. I've actually been awake a long time—I was just lying in bed trying to remember them."

The Singer nodded and started to play a bright song that made the corners of Ven's mouth twitch with the desire to smile. "Next time that happens, hop out of bed and come directly to me," he said. "Singers are trained to help put together the pieces of invisible things, like threads of dreams, songs whose words you never really knew, and directions you only sort of remember."

"I will do that," said Ven. "Thank you, McLean."

The kitchen door banged open, and Char came into the dining area, wiping his hands on his long white apron. Char was Ven's roommate in Hare Warren.

"Well, good mornin', Lazybones," he said sourly. "You looked so peaceful sleepin' when I left for work *three hours ago* that I thought some prince might be comin' to kiss ya."

Ven laughed and tossed the napkin at him. "Good morning to you, too, Grumpy."

*Char is my best friend, at least in this place. He's had a pretty miserable life. I met him on the Serelinda, the ship that rescued me when I was shipwrecked, floating in the middle of the ocean.*

*Char was the cook's mate. He's an orphan, like most kids who work on ships. Char doesn't know where he was born, or when his birthday is. He has no parents, and no clue as to who they were. He has no idea where he is going, or what he will do when he gets there. He only knows that the captain of the Serelinda, Oliver Snodgrass, husband of our innkeeper, told him to watch out for me, and he takes that order very seriously. I try to watch out for him, too, but he doesn't appreciate it if he thinks I'm pitying him. So I don't.*

*Char works in the kitchen of the Crossroads Inn. He's an experienced cook, though it would be hard to say that he's a good one. I'm very lucky to have him as a friend.*

*I don't think I've ever met anyone more loyal than Char.*

Char picked up the remaining dirty plates and glasses from the table. "Everyone else has had breakfast. Hurry up—I saved you the last two sausages." He pointed to a lone remaining plate.

"Thanks, Char," Ven said. His stomach had been rumbling since he woke up.

He looked around at the inside of the inn as he had done outside. The empty, strange feeling that had been within the walls also seemed to have gone, replaced by a warm one. There were travelers sitting at tables closer to the bar, while others went up and down the stairs, chatting happily to each other.

In spite of his run-in with the Spice Folk, Ven felt cheerful. "Hey, Char," he said to his friend, who was taking off his apron. "After I finish my chores, you want to go see if we can get your kite up on the wind? There's a great breeze blowing."

"Sure," said Char, smoothing his wild hair. "So why are you in such a fine mood today?"

Ven shrugged. "Maybe everything just feels better than it has since we got here. It's warm, but not too hot, with a cool breeze and a clear sky. What more could you ask for? All kinds of good things could happen on a day like this. Who knows? Maybe today is our lucky day."

"Hmm," said Char. "Well, I don't think this is *your* lucky day, mate."

"Why not?"

Char pointed at the table. Ven's plate was empty.

"Augh! My sausages!" Ven exclaimed. "Where did they go?"

A loud belch echoed across the room. Ven turned around to see Ida No, the thin girl with colorless hair who had been a thorn in his side since he came to the Island. She was now a friend of sorts, but kept to herself unless something interested her.

Or if there was something to steal. Ida was an extremely talented thief.

She was now sitting on a stool by the back door, scraping her boots with a knife in one hand, and licking the fingers of the other one.

"Ida—did you eat my sausages?" Ven demanded.

"Looks that way, Polywog," Ida replied, not looking up from her boots.

*I felt the urge to slap her, as I often do. But whenever she does something to irritate me, I remember what she has also done to help me. It was Ida who actually saved the Crossroads Inn.*

*Ida's pickpocketing talents, which usually cause trouble, came in handy when we were trying to reconnect the pieces of a Rover's box that held something so evil that it had tainted the very ground of the crossroads. Rovers are an eerie, nomadic people, full* of secrets, rootless wanderers who travel the world, bringing darkness with them. Rovers' boxes are such complicated puzzles that only the Rover Masters who made them are supposed to be able to solve them.

Ida managed to put aside her serious dislike of bones, which the box was full of, and piece the lid of the box back together so we could bury it to end the haunting. So whenever she takes my things, I try to remember that she's been of great help, she's very talented, and like Char, she's an orphan with no idea even what her real name is.

Or at least I think she is. I really know very little about her. She keeps pretty much to herself and has no close friends.

That prevents me from stomping on her.

But believe me, I'm tempted on a daily basis.

"Well, that was piggish, Ida—I saw you scarf down at least a dozen of your own," Char said indignantly. He turned to Ven, who was crestfallen. "There's a little leftover porridge in the kitchen still. It's cold, but it's only a little bit lumpy."

"Great," Ven muttered.

Mrs. Trudy Snodgrass, the innkeeper, appeared at the top landing of the stairs. She was a small, roundish woman with red hair that was just beginning to turn gray around the temples. Char and all the other sailors on her husband's ships were terrified of her.

"Well, lookee here, Sleeping Beauty wakes," she said. "Glad you're finally up, Ven. I have some hinges that need fixin'. Get your tools when you're done with breakfast."

"I'm done now, Mrs. Snodgrass." Ven glared at Ida. "I'll go to the shed and get them."

Outside the inn, a loud rumbling sound could be heard. It seemed to be growing closer, gaining volume, the rattling of wood and the clopping of horses' hooves shattering the peace of the morning.

"What's all that racket about, now?" Mrs. Snodgrass demanded. The displeasure in her voice made Char shiver.

He ran to one of the front windows and peered out.

"Blimey, Ven, your day is just gettin' better by the moment," he said nervously. "I think you're 'bout to get arrested again."

# - 2 -

# A Royal Invitation

Ven ran to the window. He pushed Char out of the way and peered outside.

Standing in the crossroads beyond the inn was an enormous carriage. Its walls were painted a glossy black, with golden carvings above the door and on the wheel spokes. It was flying the standard of the king, a pale blue flag on which a silver star was emblazoned. The team of eight identical black horses pulling it was just coming to a stop, their harnesses trimmed with bells. Two soldiers stood on the boards at the back, with two more up front next to the driver. Behind the carriage were four more soldiers on horseback.

"Blimey," Char whispered again. "They must think you done something *really* dangerous this time."

Mrs. Snodgrass bustled down the stairs. She grabbed a soup ladle from Felitza, the kitchen girl who was standing there in shock, then hurried to the door and pulled it open.

The soldier standing on the porch froze, his hand in a fist at the height of her face, ready to knock.

"What in the name of all that is good is going on here?" the innkeeper demanded.

"Good morning," the soldier said. "We're here for Ven Polypheme."

"Oh you are, are you now?" said Mrs. Snodgrass, standing on her tiptoes to stare the soldier down. Char ducked behind Felitza at the sight of her face. "I thought the constable was finished harassing Ven. I'll not have you bothering my guests with trumped-up charges. You'll have to go through me if you're going to arrest him again." She waved the soup ladle at the soldier menacingly.

The soldier smiled awkwardly. "We're not here to arrest anyone, ma'am," he said. "We've come with a personal invitation from the king. He wishes to see Ven at the palace at once."

Mrs. Snodgrass's face softened, and the terrifying expression left. "Well, that's different, then." She handed the ladle back to Felitza and turned to Ven. "Seems the king wants to see you."

Ven nodded, trying to contain his excitement.

"All right then," said Mrs. Snodgrass. "But when you get back, you still need to tend to those hinges."

"Yes, ma'am," Ven said quickly. He turned to Char. "You want to come with me?"

Char shook his head. "You're the Royal Reporter. Not me."

"No, he's just the Royal Pain," called Ida from the back of the inn.

The soldier shook his head as well. "The invitation's for you alone, Master Polypheme. We'll be waiting at the carriage whenever you're ready." He backed out of the inn carefully, his eye still on the soup ladle, and closed the door behind him.

"Brush your hair," Mrs. Snodgrass said as she made her way to the kitchen. "And go put on a clean shirt. It isn't every day that one is summoned to the palace. Brush your teeth, too."

"Don't need to," Ven muttered as he headed past Ida to the back door. "Didn't have any *breakfast*."

Ida snickered and went back to scraping her boots.

---

*One of my greatest blessings—and curses—is my curiosity. It has run like fire through my veins ever since I can remember. Almost everything intrigues me to the point that I can't resist thinking about it. And when I'm feeling curious, my head itches or my skin tingles so that I look like I'm scratching fleas. It's quite annoying, but it's part of who I am.*

*As I ran back to Hare Warren, my head felt like it would explode off my neck. The king had said he would have assignments for me as his Royal Reporter, interesting places or people or things he would want me to investigate and write about in my journal.*

*But I had no idea it would happen so fast.*

*I was so excited I don't even remember what I did to get ready, though I'm pretty sure I stopped in the privy. All I know is that a few moments later I was back inside the inn, standing in front of Mrs. Snodgrass.*

*She was holding two packets of ginger cookies wrapped in waxed parchment.*

---

"If you're going to see the king, you'll be crossing over the bridge at the Great River," Mrs. Snodgrass said. She handed him the cookies. "You'll want to stop before you go across and leave these at the riverbank for the trolls."

"Trolls?" Ven asked.

The small lady pulled herself up straight.

"Of course," she said indignantly. "Every self-respecting bridge has a troll or two living underneath it. Didn't your mother tell you *anything*?"

"Trolls like cookies?" Ven asked, amused.

Mrs. Snodgrass shrugged. "Seem to," she said. "I've never heard of anyone getting eaten or disappearing who remembered to leave them some."

Otis, the bald barkeeper, looked up from washing glasses and cleared his throat.

"Superstition," he muttered as he dried off the bar with a clean towel. "Myth. Legend. Horsefeathers. Nonsense."

"*Is* it just superstition, Mrs. Snodgrass?" Ven asked. "It sounds a little far-fetched."

"Well, perhaps it is at that, young sir. Perhaps it *is* just myth and legend," Mrs. Snodgrass answered darkly. "But do you want to take the chance?"

Otis snorted in disgust. "Been traveling that road for fifty years, boy. Cross the bridge daily. Never seen any trolls."

Mrs. Snodgrass raised an eyebrow.

"Pfft! That's probably because they seen you first," she said. "Even the fiercest, ugliest, nastiest troll would be frightened off by that mug o' yours. Now get back to work."

"Hmmph," said the barkeeper. He returned to washing the glasses.

Mrs. Snodgrass waved the cookies again. "Well? Do you want 'em or not?"

Ven took the waxed parchment packages. "They certainly can't hurt," he said. "Thank you, Mrs. Snodgrass."

"One package for each time you cross. Don't get hungry and eat them on the way back."

"I won't," Ven said. *I'm already starving*, he thought miserably.

Mrs. Snodgrass took hold of his chin and turned his face from side to side, examining it.

*Exactly the way my mother used to.*

She ran a finger over the one whisker on his chin, looked behind his ears, then nodded as if satisfied. Ven turned red with embarrassment. That whisker was the first sign that his beard had finally arrived. But the fact that it was alone on his face only served as a reminder that he was far behind where other boys his age would be. It was almost unheard of among the Nain not to have a full beard by the time a lad turned fifty.

"All right then, off you go," she said, releasing his face. "Mind your manners with the king."

"Yes, ma'am." Ven turned to Char, whose eyes were as round as saucers. "I'll tell you all about it when I get back. After I get my chores done, that is."

"Be careful, mate," Char cautioned.

"I will," Ven promised. "See you later."

He hurried out of the inn where the carriage was waiting, a footman holding the door open. He climbed inside, set the cookies down on the seat, and sat down himself as the footman closed the door.

*The last time I had been put in a coach and taken to the palace I was under arrest. That coach was nothing like this carriage. The walls inside this one were painted with a silvery coating that made it very bright inside. In addition, next to the door on both*

*sides were two lanterns, unlit because it was daylight still. The*
*seats were padded with thick blue cushions and the floor with a ·*
*twisted rope rug.*

*I felt a little bit like a king myself.*

"Yah!" the coachman shouted.

The carriage shuddered, and started to roll forward.

Ven sat back against the cushioned seats and watched out the window as the inn grew smaller and the green fields all around grew wider.

He continued to watch the scenery as the sun rose higher in the sky, burning off the last of the dew. The royal carriage rumbled past other travelers, people in carts and on horseback, who all moved out of the way as the team of eight horses clattered down the road.

Finally, after what seemed like forever to Ven, they came to the Great River. Ven could hear the noise of it from a good distance away. He stood up and leaned out the window.

"Excuse me," he called to the coachman and the soldiers sitting above him. "Could you stop for a moment, please?"

One of the soldiers turned, then nodded, and the carriage rolled to a stop.

Feeling foolish, Ven picked up one of the packets of cookies and opened the door. He climbed out of the carriage and hurried down to the banks of the rushing river.

*The last time I was here, the constable had told me that the*
*Great River divided Serendair into two parts, Westland, where the*
*inn and Kingston are, and the lands beyond it to the east. Up the*

river to the north were great mill towns, where the harvest of grain is ground into flour and meal. He said that the mill towns were exciting places I should see, assuming I ever got out of jail.

I was curious to see what was up the river. I was curious to see what was beyond it on the other side as well. My skin was itching like I was covered in ants.

The river was very wide. The water moved fast, rushing in frothy currents under the bridge, where it pooled for a moment, then hurried by.

Carefully Ven climbed down the riverbank, trying to keep from slipping. He made his way to the foot of the bridge, but saw nothing that could be a sign of trolls, or anything else, living under it. He quickly placed the cookies on the riverbank next to the bridge, then hurried up the gravelly bank to the carriage again.

"I'm ready," he said to the soldier holding the door. "Thank you for stopping."

"Not a problem," said the soldier. "When you've got to go, you've got to go."

"Er, no," Ven began, but then he looked to the other side of the bridge where two more of the soldiers were coming back up the bank. He shook his head and climbed into the carriage again.

The sun was high in the sky when at last they came to the tall rocky cliffs where the castle Elysian stood. More steps than Ven could count were carved into the crags, zigging, zagging, and winding all the way up to the gleaming white palace at the top.

At the bottom of the rocky cliff, and growing up its face, stood an immense forest of trees, all reaching to great heights. Ven had seen these trees a few times before and was fascinated by them. They seemed different from normal trees, as if they had been carved from stone, except that they were green and purple and blue and brown, and hummed as if they were singing.

Jutting from the front of the cliff was a giant irregular rock formation that seemed to be naturally formed in the shape of a man's face, craggy and bearded. Ven knew this formation was called the Guardian of the Mountain. It had appeared in the rocky cliffs on the day the king had moved into the new palace. One of Serendair's legends said that the face in the cliff wall was there to watch over the new king and keep him from harm.

The carriage rolled to a stop to the sound of trumpets at the barracks of soldiers that stood guard at the base of the battlements leading up to the castle.

The door swung open. The soldier who had come to the door of the inn stood in the doorway. "You ready for the big climb?" he asked.

"Ready," said Ven.

He followed the guards up the mammoth stairway carved into the cliff, past the huge rocky outcropping that formed the face of the Guardian of the Mountain. He stopped every now and then to catch his breath and admire the view of the sea rolling in the distance, with the wide green fields and forests below.

At last they came to the top and were admitted through the palace gates.

Ven was led through the vast courtyard and into the gleaming palace, down long hallways lined with tapestries, to the throne room, where a dozen or more men and women were waiting, some examining the tapestries, others staring at the high ceilings, many of them looking bored.

In the midst of the waiting people, a man was gesturing to him. Ven recognized him as Galliard, the king's Vizier.

Galliard made his way through the crowd to Ven. He was a

tall, thin man with a hooked nose and a sour expression. He had dark eyes and long hair bound back with a tiny gold chain, and was dressed in midnight blue robes that were embroidered in all sorts of odd shapes. In his hand was a long staff of dark wood on top of which was carved an eye.

"Good afternoon," he said haughtily. There was no warmth in the greeting.

*Everything Galliard says to me seems unpleasant. But then, so does everything Galliard says to everyone, including the king. That's just his way.*

*King Vandemere once told me that Galliard was of the race known as the Kith, people who are at home in the wind, and are therefore harsh the way the wind can sometimes be. Galliard is studying to be a Vizier, an advisor of sorts. He has the talents of hearing things the wind has heard, and seeing things that are far away, so he is a very valuable counselor to the king.*

*Even if he is a sourpuss.*

"Good afternoon, Galliard," Ven said.

"The king is running very far behind on his audiences today," Galliard said. "Even I am waiting. It may be an hour or more until he is ready to see you. He left word that you should go out and amuse yourself in the gardens until you are summoned."

"Oh. All right," Ven said. "Thank you for letting me know. How do I get to the gardens?"

Galliard pointed down the hall. "Through the gates at the end." Then he turned and went back through the crowd to be nearest to the throne room doors.

Ven went down the hall to the gates leading into the gardens. He stepped through them, out of the cool shade of the building into the bright sunlight.

Beyond the entrance was a vast outdoor patio that was surrounded by rolling green lawn. The gardens, like the palace itself, were new, and all around them were dozens of workers, dressed in dark trousers, white shirts, and wide hats, planting and weeding and hoeing the beds.

Ven wandered down the path paved with stones of glorious colors. All along that path were baby evergreen bushes around which wire cages had been sculpted in the shapes of marvelous beasts, unicorns and dragons and sea serpents and lions with wings. The shoots of a few of the bushes growing outside the cages were being trimmed by the gardeners. Ven could tell that one day the cages would be taken away and the evergreens themselves would be in the same shape as the beasts.

In front of him was a central garden, like many others in the wide lawn that led to a tall wall at the edge of the cliff. Off this central garden were five smaller ones, each dedicated to one of the elements. Ven stopped in the garden that was being planted in the colors of fire, admiring the red and orange plumes of the flowers, and the bushes with crimson and gold leaves.

One of the many gardeners was shaking mulch around the flame-colored bushes.

"Enjoying your day, sir?" the gardener asked.

"Yes, thank you," Ven replied.

The man looked up from under his wide straw hat and smiled broadly. His blue eyes twinkled.

It was the king.

"Your—Majesty?" Ven asked, his voice choked.

The king put his finger to his lips.

"Come with me," he said.

Ven obeyed, following the disguised monarch through the gardens of earth, wind, water, and ether, and all the way back to the rear of the palace, where an enormous hedge maze stood.

The king glanced around and, seeing no other workers nearby, motioned for Ven to follow him into the hedge.

Again Ven obeyed, struggling to keep up with the human king's long strides as he hurried through the puzzle of green walls, around and under bushy barriers, until at last he came to a stop facing the back wall of the palace.

"Are you ready for your life to change, Ven?" he asked.

Ven inhaled deeply.

"Yes," he said without hesitation.

"Good," said the king. "Because it's about to, whether we like it or not."

## - 3 -

# The Hidden Passage

Do you know anything about music, Ven?" the king asked as he ran his hands over the stone wall.

"A little bit," Ven replied. "My family members, like all Nain, hum and chant when we're working in the factory. It's a little like being back inside the mountain again, or so I'm told. Of course, none of us know how Nain *really* live—the Polyphemes haven't lived underground in four generations. Chanting is pretty easy. You don't have to remember many words, which is a good thing, and the noise of the factory drowns out any sour notes."

"That must be nice to—hear," the king said. He grunted as he pushed on the stone. "I, on the other hand, am utterly tone deaf. If I weren't king, I could've made a fine living as a singer."

"Er, can you be a singer and be tone deaf at the same time?" Ven asked. His eyes grew round with wonder as the king's fingers sank into the stone like it was butter.

"Well, certainly. Singers are paid to sing beautifully. When they sing horribly, they are paid even more to stop. I've had a few in my court that I've paid to not even *start*, having heard them once." The king turned his hands in opposite directions.

The wall before him slid aside with a soft grinding sound.

Before them was a tall, thin slice of darkness, a black slash in the shadow on the wall in between the huge stone bricks.

"Whoa," Ven said.

The king stepped inside the slit sideways.

"Come," he said.

Someone with less curiosity in his head, or maybe just a brain in there, might have given the offer a second thought. But there was a warm tone in King Vandemere's voice, an excitement that made my skin feel like it was on fire. I didn't think about anything other than hurrying to catch up with him.

So I followed him as fast as I could inside.

With another scraping noise, the wall shut behind me, leaving us in total darkness.

Unlike humans, Nain can see pretty well in the dark. Things don't look the same as they do in the bright light of day, or even by candlelight, but the warmth that living things give off radiates like a red glow. Other sources of heat glow as well, and cold things appear darker than the air around them. So it was fairly easy to see the king as he made his way through a very thin corridor that took many sharp turns. Oddly enough, even though he is human, King Vandemere didn't have a problem seeing in the dark either, it seemed.

"What is this place?" Ven asked. "Are we underground?"

"No," the king replied, making a left turn. "We are between the walls of the first floor—the throne room is just beyond here. If I were to have had this place built as a dungeon or below the ground, everyone who worked on constructing the castle would know that it is here, since those things have to be dug out and built over. Instead, when the Nain who came from the mountains of the High Reaches to build the castle were laying the stone walls for this part of it, I asked the lead stonemason to build this place in secret for me. He sent the bricklayers away and set the walls himself. He let me help so that I would be able to find it again. We did it in a single night—mostly because the stone almost seemed to move into place by itself when he touched it. Your race has an almost magical knack with stone and earth."

"Is it a hiding place?" Ven asked, running his hand along the smooth wall in the dark.

"Of a sort, yes. It's a vault. It's not for hiding people, but for storing things. But it is so artfully designed and laid out that no one within the castle even knows it's here. All this space is missing from in between the rooms of the first floor—but even the Nain who come to court cannot tell."

"And what do you store down here?"

The king chuckled and stepped aside in the small space. "Have a look."

Stretching into the darkness was a long, straight hallway. It was the longest unbroken space Ven had seen since entering the tunnel, with no turns that he could see.

Along the walls on both sides were cubbyholes, like shelves built into the stone, some high, some low to the ground, in all sizes. Most of the cubbyholes appeared to be empty, but a few had objects in them.

The king's eyes sparkled in the dark.

"Do you remember on the day you first were brought to see me, how I told you of my own journeys at your age? How I had begun to see the magic, not tricks and illusions, but the *real* magic that was out there in the world, hiding in plain sight?"

"Yes," Ven said. "That's why you hired me to be your Royal Reporter—so I could go out and see it for you, now that you are king and can't go yourself."

King Vandemere's smile faded. "Yes," he said. "I have to be careful what I say, Ven—more careful than I have been. A king's words need to be chosen wisely, because they carry a lot of power. So remember what I am about to say, no matter what comes to pass—when I chose you to act as my eyes, I believe I made the best choice a king could have made." He smiled again at the look of confusion on Ven's face. "I have something I would like you to look into for me, if you are feeling brave enough."

"Yes, indeed, Your Majesty," Ven said quickly.

King Vandemere turned to the wall of cubbyholes and pulled out something the size of a loaf of bread. It was wrapped in burlap or some other rough cloth.

"I believe I told you what my father said to me before he died," the king said. His words did not echo in the dark space, but seemed to cling to the inside of Ven's ears. "When I told him I was beginning to see magic of the world, he told me that this magic was like pieces of a great puzzle—that if I could find the pieces and put them together, I would have the answer."

"Yes," said Ven. "I remember."

"Well, my father knew this, because he had his own little collection of pieces of this so-called 'magic puzzle.'" The king held out the object to Ven. "This was one of my father's puzzle pieces."

Ven stared at the object in the king's hands.

"Go ahead," said King Vandemere. "You can open it."

Slowly, Ven reached out his hands and took it.

*I don't know if the object was vibrating, or if my hands were just trembling so much that it seemed as if it were. But there was a hum to it either way, a buzzing feeling that made my fingers feel fuzzy.*

Slowly Ven peeled off the burlap. Inside was a small wooden box, delicately carved, with a strange round seal on the front where the top met the bottom. In the dark, Ven's underground vision allowed him to see that it was engraved, but he could not tell with what sort of inscription.

"Have you ever seen one of these before?" the king asked, tapping the seal on the front of the box.

"I don't know," Ven admitted. "I can't see it very well."

"Open the box," said the king. "That might help."

Ven lifted the lid carefully. The seal came away from the box without resistance, as if it had been broken a long time ago.

Suddenly, bright golden light flooded the hidden vault.

Ven squinted quickly to keep his eyes from stinging.

"Reach in and pick it up," the king urged.

Still squinting, Ven followed the instruction, then slowly opened his eyes. In his hand was a smooth oval object that felt like a stone, but it was translucent. It had settled from burning gold to almost blue in color, and glowed from within, as if fireflies or some other light source had been captured inside it.

"Sorry about that—I'm afraid the bright light is my fault," said the king. "For some reason, it does that when I hold it, or am close to it. But in anyone else's hand, such as your own, it is calmer."

"What is it?" Ven asked.

"I've no idea," said the king. "It came to my father on the day of his coronation, when he was crowned High King of Serendair in the old castle far to the north of here, where I was born. It arrived with all the other gifts of state, presents from the other kings, queens, and nobles on the island who ruled the subkingdoms, like that of the Nain or the Lirin. But unlike those gifts, there was no card, no sign of who sent it. There was this, however, and I think it might be a clue." He tapped on the round seal.

Ven held the glowing stone closer to the seal. In the now-bright light, he could see a strange series of symbols around the edge of the seal, forming a circle. In the center of the circle an image of a hand was engraved.

"Have you ever seen one of these before?" the king asked. Ven shook his head. "I would have been surprised if you had. The language engraved around the edge here is called Thieves' Cant. This is a token to enter the Gated City in Kingston."

Ven shuddered. "I've been outside the gates of that city," he said, remembering how nervous Char had been as they passed it. "My friend says it's a market of thieves, where you could easily lose everything you own."

"That it is," the king agreed. "Or so I've been told—I've never been inside there myself. These tokens are very valuable—they cost ten gold crowns. People purchase them on Market Day, which is the middle day of the week, at the guard stand outside the city gates, in order to be allowed inside to shop for the day."

"Why would anyone want to do that?" Ven asked incredulously.

"Because it's said that some of the most magical and exotic goods in all the world are sold there—things of great beauty and great value that you cannot get anywhere else," said the king. "And while it's possible some people lose their money there, apparently not everyone does. It is said to be a wondrous place of amazing sights and experiences. For many people, that is worth the price of admission, and the risk. This token is what lets you in, but more important, it is what lets you *out*. You are given a token like this on your way through the gates. If you do not have it when you try to leave, they will not let you back into Kingston."

"Why is there a city within the city?" Ven asked, absently scratching his hairline.

The king exhaled. "Long ago, before most of western Serendair was settled, that part of the island was a penal colony, where criminals, thieves, murderers, and thugs of all sorts were sent to live, away from the civilized towns and villages east of the Great River. Eventually, when the western part of the island was being settled, the descendents of the thieves who had been exiled there came into conflict with the law-abiding settlers. Finally it was determined that those people who were the grandchildren and great-grandchildren of the original criminals should be locked up within the heavily guarded walls of the Gated City."

"That doesn't seem fair," Ven said.

"I agree, but this was long before my grandfather was king. It was believed that while these people were not criminals themselves, as far as anyone knew, they had been living in lawlessness all their lives. The Gated City is a prison of a sort, because the people who live there are not free to leave. But they have houses, and shops, businesses, and schools, just like any other city. They even have their own laws and law enforcement, so the constable of Kingston has no right to enter there. Unless, of course, he wants to go shopping." The king tapped the token humorously.

"So do you think this gift came to your father from the Gated City?" Ven asked. He was already imagining what the stores and schools inside a walled former penal colony would be like, and his mind was racing with excitement.

"It might have," the king said. "I wondered if it was an invitation to visit there, but that was just a guess. There is a message inside the box, but it doesn't say who sent it." He held the open top of the box next to the light of the stone in Ven's hand. The radiance from the stone showed that the top was carved in symbols like the ones on the token. "This language is a series of mathematical codes. It was one of the first puzzles I ever tried to solve. My father gave it to me on my eleventh birthday to work on. Finally, after almost two weeks, I broke the code."

"And what does it say?"

The king's bright blue eyes gleamed in the reflected light, and he smiled.

"The message reads: 'The brightest light in the darkest shadow is yours.' I have no idea what that means—or what it has to do with the glowing stone. I had always planned to investigate, to go inside the Gated City while I was out traveling the wide world. But then my father took ill, and I was called home from my wanderings to be with him. He told me on his deathbed that there was a great treasure within the Market, but he was very sick, very weak then, and sometimes what he said made little or no sense.

"So I have always wondered what the strange message meant, as well as what lies beyond those gates. I've heard reports, but no one has ever really been able to tell me what it's like inside that city. I can't officially send someone in there; it might be seen as an invasion, because they have their own laws. Someday I hope that someone I trust, someone curious and brave enough will want to go in and then tell me about it. That way I will know if the things I have heard about the place are actually true." He laughed at the excitement in Ven's eyes. "Maybe that person might be able to solve this riddle at the same time."

"At your service, Your Majesty." Ven bowed slightly, as his father had taught him to do.

"I was hoping you would say that," said the king. "But remember, this task might prove a dangerous one. You should not go alone."

Ven nodded. "I have a good group of friends who might like to do a little shopping in an exotic place," he said. "None of them have any money to buy anything, so they will be able to pay attention to what's going on around them."

The king reached into the pocket of his work clothes and pulled out a small leather sack tied with a drawstring.

"I had guessed what your answer might be. Here are ten garnets, gems each worth the price of admission to the Market. Many people prefer to carry precious stones rather than coins or scrip, and almost every merchant will accept them as payment. This should get you and your friends inside the Gated City, and give you what my father used to call 'walking-around money' as well. But again, I caution you to be careful. Hang on to those tokens, stay together, and remember it is far more important for you and your friends to get out safely than to bring me any information that might risk your lives."

"I understand," Ven said, struggling to remain calm and losing the battle. He tried to keep from wiggling, but couldn't manage to stand still.

"Good." The king closed the box, wrapped it in the burlap again, and slid it back into the cubbyhole. "Take the glowing stone with you. Perhaps you will be able to find out more about it in the Market."

Ven held the translucent stone up to his eye. Inside it was a series of lines and squiggles that looked like flaws in the stone, with a larger one that was starburst-shaped, but nothing else that he could see. The light seemed to grow brighter when he held it near the king, and to dim when he moved away.

"The light stone used to glow for my father the way it does now for me," said the king. "When I was working on breaking the code inside the box, it looked the same in my hand as it does now in yours. It wasn't until I was putting it safely away in this hidden vault that I noticed it was glowing gold."

"Hmmm," said Ven. "Perhaps that's another clue to the riddle."

He opened the drawstring bag and put the stone inside. As soon as the bag was shut, the light disappeared, and they were in darkness again.

"Why did you ask if I knew anything about music, Your Majesty?" he asked as he followed the king back out of the sharply turning tunnel.

"Because the lock that opens the wall we came in is a musical one," King Vandemere said. "The holes you press to activate the lock are the musical notes that spell out 'Long live the king.' I know it's silly, but that's how the Nain stonemason set it up."

"That makes sense," said Ven.

King Vandemere stopped in the dark next to the wall where they had entered. "This is how you open it," he said, placing Ven's fingers in a series of patterns, then twisting his hands in opposite directions as he had done outside the wall. "I want you to be able to find this place if you need to, Ven. You are the one person in the world besides me now who knows it exists."

The king stopped and looked away, thinking aloud. "Understand this, Ven—because as king I cannot send you into the Gated City, you are beyond my official protection there. But you always have my refuge and aid when I *am* able to give it to you. If you want to hide something, or hide yourself, this is a fine place to do it. And if something should happen to me, make sure you get the things that are stored here out and hidden safely away."

Ven stopped, his excitement suddenly choked off.

"What could happen to you?" he asked nervously. "You're the king."

Vandemere looked at him intently. "Kings are subject to the same perils that any other person is subject to, and some that no one could even imagine. I've told you that this magic is fragile; it can easily be destroyed or, worse yet, put to evil use. And I suspect that out there in the world are forces that would like to see that happen. It's always wise to have a backup plan with something this important."

Ven exhaled. "That makes sense, too," he said.

"I have to get back into the throne room," said King Vandemere. "You should return to the garden and wait to be summoned. But just remember everything I've said to you in here, Ven, and don't be offended by anything else you hear from me today. I am doing what is best for you, and for us all. Not even a king can take away your curiosity. Trust that curiosity, and your instincts. They will both serve you well."

Ven opened his mouth to ask what the king meant, but just then the wall slid open, spilling daylight into the tunnel. The king stepped out and waved for Ven to follow, so he did, moving out of the way just in time as the wall slid shut again.

He found his way out of the maze of hedges and back into the elemental garden, where he waited for an hour or so, enjoying the sunshine, until a guard came and told him the king was ready to see him.

*I followed the guard down the long hallway to the throne room. The hall was lined with rich tapestries and ended in two huge doors, with guards on either side. My escort announced my name, and the guard on the right opened the door for me. That is a very strange feeling, to be sure.*

*Beyond the door, the immense throne room was full of people. Advisors, ambassadors, and courtiers stood in great lines on either side of the room. I had only been inside the throne room twice before, and each time it was empty. It was very strange to see it now, full of people in court clothes.*

*We passed the king's puzzle room, where I had met with him each time before. The door was securely closed. That made me sad—I was hoping to catch a glimpse of the wonderful games and amazing puzzles that the king used to train his mind in puzzling. But there was no time for that. The guard led me up the marble aisle to the dais where the king's throne stood.*

Galliard, the Royal Vizier, stood next to the throne. He was wearing the same dark blue robes he had on earlier. His expression was solemn.

In the massive chair sat King Vandemere, looking very different from when Ven had seen him in the garden. The king's hair was neatly combed, and he was wearing a dark blue velvet shirt with a white collar, and crisp black trousers tucked into black leather boots. Around his neck was a heavy segmented necklace set with blue gems that matched the ones in the silver crown he wore. Ven stopped before the throne, nervous. All the eyes in the room seemed to be drilling holes in his back.

"Ven Polypheme, Your Majesty," the guard said.

The king nodded.

"Thank you for coming, Ven," he said. "I regret having to bring you here like this, but I must let you know that I made an error in judgment when I appointed you Royal Reporter. It's an error I must correct now.

"I'm sorry to say this, Ven, but you are fired."

# - 4 -

# Out of a Job

U RK," SAID VEN.

It was the only sound that would come out of his mouth.

*I felt like I had been kicked in the stomach.*

*A few moments before, the king had been showing me the secret hiding place of his father's greatest treasures, the pieces of the magical puzzle he had hired me to find and report back to him about.*

*And now, suddenly and before the entire court, I was done.*

The king's blue eyes twinkled, but his face remained solemn.

"I'm sorry if this is a shock, Ven," he said. "Sometimes a king has to make corrections to his decisions. I hope you understand."

"Yes, Your Majesty," Ven said, but he really didn't.

"I hope you will decide to stay in Serendair for a while in spite of this," the king continued. "This is a very interesting island, and I'm sure you'll find many things here worth exploring. If you choose to do so, I will pay your rent at the Crossroads Inn. If you wish to leave, I will pay your passage home. But if you stay, I hope you'll come by from time to time to chat or for a game of Hounds and Jackals. It would be nice to see you every once in a while."

The Royal Vizier's eyebrows arched suddenly.

King Vandemere noticed, and looked his way. "Something wrong, Galliard?" he asked.

Galliard drew himself up taller, clutching his staff. It was made of dark wood on top of which was carved an eye. "I would advise against that, Your Majesty."

"Really?" said the king. "Why is that?" The Royal Vizier exhaled sharply, but said nothing. "I encourage you to speak your mind freely to me, Galliard. As my acting Vizier, you are a trusted advisor and I value your opinion."

The man bowed respectfully. "Well, then, Your Majesty, it just seems odd to me that the High King of Serendair feels the need for a—a playmate."

The young king smiled. "You are probably right, Galliard. I don't have need of a playmate. But everyone has need of a friend." He looked pointedly at Ven, who smiled weakly in return, then out at the gathered courtiers. "Let it be known that while he is no longer in my employ, that I consider Ven Polypheme my friend. He is under my protection."

He looked back at Ven. "The carriage will take you back to the inn, Ven. Good luck in your travels and all your endeavors. I will be most interested to hear how you are faring next time you come for a visit."

Still numb, Ven bowed, then turned and followed the guards out of the throne room.

They led him back to the courtyard, to the gate, and all the way down the winding, zigzagging flight of stairs carved into the mountain face.

As he was passing the left eye of the Guardian of the Mountain, he saw a sudden flicker of motion behind him.

In that split second, he could have sworn the giant face had winked at him.

He waited for a moment, but saw no further movement in the rocks. The soldiers brought him to the battlements at the base of the mountain, where his carriage was still standing. The second parchment packet of cookies was still on the seat.

The lead soldier held the door for him. Ven started to climb inside, when he heard a sharp cry. He looked up.

Gliding above him, wide and dark, was the massive shadow of a bird.

Ven's mouth fell open. "The albatross," he murmured. "What on earth is it doing here, so far inland?"

*That bird has been following me for the longest time. It appeared unexpectedly on the morning of my birthday, several months ago. That would not be strange in and of itself, but when it first appeared to me, we were both thousands of miles from here, in my hometown, the city of Vaarn, on the Great Overward, where I was born. It always seems to appear when I need help, so I was more than a little nervous now, seeing it circling above me at great height.*

Unconsciously, Ven reached up and touched the feather in his cap that the albatross had dropped on him on his fiftieth birthday. As he did, a small flock of ravens, black birds with a blue sheen to their feathers, took wing from the field, giving chase to the enormous bird.

There was something a little frightening in the speed with which the ravens took to the air. Ven wasn't sure why, but he seemed to sense the malice in their movements, as if their intentions were evil, or at least threatening to the albatross.

The giant bird beat its wings and sailed quickly away, far out of reach of its pursuers, disappearing into the afternoon sun. The black shapes banked on the wind, returning to the fields below the castle, their blue-black feathers glinting in the fading light.

The sun continued to set as the carriage made its way westward. All along the horizon the clouds had turned a bloody shade of red, stretching out across the darkening sky.

Ven fingered the packet of cookies nervously. His stomach had gone so long without food that he was no longer hungry, just feeling vaguely sick. At the bridge he stopped once again to leave cookies for the trolls, feeling much less amused than he did the first time. The first packet was still on the riverbank where he had left it, wrapped in its wax parchment.

Only a slice of sun remained when they reached the crossroads, burning gold at the edge of the horizon. Ven stepped down from the carriage, thanked the soldiers, and started for the door of the inn.

Past the crossroads he thought he saw something move. He wheeled quickly around.

"Uh—excuse me," he called in the direction of the soldiers. But the carriage was rolling away, almost out of sight of the inn.

The mist of evening was beginning to rise from the ground, leaving a low-hanging fog at the crossroads. Ven swallowed hard. When these grounds were haunted, mist had gathered here, too.

Lantern light was beginning to shine in the windows of the

inn, and smoke curled from the chimney. That light and smoke, signs of normalcy, gave Ven courage. Instead of going into the inn, he walked instead across the road toward town, to the little family graveyard that stood there.

At first, nothing seemed out of the ordinary. Behind the fence that circled the cemetery, the Snodgrass family gravestones stood in neat rows, carefully tended and adorned with beautiful flowers. Something was not quite right, however. The mist grew thicker, swirling around the gravestones, hanging close to the ground.

Near the newest gravestone, the mist hung especially heavy.

Sitting on top of that gravestone was a black bird.

With a bluish sheen to his wings.

"Get out of there," Ven said. "Shoo."

The bird just stared at him, its eyes gleaming in the last light of the sun.

Ven inhaled, making his shoulders spread so that he would look bigger. "Go on," he said, louder this time. "Get out of here, you filthy sky-rat."

The raven turned around on top of the gravestone. It bobbed its tail feathers, then turned back, staring at him insolently.

"Why, you dirty prat!" Ven exclaimed angrily. "Did you just *moon* me?" He picked up a stone from the road and heaved it at the bird. The raven fluttered up from the gravestone long enough to dodge the rock, then settled back on it again.

"Stupid git," Ven muttered. "Fine. Stay in the graveyard, for all I care. Stay here till you rot." He turned and started back into the inn.

"Er—Ven?" came a voice from the mist.

Ven froze, then quickly spun around.

Hovering in the air was the faintest image of a young man, hardly more than a boy. Ven had seen him before.

"Gregory?" he asked, coming closer. It was Captain and Mrs. Snodgrass's son, dead more than fifteen years.

"Indeed," said the shade of the young man. "Would you mind getting that filthy thing off my gravestone?"

"Not at all," said Ven. "Be right back." He jogged to the inn and opened the door.

"Murphy!" he called, ignoring the astonished looks on the faces of his friends and the guests. "Could you lend me a hand out here, please?"

The orange tabby cat stood and stretched. "I could lend a paw," he said. "But only if there's a treat involved."

"Good enough," said Ven. He waited until the cat had crossed the threshold, then closed the door behind him.

"What do you need?" Murphy asked.

"You were a champion ratter, right?"

The cat nodded. "Caught 'em on three different ships for Captain Snodgrass. Why? Is there one out here?"

"No, but I need to get rid of *him*," Ven said, pointing to the raven.

"Oh. Not a problem," said the cat. He walked over to the cemetery gate, arched his back, and hissed, a world-class sound of threat that made the hairs at the back of Ven's neck stand up.

The raven just looked at him.

Murphy blinked. Ven had never seen him look so surprised.

Like lightning, the cat launched himself, arms and claws extended, at the bird, letting loose a ferocious snarl that echoed through the night air.

With a flapping flutter, the raven rose off the stone and took to the air, spattering the ground near Ven and the cat with white droppings.

"Ugh!" Ven cried, dodging out of the way just in time to spare his hair.

"Normally I don't do birds," Murphy said, turning and heading back to the inn. "That treat better be *especially* nice."

Once the cat was back inside the inn, Ven returned to the cemetery.

"You still there, Gregory?" he called into the mist.

"Yes," Gregory's voice replied. Ven looked closely, but all he could see was the slightest outline of a head, and two eyes in the fog. "Thank you."

"You're more than welcome," Ven answered. "But if you don't mind my asking, what are you still doing here? I thought once we buried the Rover's box, you were going on to the light."

"I did, mostly," the ghost said. "But part of me still feels the need to be here, to look out for my mother."

"Mrs. Snodgrass is fine," Ven said awkwardly. "I didn't tell her about you being a—well, still being here. I don't think she'd understand. She's much better now. The evil that you said was in the box—well, now that he's gone, buried, the inn seems to be healthy again."

The eyes in the fog blinked, and faded away. Gregory Snodgrass's voice faded with it, leaving his words hanging on the night air.

*I never said the evil in that box was a person. And while it may be contained, it's not gone. It will never be gone.*

"Wait!" Ven called. "What do you mean?" He waited for a

reply, but heard nothing but the sound of the warm night wind.

W ELL, LOOK WHO'S BACK!" MRS. SNODGRASS EXCLAIMED AS SHE came to the door. "You just missed supper."

Ven sighed. "Of course I did."

"That's all right," the innkeeper said, wiping her hands on the towel at her waist. "I have some hot, freshly baked bread and soup waiting for you."

"So how was your visit to the king?" Char asked, hurrying out of the kitchen. "What happened? Where is he sending you?"

"Home, if I want to go," said Ven miserably. "Or at least out of his employ."

"He *fired* you?" Char asked. "You're kiddin'. You didn't even get a chance to mess up yet."

"It was very strange." Ven sat down at the table where Mrs. Snodgrass had put the soup and bread. "He fired me in front of the entire court, when just a little while before he asked me to look into this." He reached into his pocket and pulled out the stone the king had given him. It was glowing softly as it had in the vault between the rooms of the first floor of the castle.

Char whistled. "What the heck is *that*?"

"I'm not sure," Ven said, handing the stone to Char and reaching for his spoon. "The king thinks it may have something to do with the Gated City."

Char backed away nervously, putting the stone down on the table. "Oh man," he whispered. "Get that thing away from me, then."

"I don't think you have anything to worry about," Ven said, his mouth full of warm, tasty bread. "I'm thinking about going to visit there on Market Day, which happens to be tomorrow. The king's given me enough money to pay for all of us to go in. You can leave everything you own here, so you won't have to worry about losing it. Whaddaya think? You game to try it?"

"If you're goin' in, I'm goin' in," Char said. "Captain's orders. But I sure wish you'd change your mind. All the sailors I ever worked with are afraid of that place. I think you can lose more than your stuff. It's like they can steal your soul or somethin'."

"Sailors are a superstitious bunch," Ven said, tearing his bread into two pieces. "We should ask somebody less nervous about stuff like that—Mrs. Snodgrass?"

"Yes?"

"Have you ever been to the Gated City?"

The innkeeper stopped in her tracks. "I should think not," she said haughtily. "I'm a respectable woman. Besides, I've no time for fancy-dancy shopping and folderol. I have an inn to run. And *you* have some hinges to fix—but it will have to wait until tomorrow."

"I don't mind doing it now," Ven said, soaking up the last of his soup with the last of the bread.

"Well, *I* mind," Mrs. Snodgrass said. "The hinges are on my bed, and I'm going to sleep. Don't forget to take care of your plates."

"Maybe one of the inn's guests has been inside the city," Char suggested.

"Maybe," said Ven. He popped the last piece of bread into his mouth.

"Oh, right," said Murphy. "Don't bother to ask the *cat*. The cat knows *nothing*."

"I'm sorry," said Ven. "Do you know anything about the Gated City, Murphy?"

The cat yawned and extended his front claws.

"Let's see. Walled city, near the harbor, weekly festival." He hunched his shoulders and stretched out lazily before the fire. "Lots of rats, I would say. Thankfully, I'm retired."

Mrs. Snodgrass leaned over and scratched him behind the ears.

"You are such a lazy little beggar," she said fondly. " 'Tis a good thing I take pity and feed you. You'd starve. Famous ratter, indeed."

The cat rolled over onto his back and looked up at her. "You love me, and you know it."

"Hmmph." Mrs. Snodgrass gave his belly a brisk rub, then went back to the kitchen. "Good night, boys. See you in the morning."

"Good night," Char and Ven called after her.

Ven stood up and gathered his dishes. He glanced around the inn. Everyone had gone to bed except McLean, and Ven wasn't certain that McLean ever slept.

"Any thoughts about the market of thieves in the Gated City, McLean?" he asked the Singer, who was putting away his stringed instrument and picking up a tiny silver flute. "Have you heard any tales of it?"

The Singer paused, lost in thought for a moment.

"No tales to tell of," he said finally. "I imagine it's a spectacular place, full of bright colors and sweet smells and glorious music. That's why you must be especially careful, Ven. Outside the Gated City, those things serve to delight the heart. Within its walls, their purpose is to distract the eye. And the mind. Remember that. Don't be too free with your names, either. Keep your names closely guarded; your name is what makes you what you are, and I suspect there may be people within that place who could steal your name if they knew it. Finally, remember what I said about the things Singers can do. If there's one in the market of thieves and you need help, at least you know the Singer will not lie to you."

"That's good advice," Ven said. "Thank you, McLean. Good night."

He and Char washed their dishes, then went out the back door of the inn to Hare Warren, where the hall light was still burning.

They were too busy laughing and talking to notice the five black birds sitting on the roof of the inn, watching them until the door closed.

Then the five flew off into the night, a night now as dark as they were.

# -5-

# The Adventure Begins

The next morning I got up as early as I could. No dreams remained when I woke up, if I'd had any to begin with, so I had no trouble hopping out of bed. Sleeping in had brought me nothing but bad luck, so I figured maybe the opposite would be true if I got my hindquarters out of the blankets and hit the deck as soon as the sun was up.

On my way to the tool shed I ran into Cadwalder, the house steward of Hare Warren. Cadwalder is about fifteen, has a bristly mustache and beard, and the sallow complexion of someone who spends a lot of time in the stable and not in the sun. I nodded to him, and he nodded back, but we rarely speak. Cadwalder once tried to set me up for thievery, which led to my original arrest. When Mrs. Snodgrass found out, she chewed him out within an inch of his life. He has been very careful around me ever since. I still don't trust him, but I'd like to get to a point where we can at least be friendly to one another. Maybe it will happen someday.

As soon as I got into the inn, Mrs. Snodgrass was there to meet me.

WELL, GOOD MORNING," THE INNKEEPER SAID, SMILING. "YOUR curiosity must be well and healthy today."

"As ever," Ven agreed. "Why do you mention it?"

"I just wonder how early you would have gotten up if I hadn't told you that you were going to be working in my bedroom."

Ven laughed. "Well, I have to admit I was intrigued," he said. "I've seen very little of the actual inn. Each time I get to see a new room it's something magical. This should be an interesting job."

Mrs. Snodgrass turned and beckoned for him to follow her.

"I don't know about that," she said as she walked away down the hall. "But it's an important one."

Ven followed her all the way down the corridor that led north, out toward Hare Warren and Mouse Lodge, the girls' house in back of the inn. The door at the end of the hall had a small window in it that looked very much like a porthole. Mrs. Snodgrass took a long brass key out of her pocket and unlocked the door. Then she stepped aside, allowing Ven to enter the room first.

His mouth dropped open as he did.

Mrs. Snodgrass's bedroom, not surprisingly, was fashioned to look like the captain's cabin in the stern of a sailing ship. It had long slanted windows that resembled those in the room belowdecks of the *Serelinda* that Oliver had occupied when Ven was sailing with him. The door directly across opened onto a curved patio garden that gave the impression one was standing on the rear deck of the ship.

Inside the room, everything was as neat as a pin. The open closet revealed a series of shelves and cubbyholes in which all the linens and clothes were folded perfectly, everything inside it shipshape. The windows in the room were round like portholes as well.

But the most remarkable thing in the room was the bed.

Built of four tall, round timbers that looked like smaller versions of a mast, the bed was strung with ropes like the shrouds on a ship, with crisp white bed curtains draped from the top of the ceiling above the headboard to the posters of the bed itself. The rugs on the floor were woven in multiple shades of blue and white, making it resemble a frothy sea.

One of those rugs, however, was rolled up and stashed to the side of the room. The bed was off-kilter, standing at an odd angle in the middle of the room. And beneath the bed was a large round wooden opening, attached with hinges below the bedframe.

Mrs. Snodgrass walked over to the large wooden opening.

"The inn's safe is down below here," she said, pointing to the wooden circle above the opening. "It's triggered by a mechanism here in the bedpost." She took hold of the round spindle at the top of the bedpost on the right of the headboard and twisted it three times clockwise, two times counterclockwise, and once more clockwise. A clicking sound was heard in the floor. "But the hinge is broken. Do you think you can fix it?"

Ven knelt down and examined the wooden circle. It was an extremely clever device, one that his brother Alton, the Polypheme family's chief model maker, would have been very impressed by. He followed the curves and turns of the mechanism, finally discovering where the hinge was broken.

"Yes indeed, Mrs. Snodgrass," he said. "I think I can have this ready in an hour or so."

"Good," said the innkeeper, looking relieved. "Several of our

guests have valuables stored in the safe, and I'm sure they want to take them with them when they leave this morning."

"I'll get right to it," Ven promised. He set to work, and in a short time the hinge was repaired, oiled, and working again. The giant bed moved out of the way so that the safe could be opened. Then it slid easily back into place above the hidden circle door.

"Many thanks, Ven," Mrs. Snodgrass said. "There will be a large plate of pancakes with your name on it when you get cleaned up."

"Is Char going to make them?" Ven asked jokingly.

Mrs. Snodgrass shuddered. "No, I'm trying to reward you, not punish you," she said. "I'll have Felitza make them."

"Maybe Char can watch her do it," Ven suggested. "He watches everything she does anyway."

*Char's fascination with Felitza is something I have to admit I've never understood. While I'm no judge of male beauty, and certainly not human male beauty, Char seems to be a fairly handsome guy. He's wiry and strong and seems to have a pleasant face—at least the girls in Mouse Lodge think so.*

*Felitza, on the other hand, is not what anyone would call beautiful. Anyone but Char, that is. When Char looks at Felitza, he apparently doesn't see her rather oversized teeth, her somewhat stringy hair and colorless skin. What Char sees is another kind of beauty, a beauty he first noticed in the golden brown finish on her corn bread, along with all the other skills she has in the kitchen. Whether he is still impressed by her talent at cooking or in love with her, however she looks, doesn't really matter.*

*Because Felitza doesn't know Char is alive.*

Ven went out to the pump in the garden to wash, then came back into the inn to the dining table. By then, most of his friends had arrived for breakfast.

The first one there was Nicholas Cholby, the inn's messenger, and his roommate in Hare Warren, Albert Hio. Jonathan Conroy and Lewis Craig, who had the room next door to Ven and Char, were just finishing up and waved as they carried their dishes to the kitchen. Clemency was there as well, talking with the invisible Spice Folk, along with Lucinda, Ciara, Emma, and Bridgette, the girls of Mouse Lodge who were chatting among themselves and ignoring the boys.

At the end of the table sat Saeli, the only nonhuman besides Ven in the children's dormitories. She looked up from her breakfast as Ven came in, waved to him, and returned to her pancakes. But the vaseful of rosebuds on the table in front of her stretched, and bloomed open in hues of soft pink and white, matching the blush in her tiny cheeks.

*Saeli is perhaps the strangest person I have ever seen. I don't mean strange in a bad way; I just mean more unlike anyone I've ever met. Like me, and McLean, and Galliard, she's of a different race than most people. Saeli is a Gwadd. While Nain tend to be shorter than humans, Gwadd are much shorter than Nain. Saeli is tiny and shy, and while she has a voice, she only uses it on rare occasions. Instead, she speaks in flowers.*

When everyone had cleared out except for Nick, Saeli, Clemency, and Char, Ven leaned over the table and spoke in a low, excited voice. "Who wants to go with me to Gated City today?"

The four children stared at him as if he were daft.

"Who suddenly has nothin' left to live for in this world?" Char asked sarcastically. "I still can't believe you want to do this, Ven. The king fired you. Why do you wanna do *anything* for him, let alone something this risky? Are you crazy?"

Ven took out the stone the king had given him and laid it on the table.

"His Majesty will pay our way to go shopping for the day," he said. "While we're there, I'm going to see if I can find out something about this weird stone. You don't have to bring anything of your own into the Market. If we stay together, and keep our eyes open, we should have a wonderful time."

"I repeat," said Char, "why do you want to do this?"

"If you're not comfortable going, I understand completely," said Ven. "I'm only offering you the opportunity to see what's inside those gates. It's something I've wondered since I've been here. If your curiosity is not tickled by the thought, by all means stay home and do chores. I'm going this morning, and I have to be leaving shortly. Anyone else who wants to come, leave your stuff in your room and meet me out front. I'm going to get Cadwalder to hitch up the small cart with a horse so we don't have to walk. Who's in?"

"I'll go," said Clemency. "Sounds like fun to me."

"Me too," added Nicholas. "I finished my route already today. And by the way, Ven, I've got another letter for you." He opened his leather pouch and pulled out a piece of oilcloth sealed with wax.

"How about you, Saeli?" Ven asked the small girl as he took the letter from Nick. Saeli nodded quickly, then rose from the table and scurried into the kitchen with her plate.

"All right, then," Ven said excitedly. "We have a fivesome."

The peace of the empty dining area was shattered by a belch that rattled the windows. The five turned to see Ida leaning against the wall, staring at them. They looked at each other, then back to Ida, whose gaze had not wavered.

Ven sighed. "What about you, Ida?" he asked. "Wanna come?"

"Now I *know* you're daft," muttered Char. "You must *want* to lose everything you have, including your underwear."

Ida's insolent stare became more of a smiling sneer.

"Naw," she said. "The Gated City is boring. Been in there a bajillion times. But I'll go to town. I got lots of stuff I can do there."

"No stealing," Clemency cautioned. "I don't want to have to bail you out again this week. It's been twice already."

"You're such a liar, Ida," Char said, annoyed. "It costs *ten gold crowns* to get into the Market. You don't even own your own *name*, let alone ten gold crowns."

Ida just smirked.

"All right then," Ven interrupted. "I'm going to read my letter. Then, anyone going to the Market, or to town, meet me at the crossroads in ten minutes."

He looked down at the folded piece of oilcloth in his hands. It was sealed with a blob of blue wax and stamped with a coat of arms, the Polypheme family crest. He turned it over.

Written across the front was his name and that of the innkeeper. Ven's hands shook as he recognized the clear, simple handwriting.

It was his mother's.

---

*Charles Magnus Ven Polypheme*
*In the care of Mrs. Gertrude Snodgrass*
*The Crossroads Inn*
*Serendair*

---

"Oh boy," he muttered.

I have to confess, I try not to think about my mother. It hurts too much.

That "another story" I mentioned earlier, about how I came to be here, is sort of complicated. On my fiftieth birthday, I was minding my own business, headed for work on the docks of Vaarn, my hometown, to my family's shipbuilding factory. I was pretty excited.

Then, in the blink of an eye, everything changed.

The albatross that for some reason keeps following me appeared for the first time on that day. It flew over and dropped a feather on my head, and from that moment on, my ordinary, boring life became one of constant change, both exciting and dangerous. I was sent out on an Inspection of our newest ship, the *Angelia*, which was then attacked by Fire Pirates. In the chaos that followed, both our ship and the pirate ship exploded—my fault, by the way—and I found myself on this wonderful, horrible adventure that now is my life. I have to say I am enjoying it most of the time, especially since I got a letter the day before yesterday from my father, telling me that everything was fine at home, that the crew of the *Angelia* had survived, and giving me his blessing to find my way in the world. I had adventure awaiting me, a nice place to live, great friends, and an exciting job—until yesterday, anyway.

But the one thing I haven't been able to put out of my mind is my mother.

My mother is not the sweetest person in the world, though she can be very kind. She is mostly businesslike, keeping track of a family of thirteen children and a good many of my father's employees, some of whom are upworld Nain, like us. She is the busiest person I have ever met, and is quite insistent on us always being on time and prepared for whatever we are doing. Most often she becomes annoyed if we are late for tea, which happens on occasion when things don't go well at the factory. For all that men who sail the seven seas fear Mrs. Snodgrass, she is nowhere near as scary as my mother can be if her tea is allowed to get cold. And when one person is late, we all wait, so by the time whoever had an emergency at work or got caught up in something gets to the table, the only thing colder than the tea is my mother's stare.

*So this is the reason that I get cramps in my stomach every time I think about my mother. All the while I have been away from home, I have kept imagining my teacup sitting empty on her table. I can see in my mind the expression of pain on her face. I know how confused her orderly life must have become when I never came home from the Inspection on my birthday.*

*I know she is sad. For weeks she thought I was dead.*

*I know she misses me. I'm her youngest.*

*And it makes me sick.*

He clenched his teeth, worked up his courage, and broke the seal on the letter.

As he unfolded the oilcloth, a piece of waxed paper scrip fell out, in the amount of one hundred gold pieces. Scrip was the money sailors and merchants who sold goods to them exchanged rather than using gold or gems, the way everyone else did.

Ven's eye went to the letter. It contained a brief paragraph at the beginning and the end, with a long list of items in between, carefully printed in his mother's neat hand. He read the first few lines, then blinked in surprise.

*Ven,*

*Glad to know that you are alive and well. Please make certain you are minding your manners and behaving appropriately. Be especially sure to:*

*1. Make your bed every day.*

*2. Wash well, with special attention behind your ears.*

*3. Say "please" and "thank you" in all situations.*

*4. Remember your lessons.*

5. *Use your head.*
6. *Keep your elbows off the table.*
7. *Cover your mouth when sneezing or coughing.*
8. *Hold the door for others.*
9. *Pitch in with chores around the inn.*

The list continued on for over one hundred items. Ven scanned them quickly, his worry turning to annoyance as he continued to read. Each item on the list was a directive for his behavior, the same orders she had been giving him every day of his life from the time he could remember.

*There was no mention of anyone at home, or how things were in Vaarn. No news, no sign of worry or relief in discovering I had survived, outside of "glad to know you are alive and well." Fire Pirates never leave anyone they attack alive. Everyone in Vaarn must have believed me dead, and yet my mother did not seem particularly overjoyed to know I had escaped with my life, and was now safe in Serendair, making a name for myself.*

*All she wanted to make sure of was my good behavior in her absence, since she wasn't there to correct me herself.*

*I felt about twenty years old. [Five in human years.]*

He sighed in disappointment and skipped to the bottom of the list to the last paragraph above the signature.

*Here is some money to repay the kindness of Mrs. Snodgrass and anyone else who has helped you in the course of your misadventure.*

*Please make sure you have repaid anyone you owe. If you need more, please write with the amount and I will send it.*

> *Your*
> *Loving Mother*

*P.S.—Make sure to wear clean clothes always. No one of any worth wears dirty clothing.*

The front door of the inn opened. It was painted with a golden griffin, and from where he stood, it looked as if it were holding hands with Char, whose fingers rested on the door handle.

"Ya comin'?" his friend demanded.

"I'll be right along," Ven answered. He scraped the remains of the wax seal into one of the candles on the table, then folded the oilcloth and stuffed it into his pocket. He shook his head as if to shake off his annoyance, then hurried out of the inn with Char and headed for the crossroads.

The other four children were standing in front of a very small cart, hitched to Breeze, one of the oldest and most feeble of the horses in the stable.

"Well, you can see ol' Cadwalder is feeling remorseful for all his bad deeds," Char said.

"At least it's a cart, at least it's a horse," said Ven, climbing in. "All ashore who's goin' ashore."

They piled in the cart one by one, and Saeli, who could speak to animals, gave directions to Breeze. The cart lurched forward on its bumpy wheels and began rumbling down the road to town, slightly off-kilter.

The morning was bright, and with the exception of Ida, every-one was laughing and chatting away, the excitement of the adventure beginning to grow. They fell silent as they passed the White Fern Inn, the place where Maurice Whiting, the man who had worked with Cadwalder to have Ven arrested, lived. Mr. Whiting kept vicious guard dogs, but not a sound could be heard in the yard as their cart rolled by. Everyone breathed a sigh of relief when the pristine white inn was no longer in sight.

After about an hour the shining gates of the city of Kingston came into view.

Ven turned to the others.

"All right, this is how it's going to work," he said. "Saeli, Nick, Char, and Clem, you go to the booth in front of the Gated City and buy our tokens. See if the money changer will give you gold crowns, silvers, and coppers for the leftover value in the gems. Ida, once we get to town, you're on your own. No one's going to be able to help you if you do something stupid, so try to stay out of trouble. We will meet you back at the fountain in the center of town when the Market warning bell rings an hour before the gates close. I'll meet up with the rest of you at the gates just before nine o'clock, when they open."

"And where are *you* going?" Char demanded. "You better not send us into that city and not show up."

"I'll be there when the gates open," Ven promised. "I just have something to do first."

# ~ 6 ~

# The Abandoned Pier

At the north end of the town of Kingston, the neat cobblestone streets gave way to hard-packed sand dotted with shells. This section that had once been part of the harbor was empty now. Broken boats littered the beach, and an abandoned pier stretched out into the water like a bridge to nowhere.

The pier had a good many holes and missing boards, so Ven was careful as he walked to the end of it.

"Amariel!" he shouted over the water. "Are you there?"

Only the slap of the sea wind and the screams of the gulls answered him.

*So I waited. Whenever I came to see her, I was never sure whether she would be there, and if she was there, whether she would be in the mood to speak to me. Amariel is hard to predict. From what she tells me, I think all merrows are.*

*So I waited.*

Finally, the head of a young girl broke the water, her dark hair streaming. She had a pleasantly angled face, with bright green eyes that gleamed with the same curiosity that Ven's did. On top of her head was a delicate red cap laced with pearls. She surfaced just as Ven started to call again.

"Amari—"

"There's really no need to *shout*," she said, clearly annoyed. Then her eyes gleamed a little brighter. "What are you doing here? Are you ready to come explore the depths with me, *finally*?"

Ven sighed. It was the same question she always asked him. He gave her the same answer he always did.

"I wish I could," he said. "But I have to do something in the Gated City today."

Amariel leaned back in the water, and as she did, a huge tail of magnificently colored scales crested the waves where her legs would normally be. "Of *course* you do. You always have something more important that keeps you from coming with me. So what do you want?"

Ven pulled the translucent oval stone that the king had given him out of his pocket. "Have you ever seen anything like this before?"

The merrow swam closer, and Ven held the stone down so she could get a better look. It caught the morning light and gleamed in much the same way it did in the dark.

Amariel stared at the stone for a moment, then shook her head.

"There are some rocks, plants, and fish in the depths that glow like that," she said. "They are a source of light deep in the ocean where the sun can't reach. But that doesn't look like something from the sea."

"I didn't think so," Ven said. He looked at the stone again, then put it back in his pocket and buttoned it for safekeeping.

"But I thought I would ask you, anyway. You know a lot of interesting things that nobody else I know does. And I just wanted to say good morning."

"Oh," said the merrow. "Well, good morning. And goodbye."

"Wait!" said Ven as she started to dive. "Do you know anything about the Gated City?"

The merrow looked at him oddly. "That city?" she asked, pointing behind him.

Ven glanced over his shoulder. In the distance the high wall and guard towers were visible. "Yes," he said. "That city."

"Oh—well, yes, actually, I do," the merrow said. "There's a wonderful place to eat there in the center of town called The Mermaid's Purse that makes terrific clams. It's got a lovely view, near the eastern wall, at the top of a tall set of stairs."

"Really?" Ven asked in amazement.

The merrow's face went sour. She slapped the surface with her tail, splattering him with seawater, then waved her lower fin at him.

"What do you think?" she said sarcastically. "Do I look like I do *stairs*?"

"Er, good point," said Ven, dripping wet and feeling foolish.

He smiled sheepishly at the merrow. She was glaring at him.

The harsh cry of a seabird, high above, shattered the silence. Ven looked up as a giant shadow glided over him. The albatross was circling above; it made one last pass, then flew away out to sea.

"That bird has been following me since the morning of my birthday in Vaarn," Ven said, shaking the water out of his hair. He took off his cap with the albatross feather attached to it and shook it dry. "I wish I knew why."

"Maybe she likes you," suggested the merrow scornfully. "Birds aren't known for having the best of taste. But then, you haven't been keeping *her* waiting, I suppose."

"I really am sorry about that, Amariel," Ven said as the merrow crossed her arms. "I would love to come with you to see your world in the sea, and someday I will, if you haven't lost patience with waiting. But I have to do something for the king today. Even if he *did* fire me."

Amariel's green eyes grew wide in alarm.

"He *fired* you?"

"I think so," Ven said.

The merrow exhaled sharply, then squinted as she looked at Ven.

"Are you all right?" she asked. "You don't look burned at all."

"No, I mean he told me in front of a lot of people that I don't have a job with him anymore," Ven said. "But before he did that, he asked me to find out the story of the stone I showed you. So I'm going into the Gated City today, where it seems to have come from. It's Market Day, the only day of the week you can get in *and* out of the city."

He stopped talking. Amariel was staring at him in confusion.

"I didn't mean to be stupid about the stairs," he continued. "But I didn't know if perhaps you had decided to give your cap to someone and grow legs. Didn't you say merrows could do that if they wanted to explore the dry world?"

"Yes," the merrow said disdainfully. "But only *stupid* merrows. It's supposed to be a human man that you give your cap to, and my mother says merrows who do that are kept like slaves by the men after that and go all boring and *human*, forgetting about the sea. Ugh. Believe me, there's nothing so interesting to me in the dry world that would make me do *that*."

"Well, then, I'm glad," said Ven. "I wouldn't want you to change at all from the way you are. Even if I do get splashed occasionally."

The merrow's face softened a bit.

"Well, I guess I do know one thing about the Gated City," she admitted. "Remember Asa the fisherman? The one I told you about who can cut gills for you when you're ready to explore the depths?" Ven nodded. "Well, Asa says there are underwater caves farther up the coast that lead in and out of there. But he warned me never to go near them. I guess the people who live in that place aren't especially nice—like pirates."

Ven shuddered. He had met pirates.

"Well, that's good to know, anyway," he said. "Thank you very much. I'm glad I asked you."

"Good luck," said the merrow, preparing to dive. "Stay away from pirates, even if they're on land."

"I will try," Ven promised.

"Goodbye," said the merrow.

"Goodbye," said Ven as she disappeared below the waves again.

He waited until he could no longer see any sign of the beautiful multicolored scales, then shook himself dry one more time and headed back to the gates in the middle of Kingston.

He did not notice the quick sparkle of rainbow color that glinted eerily behind him, from the other side of the Market wall, in the morning sun.

V EN, WHERE THE HECK HAVE YOU BEEN?" CHAR DEMANDED AS Ven approached the booth at the main entrance to the Gated City. "We thought you might have been stolen before you even got in there."

"I'm fine, and I'm sorry," Ven said. "Did you get the tokens?"

"We did," Clemency said as she and Saeli held up five long

ribbons on which round medallions had been strung.
They passed them out, Saeli choosing the one with
the bright blue ribbon that matched
the big bow in her hair. Ven took the
one Clem handed to him and examined it quickly.

The token on the ribbon was exactly
like the one that had formed the seal on the
box that was sent to the king's father.

"The gems the king gave you were more
than enough to get us in," Char said, handing
Ven three gold crowns. "There's enough
here for a right fine noon-meal, and maybe
even a little shopping."

"The king called it 'walking-around money,'"
Ven said absently, looking up at the guards with
crossbows manning the tall walls that encircled
the city. "If we keep our wits about us, we should
be able to learn something about the king's stone and have a fun
day at the same time. We need to each take a certain number of
stores or booths or whatever they have inside there, and look
through all the wares. Maybe we will see something like this,
something that glows, or has cracks in it. Look high and low, in
the bricks of the buildings or the cobblestones of the streets. If
everyone looks at something different, we have the best chance
of seeing a clue. We can divide it up by direction points—I'll
take the north, Char can take the south, Clem the east, and Nick
the west. Saeli, you watch the ground, since you're closer to it.
You might see something we wouldn't."

"We just need to be sure we stay together," said Nick. "If we
get separated, we may be done for."

"Shhh," said Clemency. "The guard is climbing up onto the podium." She pointed to an elevated spot to the left of the main gate.

Ven turned to see a soldier dressed in the colors of the town guard of Kingston step out onto the elevated ledge and over the crowd that had gathered, waiting to get into the Gated City.

"Good morning," he said. "Today, as I'm sure you all know, is Market Day. Here are the rules. First, no one enters the Gated City without an official token. Tokens can be purchased at the booth below. You can enter and exit the City as many times as you like, provided you have the token with you. If you do leave, and do not have the token when you return, you will be denied admittance.

"Next, be aware that the Market closes three fingers before sunset," he continued. "An hour before that, a warning bell will sound once. This is the signal that you should bring your shopping to an end and make your way to this gate. You must be on the Kingston side of the gate when the final Market Day bell sounds, or you will be forced to remain within the walls of the Gated City until the next Market Day, one week from today. On that day, you can present your token and you will be let out before anyone else enters." His eyes narrowed. "If you can survive that long.

"Finally, when each of you purchased your token, you were warned of the risks of entering the Gated City. This place was founded as a penal colony for thieves and criminals of the worst sort. And while that has not been the case for many centuries, we make no guarantees as to your safety or the safety of your possessions. You're on your own. If you do not wish to abide by these terms, you can return your token for a refund from this moment until the opening bell sounds. After that, no refunds will be given."

"Are you sure about this, Ven?" Char asked nervously. "It's not too late."

"You can stay if you want," Ven replied, struggling to keep his curiosity from overwhelming him. "I can't wait to see what's on the other side of these gates."

"One last warning, folks," the main guard said as the hands of the clock in the tower moved toward the top of its face. "For your own safety, stay in the middle of the Outer Market and as far away from the Inner Market as you can. There is nothing of any value to good, law-abiding citizens in that place anyway."

With a harsh clang, the brass bells in the high tower just beyond the wall began to ring the hour nine times. As the sound of the last note died away, there was a blare of trumpets and a roll of drums.

The three guardians of the gate stepped forward with great ceremony. They inserted enormous keys of black steel with many teeth into the lock of the gate. They turned them several times in different directions, then stepped back.

Slowly, the huge gates began to swing open.

The crowd squeezed forward. Each person struggled to get as close to the entrance as he could.

"Hang on to those tokens, now," the guard warned as the crowd swelled toward the gate. "Remember, if you lose it, you'll be living in there forever."

The five friends looked at each other. They quickly checked the tokens around their necks, then followed the crowd that was pressing through the opening into the Outer Market of the Gated City.

# -7-

# The Market of Thieves

Beyond the gates was a sight like none I had ever seen before.

Kingston is a pretty town, with well-kept gardens and fountains that spray colored water. The buildings are tidy, as are the streets, from the base of the statue of the king's father in the square to the cobblestones at the edge of the fishing village where the streets end. It's pleasant on the eye, certainly more clean and neat than the messy port city of Vaarn where I was born. Everything in Vaarn is coated in soot, much of it from my father's own factory, and the salt of the sea wind.

Stepping into the Outer Market of the Gated City, however, was a little bit like being slapped across the eyes by a rainbow of light and color.

Past the red stone of the towering wall was a carnival, a bazaar of some of the most spectacular colors, sights, smells, and sounds that I could ever have imagined. Within the square inside the gates were many festival booths, all trimmed with brightly flying flags in scarlet and gold, purple and azure silk, dancing merrily like kites in the breeze. The booths themselves were formed of colorful fabric as well, each one a different shade, many of which I had never seen. Some of them were just beginning to be opened for business.

In the center of the square were pit fires over which food was roasting, filling the air with smells so tempting that my mouth began to water. In one pit a whole ox was turning on a spit. In another a woman was grilling long skewers of fruit. And in the center of yet another pit fire was a giant pumpkin shell, large as the cart we had come to town in. The top of the pumpkin had been sawed off, and thick orange soup was bubbling inside it, sending the smell of cinnamon and nutmeg into the air around us.

"IS IT TIME FOR NOON-MEAL YET?" CHAR MOANED, CLUTCHING HIS stomach. "I gotta have some of that soup."

"Three more hours," said Clemency.

"But you can always eat early," said Ven. "What difference does it make what time it is? We're in the market. We can do whatever we want." Saeli nodded in agreement.

Ven's skin was itching so much that it felt like it would peel off his body. He turned around slowly, trying to take in all the sights.

The brightly colored booths were set up in a series of circles, almost like streets. The pit fires and other places where food was being sold were mostly in the inner circles. Tents and booths with wares for sale seemed to be in the outer circles, some of them flying colorful flags, others with brightly painted maypoles or wooden signs in front. Ven's eyes were flooded with all the colors.

Just then he heard McLean's voice in his head.

*I imagine it's a spectacular place, full of bright colors and sweet smells and glorious music. That's why you must be especially careful, Ven. Outside the Gated City, those things serve to delight the heart. Within its walls, their purpose is to distract the eye. And the mind.*

He unbuttoned his shirt pocket and took out his great-grandfather's jack-rule. It was his most treasured possession, a folding measuring stick with a knife, a magnifying glass, and other tools that had been made in the underground kingdom of the Nain almost a thousand years before. Carefully he extended the lens and looked through it.

Past the circles of colorful booths were buildings surrounding the square. The buildings on the closest street were beautifully kept, with window boxes full of flowers, carefully tended gardens, and neatly shingled roofs. They stood side by side, sharing walls, with occasional alleys between them.

When Ven looked closer, however, past the first row of houses and stores, he could see that the streets and buildings quickly lost their colors, fading into gray. It looked like a mist was hanging around them, making them hard to see. The shutters on the windows were more often broken or missing, the paint on the doors peeling.

What caught his eye most of all, however, was what was *over* the buildings of the Gated City.

Suspended in the air above the streets, attached to the roofs of the houses that stood side by side, was a second sidewalk. Wide ladders led up to it at each alleyway. Above the roofs, people were walking on the elevated footpath, greeting each other in passing as if they were on the ground below. The street in the air stretched all the way into the Market as far as he could see.

Ven was suddenly nervous. He folded the jack-rule and looked back at his friends. Everyone was watching him. They all still had their tokens around their necks, as did he.

"Where to first?" Char asked.

"Let's go to the center of the square," Ven suggested. "We'll start by just looking around to begin with." He put the jack-rule away and headed into the middle of the Outer Market. The other four children nodded and followed him.

Past the pit fires where the food was roasting were other types of fires, over which other types of pots were hanging.

At one, a tall, thin woman with red hair and a colorful apron was dipping an enormous spoon with a tin cup in its bowl. When she lifted it out of the pot, the cup had been plated in gold. Two men were striking coins in silver, copper, and a strange blue metal in a forge and cooling them in another of the pots. A third pot seemed to be a giant cauldron of medicine. Six men in brightly striped shirts with hair and skin that matched were bottling the contents of that pot, each with a long-handled ladle. Ven noticed that every time one of them poured what was in his ladle into a bottle, the color was different.

Some of the townspeople who had entered the gates with them were wandering around much like they were, taking in the sights with wonder. Others, who had obviously been to the Market before, hurried to certain booths and shops.

All around them the air was filled with delicious smells. Beyond the roasting food there was the scent of heavy spice and rare perfume, making Ven's head spin. And, as McLean had predicted, there was music playing everywhere, the sweet sounds of flutes and harps with drums keeping time.

Saeli grabbed his sleeve and tugged at it.

Ven looked where she was pointing. In the center of the closest ring of booths was a carpet weaver. Beautiful rugs in all shapes and sizes hung on bamboo frames around his tent. Many of them were tapestries showing great stories of history. Some of them seemed to be changing patterns as the stories progressed. The patterns on others were changing color in the sun. Out in front of the booth a small carpet was hovering in the air.

Flying by itself.

The weaver ignored them as he continued with his work. Sitting on the ground in front of the booth was a strange-looking man with a long black mustache and eyebrows that looked like woolly caterpillars were eating his forehead.

On the ground in front of the strange man were brightly colored balls, sticks, and unlit torches. His hands held long thin clubs, which he started to juggle. Just as he did, the carpet swooped down from the air and started to interfere. It dived at his head, and flew in between his hands, as if it were trying to make him drop the clubs. The man pretended to swat it away, but Ven could see it was all part of the act.

He looked over his shoulder nervously.

As McLean had warned him, many townspeople were around the booth, watching the show, some of them standing very close to him. Mixed in with them here and there were people without tokens. Ven realized they must be inhabitants of the city, rather than shoppers.

In spite of the bright clothing many of the Gated City's folk wore, there was a raggedness, an edge to them that worried Ven, a sort of toughness beneath the color. He felt for his wallet and was relieved to find it was still within his pocket.

"Come on," he urged the others. "This is a great way to get pickpocketed. Let's see if we can find something that looks like the king's stone. Let's keep to each of our directions and keep our eyes open."

They walked farther across the square, where a glistening carousel was being prepared. Instead of horses, however, the figures on it were mythical beasts, beautifully carved, painted, and trimmed with what looked like jewels on their saddles. Nearby were two huge swings, strung with heavy rope and shaped like griffins, their bodies hollowed out for seats. Their red and black wooden feathers gleamed in the morning air. Two men in orange shirts were checking the ropes.

A pretty young human woman with dark brown skin who was polishing a silver dragon on the carousel looked up at them and smiled. She pointed at a ferocious wooden blue-green sea monster with one hand and a golden flying lion with the other.

"Care for a ride, gentles?" she asked sweetly.

"No, thank you very much," Clemency said quickly, snagging both Char and Nicholas by the shoulders and pushing them ahead of her.

"Clem, what was the point of paying all that money to come into this place if you're not going to let us have some fun?" said Nicholas, sounding cross.

"Yeah, we'll probably never get to come back here *ever*," said Char.

"Aren't you the one who told me to stay away from this place our first day in town?" asked Ven, amused. "If I recall, you said you never needed to buy anything so badly to risk being stripped of everything you own."

Char came to a halt in front of another booth, a sort of wooden kiosk with purple draperies that was full of golden cages.

"Well, I don't have anythin' I own here, anyway," he said, staring inside the booth. "'Cept for my clothes, everythin' on me was paid for by the king. An' nobody'd want to steal *my* clothes. I think they're older than all of us put together."

Each of the golden cages contained animals of some sort, but they were different from any Ven had ever seen. There were snakes that seemed to be made of jewels, except that they were moving, their silver forked tongues darting. Fish swam in round glass bowls, glittering metallically when the light hit them. Turtles with shells that looked like they were formed of marble lazed in the morning sun. A flying squirrel leapt from side to side in its small cage. A white-coated raccoon with a silver mask and black claws appeared to be making a chain out of yarn with its claws. And in the back of the kiosk, a brown bear with an elongated snout and strangely human paws was sweeping up under the cages with a broom, a chain shackled around its ankle.

The smallest of the cages held soft, furry creatures with glossy coats, tiny claws, and large eyes and ears. Their fur was striped silver and black. They were sleeping, curled up together.

In another larger cage was an odd-looking bird. It had a large curved beak and skinny legs that ended in large feet. It seemed to Ven that its torso was, like the bear's paws, almost human except for being small and covered in red feathers.

In still another cage was a tiny animal that looked like a puffy monkey. The misery in its eyes was unmistakable.

To his left Ven heard a choking sound. He turned quickly and saw Saeli moving closer to the cages, a look of horror on her face.

Within the booth behind the cages was a tall, thin man in a soft-sided top hat with a ratty brim. The man's similarly ratty hair stuck out from beneath it. His eyes were black and twinkling; his arms and legs seemed to go on forever. He reminded Ven of a spider.

On his shoulder sat an enormous black bird with a blue tint to its feathers. It eyed them suspiciously.

As Saeli approached, the man stood up, stretched out his long limbs, and rubbed his gloved hands together.

"Well, good morning, mates," he said brightly. "Lookin' for anything special?"

"Not today, thank you," said Clem, taking Saeli gently by the shoulders and pulling her back. The small Gwadd girl continue to stare sadly back over her shoulder as they headed down the street. The man touched the brim of his cap, smiled, and returned to the depths of his kiosk.

They walked through the town square, past the circles of booths to the street where the permanent buildings stood, the sidewalks in the air above them. Here there were shops, rather than tents, that shared a long common porch, and each had a pretty wooden sign out front telling what was sold within.

They passed a spice merchant's shop with burlap sacks spilling out onto the porch, filled with fat vanilla beans and pungent peppercorns and all sorts of good-smelling herbs. Beyond that was an apothecary where tonics were being sold, a shop with nothing but fudge for sale, and a tailor who was talking to a woman in a nearby shop full of bolts of beautiful silk.

Clem stopped at a table in front of the fabric shop. "Look at this gorgeous satin," she said, running her hand over a sheet of shiny black cloth. "It reminds me of the night sky—you can almost see the stars shining in it."

"Look harder," said the woman in the shop. "You *can* see them."

The children squinted. The silky folds of the fabric gleamed, then twinkled with a million tiny sparkling lights. When they looked again, it had returned to black.

"Come on," Ven said insistently to Clemency, who blinked, then turned quickly away from the table.

"What do you suppose that means?" Nick asked as they came to a large sign hanging over a shop at the corner of first street. It read

### ARMS OF COATES

"That's odd," Ven agreed. "I've heard of coats of arms—it's like a family crest or symbol. The Polyphemes have one. But Arms of Coates?"

"Why don't we go in and see?" Char suggested. "I wouldn't mind being inside about now. All these people millin' around are making me skittish."

"Good idea," said Clemency. She climbed the wooden steps up to the store and held the door open for the others.

As they stepped inside they froze in fear.

## - 8 -

# The Arms of Coates

BLOCKING THE DOORWAY WAS A GIGANTIC GUARD DOG, LARGE enough for Char to have ridden it like a horse. His shaggy coat was brown with black streaks starting at his gigantic jaw that ran from his ears to his tail. The teeth that protruded from that jaw were the size of Ven's thumbs.

*I suddenly wished I had put Saeli behind me. Her entire body would have fit easily down his throat.*

*The muscles under the dog's smooth hide were as big as dinner plates, and tense. His paws were larger than my hands, and the skin of his brow, if that's what dogs have, was hanging down around his eyes.*

*Which were staring intently at us.*

*Behind me I heard Nicholas start to breathe shallowly. I knew without even seeing him that he was white as a sheet. Nick had a bad run-in with dogs just like this and had almost been torn to pieces.*

*I was looking around for a broom, a pole, anything to use when the dog attacked. But it didn't. It stared at us for a long moment, leaned forward and sniffed at Saeli, then turned around and walked back to the store's counter, where it settled back down on a rag rug.*

*Tufts of dog fur exploded into the air as he hit the ground.*

A man with dark circles under dark eyes and hair that matched stood behind the counter, polishing a silver mug. He seemed amused.

"Well, well, what do we have here?" the man asked. He put down the polishing cloth and came out from behind the counter.

With him came a second dog, smaller than the first. His coat looked like butter and cream, and he had a serious face with soft brown eyes and a black nose. His ears were the color of toasted marshmallows, and he trotted toward the children and stopped in front of Saeli. He sniffed her, then Ven, then Char, Clem, and finally Nick, whose eyes were tightly closed.

Satisfied, the dog turned around and went back behind the counter.

The dark-eyed man stopped in front of them and folded his arms. "How can I help you, lads and lasses?" he asked politely.

"We're just looking," said Ven.

"Ah," said the man. "That

would be a good idea. In fact, I advise you to keep your hands at your sides at all times, please."

The children glanced around.

The store was filled with weapons and armor of every imaginable kind. Wicked-looking blades from the tiniest knife to a sword taller than Clem hung high on the walls. Beside them many other weapons were displayed—clubs and maces and crossbows, spears and daggers and axes, and some kinds that Ven had never seen.

Along the walls of the shop were suits upon suits of every kind of armor, some made of shiny metals, others of leather or dull steel rings, shirts and sleeves and gauntlets.

*The man could have started his own war with just the arms and armor in his shop.*

The store owner walked slowly around them, then went over to the window and looked outside onto the market street. He closed the door, turned back, smiled brightly, and bowed to the group.

"Allow me to introduce myself—Mynah Coates, at your service," he said smoothly. "And who might you fine young'uns be?"

"Just shoppers," Clemency said, interrupting Ven.

Mr. Coates nodded. "And how did you get into the Market? They don't usually let children inside."

"Our money was as good as anyone's, I guess," said Char.

"Hmmm." Coates looked out the window again.

"Are you looking for someone?" Ven asked, suddenly nervous.

The man just continued to watch out the window. Finally he turned around and smiled.

"Is there anything in particular you were looking for here?" he asked. "I think most of the items are out of your price range, but I could be wrong. If you can afford to buy Market tokens, perhaps you are wealthier than you look." He stepped away from the window and headed back to the counter.

"Mostly we were just curious to see what your sign meant," said Ven. "Sorry to disturb you—and your dogs. I guess we can be on our way now."

"Oh, Munx wasn't disturbed," said Coates, picking up his polishing cloth and returning to his work. "He was just doing his job—he's my doorbell."

"What's the other one's name?" Clemency asked.

"Finlay," Coates replied. "He was just doing his job as well."

"What's Finlay's job?" asked Char.

The man's dark face lost its smile as he polished. "He makes certain no one brings anything in here that shouldn't be in here." He gestured, without looking, to the walls and the deeper recesses of the store. "While you're here, why don't you look around? There are many beautiful pieces. Just don't touch anything, please—for your own sake as well as mine."

Nick, Char, and Ven looked at each other, and Nick shrugged.

"Can't hurt," he said. The others nodded in agreement.

As they wandered around the shop, Mr. Coates continued to work on his mug. They passed cabinets full of rings with tiny spikes extended, decks of cards and hair combs, pots and glasses and articles of clothing, all of which seemed to have been designed as weapons. All the while they kept their hands at their sides, fearful to touch anything.

Finally Nick stopped in front of a case where a strange metal glove was displayed. Ven stopped, too; there was something about it that made his curiosity burn so wildly that his ears turned red.

"What's this, Mr. Coates?" he asked.

The dark-eyed man put down his cloth again and came over to the case. He took out a ring of many keys, unlocked the glass door, and put the glove on the top of the case.

"Try it on," he said.

"Are—are you sure?" Ven asked.

Mr. Coates chuckled. "*I'm* sure—the question is, are *you* sure?"

Ven thought for a long moment. "No," he said finally. "I'm not sure."

"That's wise," said Coates. "You can never be sure in this place. Now, do you want to try it on, even though you're not sure?"

Ven inhaled deeply. "Yes."

"Of *course* he does," Clemency said to Saeli, who sighed.

Mr. Coates handed him the giant glove.

Slowly Ven slid it on.

*When I put my hand inside it, I felt the strangest sensation—like I was suddenly older, or more powerful. Or maybe it was just that I felt safer, even if I also looked foolish. It's pretty silly for a Nain boy to be wearing a heavy armored gauntlet, something human soldiers use to keep their sword arms from being hacked open.*

*But no matter how it looked, it felt wonderful.*

"Do you want to try it on, too?" Coates asked Nick, who nodded excitedly. After Nick tried it, Char and Clemency each took a turn, while Saeli shook her head vigorously when offered the gauntlet.

Finally, when Clemency was done, Coates put the gauntlet on his own hand. He smiled at the children.

Then he flicked his wrist.

With a *snap*, a shiny metal blade leapt out of the gauntlet.

The children jumped away from the display case.

Coates chuckled. He flicked his wrist again, and the blade disappeared. Then he turned his hand over, made a fist, and appeared to punch the air.

A wide metal spike appeared, with two sharp points, out of the knuckles of the gauntlet.

"In addition to its obvious advantages, this is also useful, when used with its mate, to climb walls and stony cliffs," he said. Another turn of his hand, and the spike was gone.

Finally, he held out his palm as if to shake hands, and extended the thumb. Then he passed his index finger over the tip of the thumb. A tiny flame appeared.

"Flint and steel, good for lighting campfires," he said.

"Whoa," Char whispered, his eyes wide.

Mr. Coates took off the gauntlet and set it down on top of the display.

"That's only a few of the functions," he said as he put his keys back in his pocket. "You're welcome to examine it—you can't trigger the knives or the flame unless you are wearing it." He went back behind the counter and returned to his work.

The boys turned the glove over and began to check out each of the joints, while Saeli and Clemency looked at cases filled with oil lamps, saddles, books, dolls, and hair ribbons, each apparently deadly. Ven could find the slits where the knives had emerged, but Mr. Coates was correct—there were no visible trigger mechanisms that he could see.

He decided to look closer. He unbuttoned his pocket and took out his great-grandfather's jack-rule.

His father's voice rang in his memory, words Pepin Polypheme had said to him on his fiftieth birthday, and later in a letter telling him to follow his dreams.

*Magnus was the youngest in his family, you know. As was my da, as am I. So it's only right that his jack-rule go to you now, Ven. The youngest may be at the end of the line for everything from shoes to supper, but often we are at the head of it for curiosity and common sense. Use it well—it was calibrated precisely to the Great Dial in the Nain kingdom of Castenen, and so it will always measure truer than any other instrument could. It also contains a small knife, a glass that both magnifies and sees afar, and a few other surprises—you will just have to discover those for yourself. If you see things as they appear through its lens, you are taking measure of the world correctly.*

Ven extended the magnifying glass and peered through it at the gauntlet.

He was examining the slit in the gauntlet's wrist when he noticed Mr. Coates was standing over him again, looking at him intently.

"Is that a Nain jack-rule?" the merchant asked softly.

"Ye—yes," Ven answered.

"May I see it?"

*I didn't know what to do. Ever since my birthday, when my father put it in my hand, it had never been off my body, except once to save a tangled kite, and then only for a moment. I had not let it out of my control at any moment. Not while I was floating, shipwrecked, on the sea, or in jail, or even in the presence of the king. I felt sick in the pit of my stomach at the thought of handing over one of my family's greatest treasures to a maker of weapons in a market of thieves.*

*But I also knew as surely as I knew anything that if Mr. Coates*

*wanted my jack-rule, he could take it, whether I refused to give
it to him or not.*

"Please be careful," Ven said awkwardly as he handed the tool
to the merchant.

"Of course," said the dark-eyed man. He opened the measuring tool slowly and examined it, turning the hinges with ease and
familiarity. He extended the telescope and the tiny knife, then
folded it up again and handed it back to Ven.

"I don't suppose you want to sell it, by any chance?" Coates
asked, but with a chuckle in his voice that showed he already
knew the answer.

"I couldn't," Ven said. "Family heirloom."

"Of course," said Coates. "It's a thing of beauty. I've never
seen a real one before, just drawings in books and a few fakes."

Ven blinked in surprise. He had no idea humans had ever
heard of Nain tools. He watched Mr. Coates look out the window again. "Well, we had best be going," he said. "Thank you
for showing us your weapons—they are amazing."

"You're welcome," said Coates.

"Just out of curiosity—how much is the gauntlet?" Ven asked,
knowing that the answer would be far more than he would ever
have.

*Especially now that I no longer had a job.*

"Are you looking to trade?" Coates asked, amused.

"No," Ven said quickly.

"Didn't think so," said Coates. He glanced out the window.

"Why do you keep doing that?" Char demanded. "What's goin' on outside that you're looking at?"

Even as the words were leaving his lips, it was clear that Char regretted them. The shop suddenly went silent. Ven, Nick, Clemency, and Saeli all held their breath in shock.

Coates turned around and regarded Char thoughtfully. He walked slowly over to the cook's mate, who started to tremble, and patted him on the shoulder. Then his hand went a little farther down Char's back.

When he took it away, there was a small black circle of felt on his smallest finger, no bigger than his fingernail.

"What's that?" Ven asked.

Coates exhaled. "A mark. You have one, too, no doubt. Turn around."

Ven tried to look over his shoulder as he spun, but saw nothing. Coates reached into the folds of his shirt collar and removed another felt circle, this one white. Nick and Clemency examined each other's backs, removing similar circles.

"They must have thought you had something especially valuable," said Coates to Saeli. He held up two he had taken off her.

"What does this mean?" Clemency asked, her voice shaking.

Coates sighed. "That the people who go about the market, marking the, er, guests, guessed you had something worth stealing," he said. "But white marks are minor; if you had a red one, now, then you would be a prime target."

"An' how about black?" Char asked.

Coates laughed. "That means they determined you had nothing of value to steal."

"See?" Char said, turning to Ven. "I *told* you nobody'd even want my clothes."

"I thought someone might try to pickpocket one of us," said Ven. "But I didn't expect it would be this bad."

Coates went back to the front of the counter, stepped over Munx, and came back a moment later with a handful of black circles.

"You're in a market of *thieves*," he said. "What *did* you expect?" He stuck one on Ven's back, then turned Nicholas around and affixed one to his shirt. "Why *are* you here, young'uns? Beggin' your pardon, but it doesn't make sense that children who have little or no worldly goods are able to come up with the scratch to buy a token." He patted the ribbon around Clemency's neck as he put a black felt circle on her back.

*I wanted to trust him. I wanted to believe that this kind man with the gentle dogs was a good man, someone who could help me find the answer to the king's question about the translucent stone. He certainly had been polite. But then, so had the woman at the carousel, and the man with the weird animals, and virtually everyone else we had met in this strange, magical, threatening place.*

*A place where unseen strangers had marked us for theft.*

*I had no idea what to think. I was less sure of anything in the Gated City than I had been before I came.*

*Then I remembered what my father had said.*

*If you see things as they appear through its lens, you are taking measure of the world correctly.*

*Trust that curiosity, and your instincts, the king had told me. They will both serve you well.*

*I decided to give it a try.*

Ven opened the jack-rule once more and took a look through the glass.

He tried not to be obvious, looking at the gauntlet one last time before casually lifting the lens and training it on Mr. Coates. He aimed it for his eyes, and when he looked through it, he thought he could see something deep within them, something simple and plain, without reflection or cloudiness hiding secrets. He couldn't be sure, but he thought the look in those eyes was very much like the expressions he saw in the eyes of his parents, or the captain, or Mrs. Snodgrass, or the king.

He wasn't certain why, but it seemed enough.

Ven drew forth the king's stone and handed it to Mr. Coates.

"Do you know anything about this?" he asked.

The weaponsmaker took the glowing oval and examined it for a long time. Finally he handed it back.

"Not really," he said. "If I were a jeweler, or an alchemist, I would say it looks like an instrument used in an assay, to measure or weigh something of value. But to me the markings look like a map of some kind." He went back to the window and looked out again.

"I hadn't thought of that," Ven admitted.

"What do you see when you look at it through the jack-rule?" Coates asked.

Ven looked at Char, who shook his head. "I—er, haven't tried," he said. "Yet, that is."

Coates nodded, still looking out into the street. "Well, you might want to."

Quickly Ven extended the magnifying lens and held up the stone to the light. He examined the strange cracks within it.

For a moment they looked like nothing more than flaws in the stone. Then, just as he was about to put the jack-rule away,

Ven blinked. In his mind he saw the image of dark tunnels, twisting and turning in many directions. It made his head hurt.

Then the picture faded.

"I saw tunnels," he said. "Seemingly endless. Does that mean anything to you?"

Mr. Coates came back to the middle of his shop.

"No," he said. "The only tunnels I know of in the Outer Market are the ones that lead out to the harbor."

"You know about those?" Ven asked, amazed.

"Of course. Everyone does."

"Well, then what's the point of the wall around the city? If anyone can get in or out at will, why all the guards and the locks?"

Coates's expression grew serious. "You're leaping to a lot of conclusions, young'un. There are many layers within any prison; remember that. It all depends on who's guarding what. Not just anyone can go at will out of the harbor tunnels, believe me. If they could, I—" He stopped, then coughed. "I'm sorry I can't help you further, and I wouldn't just be asking anyone about that stone if I were you, unless you don't mind losing it. Perhaps you should go to Madame Sharra, if you can find her, and see if she tells you anything about it."

The children looked at each other.

"Who's Madame Sharra?" Ven asked.

"She's a seer, a fortune-teller of sorts," said Coates. "A Reader, I think she is actually called. You can't always find her when you want to, though many try, believe me. Her deck is one of the most powerful means in the world of predicting the future, finding the past, or seeing your way clear in the present, or so I am told. She might see something about that stone if she does a reading for you."

Ven exhaled. "So I can trust this Madame Sharra? I could ask her about the stone?"

Coates's eyes grew blacker. "You can trust no one in this place, lad. *No one*. Remember that."

"Not even you?" Clemency asked softly.

Coates looked suddenly tired. *"No one,"* he said to Clem. Then he turned back to Ven. "I would not *ask* Sharra anything, lad. A lot of people do, and I imagine she learns a great deal more than she needs to that way. I would see what she has to say to you first before you tell her too much. *If* you can find her. She's found only when she wants to be. Her booth is across the square, by the fountain, between the toymaker and the dream seller."

"Did you say *dream* seller?" Char asked. "How can you buy a dream?"

"You can buy anything in the Gated City, lad," said Coates. "If you are willing to pay the price." He glanced out the window one last time. "I think it's probably all right for you to go. Those that mark the guests should be done by now. If you keep the black circles on your backs, the second team won't pay any mind to you."

"Thank you," said Ven sincerely. "I appreciate all your help."

Mr. Coates smiled. He picked up the gauntlet and looked at it for a moment, then held it out to Ven.

"Here," he said. "Take this. I suspect you will find a use for it someday."

"I couldn't," Ven said. "I can't pay for—"

"It's a gift," Coates said. "For showing me the jack-rule. But don't wear it—put it in your pack. It's a tool, and a piece of protective garb. But it's also a weapon. You don't want to be carrying a weapon, visible or otherwise, in this place. Even the youngest infant who lives within these walls is better with any weapon than you would be. You should never look more ready for a fight than you are, young'uns. It's the best way to get yourselves killed."

He went behind the counter and came back a moment later with a piece of burlap and a length of string, with which he wrapped and tied up the gauntlet. Then he handed it to Ven.

"That's good advice," Ven said. "Thank you—and thank you for the gauntlet. We will try to use it well."

"I have no doubt," said Coates. "Good luck to all of you." He walked over to the door and opened it.

Ven, Nick, Char, and Clem started through it; then Clem turned quickly around.

"Where's Saeli?" she asked.

"Here," came the rough voice that they almost never heard come out of the small Gwadd girl. The children looked into the back of the shop, from where it had come.

Saeli was sitting on the floor, one arm around Munx, rubbing Finlay's stomach in much the same way Mrs. Snodgrass had rubbed Murphy's the night before. Finlay had pulled the blue ribbon from her hair with his teeth and was playing with it, making the little Gwadd girl giggle.

"Seems my doorbell is broken," said Mr. Coates. "All right, miss, off with you now. A few more pats and both of them will be of no use ever again." He smiled as Saeli leapt up and hurried through the doorway, then called one last piece of advice as he closed the door behind the children.

"Stay together, and watch your backs."

Ven lingered on the porch step long enough to hear the words the weaponsmaker muttered to himself once the door was closed.

"Everyone else in this place certainly is."

# The Fortune-teller's Tent

W HEN THEY STEPPED BACK OUTSIDE INTO THE MORNING SUN-light, the Market was in full swing. The shops were busy, all the booths now fully open. Bright music filled the square, and the colored banners flapped merrily in the breeze. Over the laughter and chatter of excited voices came loud shouts.

"Pearls from the deepest depths of the ocean, perfectly round, perfectly white!"

"Ambergris, frankincense, sandalwood, myrrh, sweet perfumes to sweeten your dreams! Get 'em here!"

"Spidersilk! For anything you need to trap. Step up, now!"

"I think this place has an unfairly bad reputation," said Clemency, looking around in wonder. "Look at all this amazing stuff! And the people aren't anywhere near as bad as they've been made out to be."

"You're cracked, ya know that?" Char muttered, stopping to look at the booth of a candy seller in the middle of the square. Great billowing clouds of spun sugar were twirled on sticks next to lollipops that sparkled in colors they could almost taste. "One o' the *first* lessons they teach you in Don't Be An Idiot School is you can't trust anybody in a *thieves'* market. Didn't you hear Mr. Coates?"

"Well, if you can't trust anybody, what about Mr. Coates?" demanded Clem. "He seemed very nice, and very honorable."

"I thought so as well," said Ven. He understood what Clem meant—there was an excitement in these colorful streets he had never experienced, a fascinating display of exotic things that seemed almost as if they had come from his dreams. And the people were beautiful, polite, and kind. His curiosity was burning like wildfire, making him want to investigate every booth, every shop, every alleyway. At the same time, he was listening in his head to all the warnings he had been given. "But Char is right. Even Mr. Coates told us to be on our guard."

"Potions!" shouted the man in the booth next to them. "Tonics for all occasions and needs! You, young folk! What sort of elixirs can I interest you in?"

Saeli stopped in front of a long table that was just below her nose. The rest of them came to a stop as well.

From one end to the other was a tablecloth of sky-blue silk embroidered with gold thread ending in sparkling tassels. Set out on the table was a vast array of bottles, in all shapes and sizes, some clear glass, others solid. The clear bottles all seemed to contain different colors of liquid, some of them with tiny specks of silver or what looked like pearls floating in them.

"What do you have?" Clemency asked, looking like she wished she hadn't.

The potion seller, a bald man with a thick black beard, opened his hands wide.

"Ah, now, miss, as you can see, we have just about anything you could imagine and your heart might desire. You want to be taller, thinner, more beautiful? You want to be stronger, sleep better at night, or go without sleep at all? You want to be able to speak to animals and have them understand? You want to grow a third hand, or an eye in the back of your head, or sprout wings on your feet? You want to make your enemy's ears seal shut, his nose grow a foot long, or his mouth vanish? You want to find something that you lost long ago, have a wish come true, find true love?" His dark eyes sparkled. "Everyone wants that one. Can I interest you in a fine potion to make someone fall in love? It can work on anyone, no matter how reluctant."

"Really?" asked Clem.

"Yes, indeed," assured the man. "Would you like one?"

"Maybe for Char," Clem said, poking him in the ribs. Char scowled at her.

"Char doesn't need that," said Ven merrily. "He's already got Felitza."

"Not for him," Clemency said. "For her."

"How much is the one that makes someone's mouth vanish?" Char asked.

"Twenty gold crowns," said the man. Char sighed, looked at Clem, then shook his head.

"Wouldn't you like to be able to speak with animals, little girl?" the potion seller asked Saeli. "I can sell you a potion that would make it possible."

Saeli just smiled, and the other children laughed.

"Come on, let's keep looking around," said Ven, walking away from the potion booth. "Let's see if we can find the fortune-teller."

They walked past kiosks where giant puppets shaped like butterflies and birds were being sold, past muffin sellers and men wandering the streets with large barrels of roasted turkey legs. Char clutched his stomach again.

"As soon as we find the fortune-teller, I'm gettin' somethin' to eat," he muttered. "This is torture, bloody *torture*."

"Whether we find her or not, we'll have noon-meal after this," Ven promised. "Even though you would still be serving breakfast if we were back at the inn."

They passed a large booth above which colorful kites were fluttering in the air until they came to a huge fountain, splashing silvery water at its edges.

In the center of the fountain was a large display of what looked like dollhouse-sized cottages, stores, taverns, and houses. They formed a street scene very much like Kingston or Vaarn, with hundreds of little human figures positioned in the sorts of places they would be if it were a real city. Groups of toy women carrying baskets seemed to be talking together, toy men on rooftops appeared as if they were fixing the roofs, hammering with toy tools. Mechanical merchants showed their wares to toy shoppers. A tiny wooden goose girl drove a flock of even tinier wooden geese through the streets. All the figures were moving and making sound, apparently powered by the force of the fountain's splashing water.

Many bright coins sparkled at the bottom of a deep channel filled with water around the outer ring of the fountain.

"Do you think this is the fountain Mr. Coates meant?" asked Nick, staring at it.

Clem glanced around. "I don't see another one."

Saeli pointed ahead of them.

"Dream seller," she said in her low, scratchy voice.

The others followed her finger.

A booth formed of deep blue silk stood to one side of a round black tent, its drapes pulled back and tacked with filmy fabric that resembled clouds. Hints of fog swept out from beneath its drapes, and above the doorway a moon-shaped sign read DREAMS.

"Well, there it is, if you're still interested," Clemency said to Char.

"I never said I was interested," Char replied curtly. "I just don't get how you buy a dream. I bet these people would sell a burp if they could get hold of it. And some fool would *buy* it."

"And there's the toymaker," Nick said, pointing to the other side of the black tent. "So this here in the middle must be your fortune-teller, Ven."

"If she's there," Ven agreed. "Mr. Coates says you can't always find her."

"Well, if you're going to find out about the glowing stone, I don't think we have much choice," said Clemency. "Shall we go inside?"

Ven's skin was itching with excitement. "Absolutely!" he said. "Come on."

Unlike the booths to the left and right of it, the round black tent had no sign above it, nor any kind of banner out in front. Waving from the point in the middle of the top was a white flag with nothing more than what looked like a sketch of an eye. In the center of the iris was a star. A flap in the tent hung

open in the front. Otherwise there appeared to be no door.

Ven pulled the heavy flap of the tent aside and stepped out of the way for the others to enter. Saeli looked at him nervously as Nick and Clem went into the darkness, then followed them as Char brought up the rear. Ven stepped in last, letting go of the tent flap.

As soon as he dropped the flap, all but the thinnest line of light at the bottom of the tent drapes disappeared, leaving them all in blackness.

"I can't see a thing, Ven," Clem called from the front of the line. "What do you want to do?"

"I'm not sure this is such a good idea," said Nick nervously.

Ven reached into his pocket and took out the glowing stone. Its light looked a little bit like that of the moon on a misty evening.

"Is this better?" he asked, holding it up.

Once the light was out of Ven's pocket, they could see that they were in the outer ring of the tent, with black walls forming a hallway that circled around. On the black fabric of the walls were black satin symbols, letters in an alphabet or language that Ven did not recognize. There was something familiar about the writing, but he could not place what it was. The symbols were visible only when the light hit them, disappearing into the darkness when it moved on.

"I feel like I've seen this writing before," Ven said quietly. "Anybody else?"

"It doesn't look familiar at all to me," Clem said. Her voice sounded strained. "I don't think I like this place, Ven. It makes me uncomfortable. Maybe we should leave."

"If you want to leave you can, Clem. Anybody else who's nervous should go as well," Ven said. "But this seems to be my best way of finding out about the glowing stone, so I think I'll stay, at least for a few minutes more."

"Well, if you're stayin', I'm stayin'," Char insisted. "Cap'n Snodgrass told me to look out for you, after all. Can't really do that from outside."

They continued around the curving dark corridor until they came to what they thought was the place they had come in. The flap they had come in through was not visible. Instead, there were unbroken walls of fabric, and more corridor ahead of them.

"Madame Sharra?" Ven called. His voice seemed to be swallowed in the heat of the heavy black cloth.

"There's no one here, Ven," Nick said. "I agree with Clem—this place is giving me the pricklies. Let's go."

As the words left his mouth, a golden glow appeared behind the wall of fabric to their left, followed by a rainbow flash, a quick burst of color Ven had seen several times before, once while looking over the wall into the Gated City for the first time.

And once inside the Rover's box.

As quickly as it had come, the colorful burst of light was gone.

The tent wall in that place appeared to be thinner, of lighter fabric. Behind it appeared to be the shape of a very tall woman who, like the king's stone, seemed to radiate her own soft light. The image was fuzzy through the cloth, but Ven could see that her eyes were enormous. She drew aside the drape of the fabric like opening a door.

*Getting a good look at her was far more frightening than being in the dark of the tent.*

*The woman was clearly of another race, one I had never seen, not even in Vaarn, where all kinds of people pass through. She was extremely tall, taller perhaps than anyone I had seen since coming to Serendair. Her forehead was wide, and her face tapered down to a narrow chin. Her skin was gold, not like the golden tan sailors get from being outside in the sun all their lives, but gold like the color of the sun itself. But the most extraordinary things about her were her eyes. They were entirely gold, even the parts that would normally be white on a human or a Nain, with darker gold irises.*

*Her face was completely expressionless.*

*The only thing I could tell for certain was that she was watching me.*

"Madame—Sharra?" Ven stammered.

The woman's eyes seemed to cast around at each of the children. Then she looked back at Ven.

She said nothing.

Ven's skin, already tingling, stung with nervous energy. He tried to look into the dark area behind her, but saw nothing. In the glow that radiated from her he could see the black satin symbols on the tent walls to the left and right of the opening more clearly. The one on the right closest to the door seemed familiar. He concentrated, trying to remember where he had seen it. When he did, his eyes opened wide.

"I know where I've seen that symbol before," he said to Char, who was standing beside him, trembling slightly. "That's the same writing I saw on that thin stone in the Rover's box."

Before Char could answer, the woman's long arm shot out from behind the drape. She seized Ven by the collar of his shirt in a grip stronger than his brother Luther's.

And dragged him into the depths of the tent.

With a soft *whoosh*, all the flaps of the tent slammed shut, plunging the remaining children into darkness where they stood.

# ~ 10 ~

# Madame Sharra

Tell me," commanded the golden woman.

Her voice was soft and clear, with a low music in it, like the song of the wind on an especially dark night. It sounded like it came from another place, another time.

It was also as sharp and deadly as the weapons in Mr. Coates's shop.

From behind the tent walls Ven could hear his friends panicking, calling to him and to each other. Their voices were muffled by the fabric as they stumbled around in the dark.

"Please," he said, his throat tight and dry in her grasp. "I don't know what you mean. Please let me go."

The tall woman's deadly grip tightened, choking off the air in his throat.

*"Where did you see it?"*

Ven's mind was starting to darken. He felt like he was about to pass out. He struggled to remain conscious, fearing what would happen to him and to his friends if he didn't.

"The stone?" he asked woozily.

The golden eyes narrowed.

Ven did not know what to say, but he knew that his life was hanging in the balance now. He decided that a woman who could see the future could also tell if he was lying, so he took his chances with the truth.

"I—I saw something—inside—a Rover's box—" he stammered, his voice coming out in a rasp. He struggled to breathe, but each breath hurt worse. "It was a—a—thin stone—or something like it—sort of gray—with what looked like a picture of a keyhole on it. It—it sparkled—the same way your tent did—when we first—came in—"

"*Where?*" the woman demanded again.

"At the—crossroads," Ven whispered. "Outside—Kingston. The box is closed—now—and buried."

The air rushed back into his lungs as the woman released him.

Ven's hand went to his neck. He rubbed his throat, trying to soothe the sting out of it.

The tall golden woman turned away for a moment, and extended her hand. In it was a thin tablet of stone, about the size of Ven's palm. It was inscribed with the same symbol that was on the flag above her tent, an eye with a star in the iris.

"Give this to the others," she ordered. "Tell them to go find food. Give this to the soup seller, and they will not have to pay."

Ven looked down at the stone in his hand and blinked. "Uh—"

"You came here for answers," the woman said. "You will not be able to hear them spoken above their noise. Tell your friends to wait for you at the fountain when they are done."

"For—for how long?"

"If you still have not come when the warning bell rings, they should make their way out of the gate," said the tall golden woman. "If you still wish to know what you came here to learn, send them away. Now."

I have never been more confused than I was at that moment. A few seconds before I was fairly certain I was going to die in her grip. Now she was giving me a marker so that my friends could get food in the Market without paying for it. In the back of my mind I wondered if I should run, but I wondered if I would get out of the tent alive.

So I decided to do what she said.

And that I really needed to speak to the king about these assignments he sends me on.

If I lived, that is.

"All right," Ven said.

The woman held the tent flap open.

Ven stepped out into the darkness of the outer tunnel and held up the glowing stone. "Char, Clem," he called quickly. "Saeli, Nick, here!"

A moment later all four of his friends appeared, the girls from the left, the boys from the right.

"Blimey, Ven, what happened to you?" Char demanded. "Let's get the heck out of here."

"Calm down," Ven said. "I'm not done with my reading. Here, take this to the food vendors and get that early noon-meal you've been craving. If you show it to them, you won't have to pay."

The cook's mate shook his head in disbelief. "I was wrong," he said. "I must've bought a dream and didn't know it. This one's a doozy. Wake me up."

A vertical line of light appeared in the tent wall in front of them. Ven took hold of the flap and opened it easily. The blindingly bright light of day spilled into the dark tent.

"Go on," he said. "Meet me at the fountain when you're done. If you hear the warning bell, and I'm not back, get out of the Market, and tell Mrs. Snodgrass what happened to me."

One by one, his friends filed out of the opening, looking back at him nervously. Char went through last.

"You sure about this?" he asked.

"No," said Ven. "But go anyway. And take this." He handed Char the wrapped gauntlet, then dropped the tent flap and was back in the darkness once more.

In the center of the tent, the glow returned, joined by more tiny lights. The tent flap in front of him opened, allowing him into the inner chamber. Ven came inside.

The golden woman now sat behind a table made of glass, with smaller movable tables above it, also of glass. All around her inner chamber were candles of different heights, their wicks gleaming with warm flame, releasing a woody scent into the air. The odor of the candles made the thickness that had been hovering in Ven's head disappear, leaving his mind clear.

Beside the table was an hourglass taller than Ven, filled with pure white sand. Ven had seen hourglasses many times, but this one was far larger and more strangely shaped than any he had ever encountered. From the upper bowl a long thin pipe of sorts protruded, like the spout on a teakettle.

In front of the table was a plain black stool made of wood.

"Sit," said the woman.

Ven bowed as politely as he could, considering he had been dangling from her grasp, choking to death, a few moments before.

"First, before I do, are you in fact Madame Sharra? I need to be accurate for my journal."

The thin golden woman smiled slightly for the first time, and nodded once.

"Thank you," Ven said. He sat down on the black stool before the table.

"What do you seek to know?" Madame Sharra asked. Her dark gold eyes glinted in the dim light.

Ven thought about what Mr. Coates had said. "What can you tell me?" he asked in return.

The fortune-teller smiled more broadly. She nodded at the hourglass. "Touch the upper bowl," she directed.

Ven reached out and let his hand come to rest on the hourglass. It was warm and felt tingly beneath his fingers. Then he put his hand back in his lap.

Madame Sharra took hold of the hourglass by the golden handle at the thinnest part of the middle. She shook it slightly, then turned it as if she were going to flip it over. Instead, she poured a generous amount of sand from it onto the glass table through the spout. Then she passed her hand over it.

Before Ven's eyes, the sand took on the shape of an eye.

"Someone is watching you," Madame Sharra said.

"Well, yes," Ven said, trying not to sound disrespectful. "We're in a thieves' market. Apparently everyone is watching everyone."

The golden-eyed woman did not break her gaze away from his. Instead, she passed her hand over the sand again, and this time it took on the shape of a bird.

"Someone is watching you *from afar*," she said pointedly.

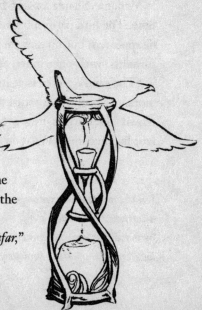

"Oh! You mean the albatross! Yes. That bird is very odd—she's been following me since my birthday, all the way from Vaarn," Ven said. He started to explain to the fortune-teller about how the albatross saved him from the sea by flying in great circles around him when he was adrift, but then shut his mouth quickly. Mr. Coates's words came back to him.

*I would not ask Sharra anything, lad. A lot of people do, and I imagine she learns a great deal more than she needs to that way. I would see what she has to say to you first before you tell her too much.*

The fortune-teller shook her head.

"The bird is just a messenger, the eyes of someone else far away," she said in her dusky voice.

For a moment the only sound inside the dark tent was the whispering of the candle flames.

When Ven could speak again, his voice was higher than it usually was.

"Who—who is watching me?"

Madame Sharra passed her hand over the sand one more time. The bird pattern broke into many tiny such patterns, then disappeared, but no new image emerged. The sand settled into formless swirls once more. She exhaled.

"The sand's power is at its end for you. If you wish to know more, you will have to ask the deck. That will require a gold crown." Her brows drew together when she saw how white Ven's face had become. "What do you fear?"

*I was too upset to remember I shouldn't be asking too many questions. For a long time I had thought that the interest the bird took in me was something special, something that helped keep me from harm. And now I was hearing that perhaps the* albatross was nothing more than a spy for someone keeping track of me from far away.

As disturbing as it felt to discover white circles on our backs, that feeling could not begin to compare to how nervous I was now.

---

"What—what does the person who is watching want from me?" Ven asked, his voice still shaking. "Am I in danger?"

The fortune-teller shrugged slightly. "Has the bird done more to help you, or harm you?"

Ven considered. "The albatross has done *nothing* to harm me," he said after a moment. "Everything she's done has helped me in some way. She saved me from drowning by alerting Amar—" He stopped. "She's just helped me, never harmed me, at least as far as I know."

Madame Sharra nodded. "Then either the person who sent the bird is trying to protect you, or wants to keep you alive until he can kill you himself. Or herself."

"Great," Ven muttered.

"Do you wish me to read the scales for you?" Madame Sharra asked, brushing the sand into a small pile. She snapped her fingers, and the sand caught fire, then vanished in a puff of smoke.

Ven's dismay vanished with it as his curiosity roared back, making him itch.

"Scales?" he asked.

The fortune-teller took hold of the two movable pieces of glass and swung them carefully into place above the glass table.

"The gold crown rests in your left hand, palm up, on this surface," she instructed as she moved the first glass piece into place. "Your open right hand rests here, palm down." She positioned the second piece below his hand. "Here they must remain. You may not touch the scales with anything except your breath. If you do not heed this warning, you are risking a tear in the fabric of the world. And your life. Do you understand?"

Ven hesitated. He was not certain that anything was worth the risks Madame Sharra had just stated, but his insatiable need to know the answers won out. *I can hold my hands still*, he thought. *It can't be that hard.*

"Yes," he said finally.

"The gold crown," said the fortune-teller.

"Oh! Yes, sorry." Ven dug into his pocket for the small leather wallet. To his relief his money was still there. *Thank you, Mr. Coates*, he thought, wondering if the black felt circle was still on his back. He put his left hand, with the gold crown in the palm, on the left piece of glass over the table, and let his right hand rest on the other piece.

Madame Sharra closed her eyes.

A breeze whistled in from beneath the drapes of the tent, snuffing the candle flames. It rustled through Ven's hair, making him suddenly cold, even on this warm summer day.

In the darkness Ven could see nothing but the faint golden glow that Madame Sharra herself gave off.

Until she spread her hands across the glass table beneath where his own rested.

*Fanned out on the lower glass table was a deck of what at first I thought were tattered cards. Then I looked closer.*

*The objects were oval, and about the same size, but irregular. Their edges were finely tattered, and their surfaces were scored with many fine lines. At first they looked a little bit like giant* fish scales, with a slight curve that made one side a little bit concave and the other convex. In the dim light they looked gray, like the stone in the Rover's box had—now I understood that it was one of these things, not a stone at all. One that lay closest to her hand seemed far older than the rest.

When I glanced at them all together, it seemed to me that there were fine drawings on each of the scales, but when I looked closer, I saw nothing.

It was hard to see anything in the dark, with only the tiny orange glow and the smoke from the candle wicks.

Suddenly, one last candle sparked with light before it winked out.

That candle cast a tiny beam onto the table. Colored light, the same rainbow sparkle I had seen the first time I walked past the Gated City, and in the Rover's box, exploded from the cards.

I shut my eyes quickly. Then I opened them again.

When the light passed over the surface of the scales, it looked like it was passing through a prism. Rainbows danced on the table below the glass pieces where my hands were resting, then disappeared into the darkness.

The scales went gray once more.

"Did these come from a—a giant fish?" Ven asked, his eyes still stinging.

Madame Sharra smiled, her eyes watching him sharply.

"Dragons," she said.

"Dragons?" Ven repeated. "These are *dragon* scales?"

"What other sort of scales do you think would hold the power to see the future?" the fortune-teller asked. Her glance was still sharp, but her tone was amused. "They are ancient, from the Before-Time, when the world was new."

Madame Sharra passed her hand again over the array of ancient dragon scales.

"You may select two of the scales, or three, to be read for the price you are paying. The choice is yours. The first scale will tell you about yourself, where you are at this moment in Time. The second will tell you what is coming. And the third, should you choose to accept it, is a gift. It could be a gift of great power."

"Why would I not choose to accept a gift?" Ven asked.

"Most people who seek me do not choose the third scale, for they are unwilling to risk the possible negative aspect of it," said Madame Sharra. "Choose wisely—great power is backed by great consequence. Only you know if you are willing to pay the price for it."

*Suddenly I wished I was home. I wished I was in bed, in the small room I shared with my brothers Leighton and Brendan, who work in the areas of Pitch and Varnish and stink up everything I own. I wished I was working in the nastiest place in my father's factory, or even back in school. When I realized I was wishing for that, I knew how desperately I didn't want to be here.*

"Do I have to decide now?"

Madame Sharra smirked. "When else would you decide?" she asked. "No one who seeks me knows whether he will ever find me again—all you have is this moment. And who knows? You may not even have that if you tarry."

The light glowing from within her began to dim.

"All right," Ven said quickly. "What do I do?"

The fortune-teller rested her hands in front of her.

"Choose whichever scale you wish," she said. "Your hand remains on the glass. Let it come to rest above the one you wish me to read."

Ven slowly let his breath out, trying to concentrate. The cards all seemed about the same, except for the very old one. He thought about it until he realized he was getting nowhere. Then he just pointed to one of the scales in the middle of the outspread deck without taking his hand off the glass.

"That one," he said.

Sharra pulled the one he had chosen from the deck, then passed her hand over it. The card sparkled with the same rainbow flash, and in its light, a picture appeared briefly, little more than an engraved sketch. The edges of the scale glowed pale blue.

"You have chosen the Windmill," she said.

As the words came out of her mouth, the picture on the face of the dragon scale was instantly clear to Ven, a mill on a river with four sheets on blades, turning to grind grain. Then, within the same instant, it was gone.

"What does that mean?" he asked nervously. "Where is this windmill?"

The golden woman shook her head.

"Some of the scales refer to people or things that actually exist, while others are merely representations of something. The Windmill is such a representation. Drawing it first means that at present, you live in a constant state of change. It means that you are someone who unifies diverse people and things. Also that you are transforming, growing and changing." She smiled slightly. "Though you may also run into an actual windmill in your travels. One never knows."

"Well, my friends are an odd group," Ven admitted. "And I certainly am changing. Is this a bad card to draw?"

"The scales do not determine what is bad and what is good. They only declare what *is*," said Madame Sharra. "Before you know where you are going, you must see where you are. Make your second choice. Let us see what is coming for you."

This time one particular card seemed to jump out at Ven.

"That one," he said, pointing, being sure not to take his hand from the glass.

The golden woman passed her hand over the card. It stopped in midair. Ven saw the expression in her eyes change.

"How unfortunate," she said.

## - 11 -

# The Reading

ALL THE COLOR DRAINED FROM VEN'S FACE IN THE DIM LIGHT OF the tent.

He leaned forward to better see what was below the fortune-teller's hand.

The ratty gray scale gleamed brighter for a second, glittering in a rainbow sparkle. The edges glowed with a faint violet light.

On its surface was the sketchy image of a woman in rich robes on a throne, a crown on her head and a sinister smile on her face. In the fleeting moment in which Ven could see the image, the woman seemed ordinary in every way but one.

Her hands, which rested on the arms of the throne, ended in long, cruel-looking talons.

"The Queen of Thieves," Sharra said. Her hand moved away, and the image faded into dull gray again.

"Is—is there such a person?" Ven asked, his voice shaking. "Or is that just a representation, like the Windmill?"

"Both," said Sharra. "The Thief Queen signifies a change of possession. Either you will be gaining something, or losing it."

Ven's stomach turned over, and he felt suddenly like he was going to vomit. "Which one? Can you tell?"

Madame Sharra's smile broadened. "The Queen of Thieves only rarely gives; she most often takes," she said, resting her hands on the table in front of the array of scales. "But again, one never knows until it happens."

"But there is also a person who is the queen of thieves?"

The smile faded from Madame Sharra's face.

"Deep within the Market, past the keyhole gate, is a very different world," she said softly, her tone serious. "It is a place that has lived by its own code of lawlessness since the sands of Time began running through the Great Hourglass. It is an evil and dangerous place, even by the standards of the Gated City. There are many guilds, many families of powerful thugs and cutpurses, burglars and assassins within the walls of the Inner Market, but none is as powerful as the Raven's Guild. Their hideout is Raven's Nest, a place of great darkness, where the most unholy of actions are taken, where the secrets are more deadly than can be imagined.

"That guild has ruled the Gated City since it was founded—and a woman has always ruled that guild. The crown and scepter pass from taloned hand to taloned hand, often mother to daughter. But sometimes a woman of greater skill and even less conscience than the reigning queen takes over the throne and starts a new dynasty. So while your selection of this scale merely means that you will be losing, or gaining, something important to you very soon, there also is such a woman—and she is someone you will wish to steer clear of. I suggest you keep as far away from the Inner Market, and the keyhole gate, as possible. Finish your business, whatever it is, then leave this place, and do not return unless you have to."

"I will," Ven promised.

"Do you wish to draw a third time?" Madame Sharra asked.

"Remember the risk—great power is backed by great consequence. Only you can know if you are willing to accept a heartbreaking outcome in return for such a gift."

What a choice.

I had just heard about the worst news I could imagine—that most likely I was about to lose something valuable. I don't own many things of value. I felt to see if the jack-rule was still there, fearing Mr. Coates might have picked my pocket. It was still there, for now at least.

And I was nervous. I was sweating from every pore, even at the roots of my hair.

But even as nervous as I was, my stupid curiosity was raging. I wanted to tell the fortune-teller I was done. I wanted to tell her I couldn't risk the consequences that might come with a gift granted by ancient dragon scales with the power to see the past, present, and future. I wanted to get up, thank Madame Sharra, and leave with as much of my sanity intact as I still had.

But I couldn't.

Ven's right hand shot out and stopped on the glass over a scale.

"That one," he said. He closed his eyes and swallowed, a sore knot tight in his throat.

The golden woman passed her hand over the scale. The rainbow light flashed, then settled into a violet glow at the tattered edges.

She inhaled, then stared at the scale. She said nothing.

The purple edge of the scale continued to glow.

Ven was silent for as long as he could be. Finally he couldn't stand it anymore.

"Well?" he said, trying to keep his voice calm. "What scale did I pick? And what's going to happen to me now?"

Sharra raised her eyes and met his for a moment. Then she passed her hand over the scale once more, and another rough image appeared, the picture of an hourglass in front of which a pair of scissors was stretched, a thin thread in between the blades. Then, as with the other scales, the image vanished.

"You've chosen the Time Scissors," Madame Sharra said. Her tone was solemn. "I have never had this card selected before—throughout all of history, it has rarely allowed itself to be chosen."

"Allowed itself?" Ven began, then caught the look in the fortune-teller's eyes. "Never mind. What does it mean?"

The golden eyes went to his right hand.

"Look at your palm," Sharra said.

Ven turned his right hand over.

On the palm was a faint version of the same image he had just seen, as if it had been painted on there in very weak watercolors. Ven flexed his hand, but the image remained.

"You have received a very precious and dangerous gift," said Madame Sharra. "All of Time, as it passes, is woven into a giant tapestry, like the threads of a carpet. That tapestry is called history; it is the record of what has gone before, of what has happened in the Past. Good or bad, whatever is woven into the tapestry of history cannot be changed by mortal man, though often it is wished that such a thing could happen."

Ven nodded. He had wished such things himself many times.

"The selection of the Time Scissors, however, grants some-one the power to undo one of the threads of his own Past. This gift will allow you to change something you have done, but only once. It is a power you should use with the greatest of caution, because once you change the Past, everything that has come af-ter that thread will be changed as well. I suspect you will con-template doing it many times before you actually decide to do it, if you ever do. Remember, the longer ago the time thread was woven in history, the more will change if you undo it. Your reading is now at an end."

The gold coin in Ven's left palm vanished.

The image of the hourglass and scissors faded until it was lit-tle more than a slight stain in his right palm.

*I'm not sure how long I sat there, staring at my hand, but when I looked up, Madame Sharra was watching me. Her eyes glowed in the darkness of the tent.*

"Go now," she said. "Your friends are waiting."

Ven rose from his chair. "Where does the power come from that allows these things to happen?" he asked, his hands still shaking. "How can a gold crown buy the ability to undo a thread of Time?"

Madame Sharra passed her hand over the deck and gathered the scales into a pile.

"The power comes from the scales, not the gold crown," she said. "The gold crown is for me. Even mysterious fortune-tellers of an ancient race need to eat from time to time."

In spite of himself, Ven smiled slightly.

"Most of the scales in this deck were given freely by the dragons they came from to do something very noble, something that saved the world," Madame Sharra went on. "Each scale came from a different dragon. A little bit of each dragon's magical lore, the power it could use that came from the earth itself, is still in the scales.

"Each time a new dragon is born in the world, the scales grow in power. That has always been a rare event, but it is even more so now. That power dwindles as each dragon dies as well. One day, as man or Time finally destroys the dragon race, the scales will be nothing more than cards with images on them no one can see any longer."

A stiff breeze blew through the fortune-teller's booth. The tent flap behind him opened.

"Thank you," Ven said awkwardly, still in a daze. "I didn't learn the answers I hoped to discover, but it was an—interesting experience."

"Sometimes the answers we seek are not the ones we need to hear first," said Madame Sharra. "All questions are answered, one way or another, in time."

"I guess so," said Ven. "Thank you."

The fortune-teller nodded.

Ven stepped through the tent flap and followed the light under the fabric walls until he found himself out in the bright light of the Market again.

He paused at the door of Madame Sharra's tent long enough to look at his palm. The faint stain of the Time Scissors was still there, all-but-invisible in the sunlight. Ven stared at it for a long moment, then walked away from the tent, struggling not to look back over his shoulder.

He came out between the booths of the dream seller and the

kite maker, through the bright colors and the sound of merriment and music, to find Char sitting at the edge of the splashing fountain. The burlap-wrapped gauntlet was slung securely over his shoulder. Char leapt up and ran to him.

"How was the soup?" Ven asked.

"Didn' get none," Char said. "You all right? Gah, Ven, you were in there a ghastly long time."

"I'm fine," Ven said. "Why didn't you get something to eat? You've been starving all morning."

"Been waitin' for you," Char said. "I figured we'd go to the pumpkin and get some together once you came out."

"No need for that," Clemency said as she, Nick, and Saeli joined up with them. Ven noted with relief that they all still had their tokens. Clemency handed a hollowed-out gourd full of squash soup to Ven while Saeli gave one to Char. Ven inhaled the aroma. It was sweet, warm, and spicy, all at the same time.

"Thanks," Char said gratefully. He put the gourd to his lips and drank greedily.

Ven tasted his as well. His mouth was filled with warm spices and sweetness with a hint of cream. As he swallowed, he felt the warmth spread through his body. "This is delicious."

"If you like that, you should try some of the wares of the street vendors," Nick said. "Especially the steak on a stake and the giant apple fritters. Come on, Ven, if you're done with the fortune-teller, can we go around and see the sights now? I'd really like to take a ride on the griffin swings or the carousel."

"Sure," Ven said in between mouthfuls of soup. "Why not?"

"Well, did you get the answers to your questions?" Clemency asked as they headed back to where the rides were. "Any luck finding out about the king's stone?"

"No," said Ven. He tossed the empty gourd into a trash barrel and watched Char wipe his lips with the back of his sleeve. "I just discovered that there are far more questions I didn't even know I had. And that we should stay as far as possible away from the Inner Market."

"No lie," agreed Nick. "If you look close just beyond the edge of the Outer Market, everything starts to look pretty shabby and drab. I can't even imagine how run-down it must be beyond the inner gate. No need to find out, I say."

"Me too," said Char as they approached the ride area. "So if she didn't tell ya anything about the stone, what *did* she tell ya?"

Ven stopped in the street. He looked around and, satisfied that no one was close enough to see, held out the open palm of his hand with the stain of the Time Scissors.

"I didn't get many answers," he said. "But I did get this."

Nick, Saeli, Char, and Clem stared at his hand, then looked up at him.

"Got what?" Char asked.

Ven looked down. The image was still there.

"Can't you see the picture?" he asked.

Saeli and Nick shook their heads. "Nope," said Char.

"What picture?" Clemency asked.

Ven looked at his palm again. The image was faint, but still clear. *Maybe only I can see it*, he thought. *That's probably for the best.*

"Step up, gentles!" the barker at the rides called out, his voice cutting through the noise of the festival. "Just a copper piece a rider!"

The friends looked over in the direction of the mythical beast rides. The beautiful young woman they saw earlier that morning was helping people onto the carousel, a flower in her hands, collecting the fares. Two burly men were pushing the griffin swings, which were twisting wildly on their ropes, high into the air amid screams of excitement. Merry music played from the carousel. The floor of the ride had lifted off the ground and was spinning high in the air.

"Come on!" Nick insisted, digging in his pockets. "I have a bunch of coppers left over from buying our entry tokens. Let's catch a ride."

The children scattered, each to his or her favorite wooden beast. Nick waited behind a rope gate for the wild red griffin swing while the others stood in the line for the carousel. Finally, when the current riders had cleared away, the young woman came up to the rope. Her smile was bright in the noontime sun.

"Glad to see you're back," she said sweetly. "A copper for the ride, please."

Nick held out five copper pieces. "Here's the fare for all of us," he said, his face turning red as the woman smiled more brightly and opened her hand to him.

"You want to ride the griffin swing?" she asked, pocketing the coppers.

"Ye—yes ma'am," Nick said awkwardly.

The young woman nodded, then took the beautiful blossom in her hand and held it under Nick's nose.

"Do you like my flower?" she asked. Nick nodded. "Does it smell pretty?"

Nick sniffed, then nodded again. Char coughed into his fist, and Ven suppressed a chuckle. Nick had the same stupid look on his face that Char got when he was around Felitza.

The burly man in charge of the red griffin swing nodded to the woman, and she took down the rope. "You can board the griffin now," she said. "Have a wonderful flight."

"Thank you." Nick scurried over to the swing and climbed into the hollow seat.

Char was next in line. "Can I ride the silver dragon on the carousel?" he asked.

"Of course," the woman said. "Any beast you want." She waved the flower in Char's face as well, then stepped out of the way so he could climb onto the dragon. Then she turned to Ven. "And you, sir?"

"I think I'll ride the winged lion, if that's all right," Ven said.

"Certainly," said the woman. She held out the flower again for Ven to smell it. It was a luscious red, with soft petals and a black center.

From behind Ven's shoulder, Clemency's arm shot out and pushed the stem of the blossom out of the way.

"Uh, Ven, don't do that," she said seriously. She pushed Ven toward the carousel, then let Saeli go ahead of her.

"What's the matter, Clem?" Ven asked as he walked over to the wooden lion with wings.

"You shouldn't be sticking your face in herbs or flowers you don't recognize," Clemency answered. "The Spice Folk use flowers and herbs for all sorts of things, mostly medicines, but for mischief as well. You need to be more careful with what you breathe in."

"You're right, I didn't even think about it," said Ven as he climbed into the lion's bejeweled saddle and took hold of the reins. "Glad you're paying attention, Clem."

"Someone has to," Clem agreed. "And I'm the only house steward here, so it may as well be me."

Smoothly, the carousel began to move, slowly gaining speed as the music grew louder and merrier. Ven held on to the lion's mane, gripping the heavy wooden sides with his knees.

Then, suddenly, it seemed to me that the animal underneath me was running. Not spinning on a giant wooden wheel of floor, but actually leaping and bounding, its wings beating as it took to the air.

I gripped it tighter.

With a whipping spin, the carousel rose up into the air. We had seen it elevate when the last group of riders were on, but it somehow felt higher now. We soared over the trees, looking down at the bright carnival below us. It was a feeling similar to standing at the top of the mast of a ship, looking down at the endless sea and the world below you, the wind rustling your hair and clothes.

I was flying.

I never wanted to stop.

The wings of the lion beat in time to the music as the carousel spun around, thrilling Ven to the bone. He could hear the excited laughter from his friends on the carousel, and the high, wild screaming of Nick as the griffin swings were pushed higher and higher by the burly men.

After what seemed like both forever and no time at all, the rides slowed to a gentle stop. The carousel settled back onto the ground, still slowly spinning. Ven looked behind him to see Saeli's tiny face bright with excitement, her eyes sparkling, as she climbed down from the black unicorn. Even farther back, Clem was dismounting from the sea serpent, looking equally excited.

They stepped off the rides and made their way to the other side of the ropes. Ven looked over his shoulder and stopped in alarm.

Char and Nick were bringing up the rear. Nick looked like he was going to be sick, while Char's face was as gray as a dishrag.

"What's the matter?" Ven asked as the girls turned around. "You guys look awful."

"Gotta sit down," Nick mumbled. "Gonna yak if I don't."

"Here, come this way," Clemency ordered, taking Char by the arm. He seemed to be having trouble focusing, while Nick was growing paler.

"Don't your ears hurt, mate?" Nick asked Ven woozily. "That bloody lion of yours was roaring the whole time. My skull is ready to explode."

"What are you talking about?" Ven asked. "The lion didn't make any noise. You're imagining it."

"No more than I'm imaging my dragon was breathing fire," Char insisted as Ven helped him sit down on a log bench near the toymaker's booth. "I think it burnt my eyebrows off. Look." He wiggled his forehead at Ven, who rolled his eyes.

"You're right about that flower, Clem," he said. "We better get these guys some water."

"I'll do it," Clemency said. "The food sellers are right over past the fountain."

"Thanks," Ven said as Saeli sat down on the log beside Nick and began patting his hand sympathetically.

Nearby a Lirin man in brightly colored clothing was sitting, chatting with a group of children. Ven turned and watched. These were the first children he had seen since coming into the Gated City. After a moment, he realized that none of them had tokens around their necks.

These weren't visitors, or shoppers here with their parents.

These were residents of the Thieves' Market.

His stomach sank. The children were talking happily and excitedly among themselves as they settled down on the ground in front of the brightly clothed man.

They looked just like us, or at least like Clem and Char and Nick. They were all human, as far as I could see, though there might have been a little bit of Lirin mixed into the bloodlines here and there. Their clothes were fairly worn, but not as ratty as Char's were.

I'm not sure what I expected kids in a city of thieves to look like. They weren't cutting anyone's purse, or picking anyone's pocket. They were just sitting on the ground in a corner of the square, waiting for something magical to happen.

Just like we were.

Or would have been if Char and Nick weren't so sick from the ride.

The man in the bright clothes took out a small wooden chest and set it in his lap. With a great flourish, he slowly opened it and waved his hand in the air above it.

Out of the chest flew what looked like many white doves. Ven covered his head, remembering the raven on Gregory's headstone, but the doves floated up into the air at about the shoulder height of the man, in pairs. A closer look showed that they were not doves at all, but *gloves*.

Ven sat back on the log, intrigued.

The man looked down at the children around his feet.

"First, I believe I will recite the story of Ogre Bruce and the Magic Wheelbarrow," he said solemnly. He turned to the gloves. "Maestro, if you please."

The pair of gloves closest to the man swelled until they looked like hands, clapped itself, then raised up its index fingers like the conductor of an orchestra. Immediately, the other gloves scurried into position, hovering in the air. Then the first pair of gloved hands began to move, making gestures that looked like they were drawing anchors in the air.

The remaining pairs began to move in time, one as if it were playing a flute, another a violin, a third a cello. Gloves tapped out rhythms on invisible drums and strummed the air as if it were harp strings.

And as they did, from each pair of gloves came forth music, beautiful tunes in the sounds of the instruments.

Even Char and Nick looked up, entranced. But the multicolored man didn't seem to notice. He launched into his tale, an amusing story of a well-mannered ogre and his ill-tempered wheelbarrow, much to the delight of the audience of children. All the while he was talking, the hand band was providing a musical undertone that exactly matched the action of the story.

At the end, the musical gloves swept to a big finale, then fell silent.

The audience of children applauded politely. Ven joined in, only to receive a sharp dig in the ribs from Char, who was still holding his head in pain.

"He must be a Storysinger, like McLean," Ven murmured.

"*Really?*" said Char. "Ya think so? What gave it away?"

"Thank you, thank you," the Singer said to the children. "And now we will have a Gwadd tale from the Wide Meadows across the Great River, the Sad, Strange Tale of Simeon Blowfellow and the Lost Slipper."

Ven turned around to smile at Saeli. Instead he saw Clem, just retuned from the food sellers, holding two mugs of water. She was staring wildly at him.

"Ven," she said, her voice brittle. "Where's Saeli?"

# - 12 -

# A Prophecy Comes True

*If you ever need to get rid of something in your stomach that is making you sick, have a friend ask you, in the middle of the Gated City, where another one of your friends is.*

*Especially a tiny, timid one who speaks in flowers.*

*And has no thorns.*

Ven was on his feet in an instant, glancing around the crowded market square.

"Saeli?" he shouted, turning frantically and trying to see between the bodies crowding around the booths and kiosks. "Saeli!"

A split second later, the others were doing the same, spinning to see where the tiny girl could have gone. They were shouting her name, pushing through the crowd of children, looking desperately for any sign of the Gwadd girl.

All they saw was the sea of people jamming the square, paying no attention to anything but the exotic goods for sale.

Ven stumbled into the circle of sitting children, causing the Singer's story to grind to a sudden halt.

"Excuse me," he gasped, "have any of you seen a little girl? She was right here—she's about this tall—"

The children stared at him in confusion, looked at each other, then slowly shook their heads.

"Who's missing?" the Singer asked, putting his arm around a dirty-faced little girl with stringy blond hair.

"My friend Saeli," Ven said desperately, watching Char and Nick looking under the skirts of booths, while Clemency was trying to stop passersby, who mostly ignored her pleas. "She's a—a Gwadd, and she—"

A look of shock crossed the man's face.

"A Gwadd? A real Gwadd, here? In the Gated City?"

"Yes," Ven answered, his stomach knotting in fear.

"Since when? Did she come in at the opening bell?"

"Yes," Ven replied. "We all did."

The Singer shook his head sadly. "Surprised she lasted this long." He looked down at the wide-eyed faces of the children sitting on the ground below and smiled. "There's a little girl missing, my lovelies. Her name is—Saeli?" He looked questioningly at Ven, who nodded. "Go through the streets up to the First Row, no farther, and see if you can't find her, eh? If you do, take her hand, bring her here. You'll know her—she doesn't belong here."

The children nodded and scattered.

"She was here?" the Singer asked after the children had disappeared. "In the story circle?"

By then, Nick and Clemency had joined them.

"Yes," Nick broke in. "She was sitting right beside me. I was feelin' kind of sick, an' I wasn't payin' attention—"

"To the left of you, or the right?" the man asked.

"The left," Nick replied.

The Singer looked around, then nodded. "Well, if she was not on the end of the bench, but inside, she must have wandered off. Good as the thieves in this market are, you would have noticed if they reached over you and dragged her away."

"Yes," Nick said. "I certainly think so."

"So," the brightly dressed man continued as Char joined them, "you need to figure out where she went, what she would have gone back to see. What caught her eye? What entranced her earlier?"

The children looked at each other.

"Everything," said Clemency finally. "She was excited by everything. Even the giant soup pumpkin."

The man exhaled sharply, a look of sympathy on his face. He looked around again, as if he were following moths in flight, then reached into the air as if he were catching a few of them. He pulled the invisible strings together with his fingers, then looked back at the children again.

"Well, you know what they say when someone goes missing." His voice had the same ring that came into McLean's when he was speaking as a Singer instead of just as a person.

"No," Ven said quickly. "What do they say?"

The Singer smiled.

"Better call out the dogs," he said knowingly. Then he turned and walked away.

Ven, Char, Nick, and Clem stared after him as he left.

Then they looked at each other.

Without another word, they darted across the square to the First Row of shops, where the weaponsmaker's store stood.

Nick reached the steps of the Arms of Coates first, Char behind him. They burst through the door, shouting as they did.

"Mr. Coates! Mr. Coates! Help, please!"

Clemency climbed up the porch just as the fabric seller next door came to her window and peered out in alarm. Ven, puffing, came up behind her.

Mr. Coates stood in the center of his shop, his hands out in front of him. The dogs stood on either side, their ears back, their teeth exposed.

"Shhhh, now, young'uns," he said softly. "Please do me a favor and don't come slamming into the store like that—for all our sakes." He looked at the dogs, then at the weapons on the wall. Many of them were loaded and pointed directly at the doorway where they stood, like a trap about to be sprung.

"Sorry about that," Ven said. "Mr. Coates, Saeli is lost in the Market."

Mr. Coates sighed, the dark circles under his eyes deep and sad.

"I was afraid of that," he said. "Should'a known when I saw the double circles that nobody could resist a Gwadd. Highly rare and valuable, they are."

"Can we borrow Finlay?" Clemency asked urgently. "Please, he may be the only hope we have of finding her before the Market Day bell rings."

Mr. Coates exhaled again, then looked down at his dogs.

"Well, if you're gonna take Finlay, Munx is gonna want to go, too," he said. "Can't play favorites, you know. Just bring 'em home as fast as you can. Kinda need 'em around here, especially as the day goes on."

The children looked at each other in relief.

"Thank you *so* much," Char said.

"Do you have something of hers that Finlay can smell?" Mr. Coates asked. He walked over to the wall behind the counter. "Hold still a moment, please."

Char, Ven, Nick, and Clem looked at each other.

"I don't," Clemency said as the boys shook their heads. Then a thought occurred to her. "But I think Finlay does."

Mr. Coates gave the wall a solid smack. The crossbows and swords straightened back into place again.

"How's that?"

"He took her hair ribbon," Clemency said. "It's blue, and tied in a bow."

"Ah, so that's what that was," the weaponsmaker said. He rifled through his trash bin and pulled out a soggy, shredded mass of blue goop. "Don't know if any of her scent is still on it, but it's the best we have, I suppose." He snapped his fingers twice. Finlay spun around and trotted over to him. He held the slobbery fabric under the cream-colored dog's soft black nose.

"All right, then, boy, *seek*," Mr. Coates directed.

Finlay sniffed what had been the ribbon carefully. After an agonizingly long few moments, his ears went up, as did his head, and he bolted out the front door, his nose to the ground.

"Better catch up quick," Mr. Coates cautioned. "He will leave you in the dust if he gets a good trail." He tossed Ven the shredded hair ribbon.

"Thanks, Mr. Coates," Ven called over his shoulder as the other three ran out the door after Finlay. He followed them, while Munx brought up the rear, trotting in long, unhurried strides. Tufts of hair exploded into the air with every step.

Finlay dashed through the market, his long, slender body and legs slithering through the crowds easily. Nick and Char struggled to keep up, bumping into the people shopping as they ran through the crowds, with Clem and Ven farther behind.

The dog hurried across the square to some of the first booths they had visited upon entering that morning. He passed the carousel of wooden beasts, now flying high in the air above the streets again, and the griffin swings, until he came to a halt in front of a wooden kiosk hung with purple draperies.

The kiosk was closed down, the draperies pulled shut and bound with rope.

Finlay sniffed in circles, then sat down on the cobblestones of the street and gave a short bark.

"What was this place?" Clemency asked out loud as she came to a stop in front of it. "And what is Finlay telling us?"

"This was the one full of golden cages, wasn't it?" Char said, pulling on the knotted rope.

"Of course! The strange animals!" Ven exclaimed. "Saeli was so unhappy to see them in there. I'm not surprised she came back here."

"But where did everything go?" Nick wondered. "Things sure appear and disappear into thin air fast around this place."

A harsh cawing sound scratched their ears from above. Ven looked up to see a raven, possibly the one that had been on the animal seller's shoulder. It was eyeing them from atop the kiosk.

His anger exploded. He stooped and picked up a stone, then heaved it at the bird.

"You piece of dung!" he shouted. *"Where's my friend?"*

The bird cackled, then took to the air, leaving a stream of white droppings behind on the cobblestones. It caught an updraft, then banked away toward the Inner Market.

Char was struggling with the knot on the draperies.

"Can't—believe I'm sayin' this but—I almost—wish—Ida was—here," he muttered. "She would have this stupid thing untied before her heart beat twice." Nick nodded and began working on the other knots.

"Enough of that," Ven said, still angry at the bird. He got down on the ground and started to crawl under the draperies.

A strong hand grabbed him by his belt and pulled him back out again.

"*Think*," Clemency said in her best House Steward voice. She pushed him backward on the ground. "There were *animals*, and a pretty scary man, in that tent. If you crawl under, you'll have no escape route and you won't be able to see. Take a breath, Ven, and we'll get the rope untied while you do."

Ven exhaled sharply, then nodded. He stood up and brushed the dirt from himself as Char and Nick finished untying the knots and pulled the ropes away. He pulled back the draperies and went inside. Char followed him.

Inside the kiosk was dark, like Madame Sharra's tent. The golden cages were either gone or hanging open, the animals missing.

"Saeli?" Ven called. "Are you here?"

There was no answer.

He took out the king's stone and held it up. The glow filled the dark tent with shadows of cages, making eerie, crisscrossed stripes on the fabric walls.

"Saeli?" he repeated again in the ghostly light.

"Ven, here," Char said. He bent down next to a table of empty cages. "Bring the light."

Ven came over and held the stone above Char's head.

On the ground was a Market Day token on a blue ribbon.

"Oh no," Ven whispered as he picked it up. "Oh no."

A terrifying growl shattered the air. Suddenly the cages tumbled around their heads as the tables were thrown to the sides of the tent.

A brown bear dived at them from the shadows, its mouth snapping wildly. It stood up on its hind legs, then seized Char with paws that looked almost like human hands with claws, ripping his shirt as he twisted away, gouging at him with the teeth in its long, thin snout.

"Ven, run!" he screamed, trying to free his shirt from the animal's claws.

Ven spun around. There was nothing, not a broom, not anything except the cages, so he grabbed one and hurled it at the bear's head. The bear flinched as the cage whizzed past him, then dragged Char closer by the shirt, biting at his throat.

A sudden snarl came from behind Ven, and another flash of teeth and fur leapt at Char.

Ven reached for another cage, then stopped.

It was Munx.

The muscular dog seized the bear's arm in its powerful jaws, throwing his body against the bear's chest. Off-balance, the animal dropped Char and swung at the dog clinging to its arm, growling and yelping at the same time.

Munx responded with a low growl, dragging down on the animal's arm in his teeth. The bear crashed backward onto his back amid the scattered cages, the dog still on its chest.

"Get out of here!" Ven screamed to Char. He grabbed the kiosk drape, spilling dusty afternoon light into the tent. Char, stunned, shook for a moment, then gathered his wits and ran out through the drapes, followed a moment later by Ven.

"What the—?" exclaimed Nick as the two boys came crashing out of the kiosk.

"Run! Run!" Char gasped, grabbing Clem by the arm and pulling her with him away from the booth.

As the children and Finlay dashed away from the tent, some of the passersby stopped in their tracks to avoid running into them.

"What's going on?" demanded a man with a Market Day token whom Char narrowly missed as he darted across the street.

"There's a bear loose in there," Char said raggedly, gasping for breath.

"A bear?" gasped the woman with the man. "Did you say a *bear*?"

Murmurs of horror passed quickly through the crowd: *A bear? Did she say a bear? There's a bear loose! Where? Where's the bear?*

The tent flap rustled.

Gasps of anticipation and fear rang through the street.

A street vendor carrying a pole of pretzels lifted its base, spilling his wares onto the cobblestones, and held it like a weapon.

The tent flap slapped open.

Munx emerged from the tent, trotting smoothly across the street to the children.

The street vendor opened the flap of the tent wide. There was nothing there but scattered cages. He dropped the flap in disgust and looked down at his pretzels on the ground at his feet.

The sounds of shock were quickly replaced by ragged laughter as the people in the crowd went back to their shopping, some chuckling, some rolling their eyes, some glaring angrily at the children.

"Are you all right, boy?" Ven asked, running his hands over Munx's massive head, coating his palms with dog hair. The dog wagged its shaggy tail.

"Hey! You kids! You owe me for those pretzels!" the vendor shouted from across the street.

"I'll get it," said Nick, trotting over with his hand in his pocket.

"No sign of Saeli in there?" Clem asked anxiously.

Ven shook his head. "Just this," he said, holding up the token.

"Where'd the bloody bear go?" Char wondered aloud.

"All the tents and kiosks and stores in this place seem to have escape hatches and back exits," Ven said as Clemency took the token, tears filling her eyes. "Let Finlay smell that thing, Clem. Maybe he can tell us where she went."

Clem nodded, wiping her eyes with the back of her hand. She held the token down to the cream-colored dog.

"Here, Finlay," she said. "Seek?"

The dog sniffed the ribbon, then followed his nose back to the front of the tent again. He stopped, looked up, gave another short bark, then sat down, as he had done before.

"This must be where her scent trail ends," said Ven miserably. "Probably whoever stole her put her in a cage, or carried her, wherever they went, which is why Finlay can't find her scent."

"What do we do now?" asked Nick, looking around. "I'm all out of money, and all I've got is a bunch of dusty pretzels. It's starting to get on toward closing time."

"Maybe you all should go home," Ven said. "I'm not leaving without her, though. I brought her into this madness, and I can't abandon her here."

"Well, I'm not leaving either," said Clemency. "I'm her house steward, and I'm responsible for her."

"Don't even ask," warned Char as Ven glanced at him.

"I want to stay and help look for her," added Nick.

"Maybe for a little while longer, Nick," said Ven. "But I think if we don't find her soon, you should get out of here, meet up with Ida, and go to the constable. Let him know she's missing."

"I can do that, but he can't do anything about it," said Nick. "Didn't you say the king said the constable has no right to come into this place, and no power here?"

"Yeah, unless he's going shopping, that's right." Ven sighed. "All right, well, at least someone should meet up with Ida and get back to the inn to let Mrs. Snodgrass know what's going on. Especially if four of her residents aren't coming home for a week."

"Or longer," Char added gloomily.

*This is just so wrong*, Ven thought. *This is just wrong. What do I do? I wish my father were here.*

As his mind went to his father, he remembered the words in the last letter his father had sent him.

*I hope that the jack-rule survived your ordeal*, Pepin Polypheme had written. *If you see things as they appear through its lens, you are taking measure of the world correctly.*

*I haven't tried the jack-rule*, Ven thought. *I guess it can't hurt to look around with it.*

He unbuttoned his pocket and pulled out the thin folding ruler, then extended the telescoping lens.

Ven peered around through the crowd, through the booths at the shoppers and merchants and goods, but saw no sign of Saeli. Then he turned to the carousel in the distance, and sighted in on the riders aloft in the air on the wooden beasts, laughing or screaming or looking dazed. He scoped all around, but there was nothing visible. Finally he looked back at Finlay, who still sat across the street in front of the tent where the strange animals had been sold. He caught sight of the toasted-marshmallow ears up close, then a gigantic nose, then down to his soft yellow feet tucked in front of him.

In front of which a tiny smattering of dainty blue wildflowers grew in between the cobblestones.

Ven looked harder.

"Clem," he said to the curate-in-training, "come here a minute."

Clemency walked over to him, and he held the glass of the jack-rule steady for her.

"What kind of flowers are those, do you know?" he asked.

Clem peered through the lens. "Forget-Me-Nots," she said. "One of the Spice Folk is Forget-Me-Not. Her brother is Sweet William, but we call him Bill."

Ven's heart started to pound. "Forget-Me-Not," he murmured, "Forget-Me-Not!"

"Saeli!" he and Clem shouted at the same time.

"What?" Char demanded. "What's going on?"

Ven ran across the street to where Finlay sat.

"Good boy," he said, tousling the marshmallow ears. "Good boy!" He pulled the flowers from the ground and held them under Finlay's nose. "*Seek!*"

The cream-colored dog sniffed the blossoms, then took off, nose to the ground, away from the bright booths of the Market square, heading north.

Toward the Inner Market.

"Oh man," said Char as they ran to catch up, Munx loping casually behind. "I was hopin' he was gonna go the other way."

"How realistic is that?" Clem said. The dog came to a halt at the edge of the street.

"Look," said Nick. "More flowers." A tiny patch grew near a hitching post.

Ven took out the jack-rule, looking up the road deeper into the gray streets. A haze was hanging in the air, making it hard to

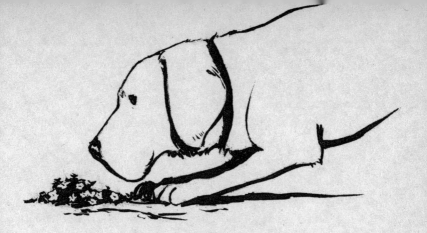

see. But sure enough, all along the street were tiny clumps of fragile blue flowers that grew nowhere else in the city.

Ven glanced to his left.

"If we're going to follow the flowers, we should get the dogs back to Mr. Coates," he said. "His shop is a few blocks over, at the First Row." The other children nodded in agreement.

They hurried back to where the pretty shops lined the edge of the market.

The door to Arms of Coates was standing open.

The woman who had shown them the silk saw them as they approached. Her face went slack; she turned and hurried back into her store, slamming the door shut behind her. The window shade went quickly down.

"What's going on here?" Nick asked nervously.

Ven ran up to the porch and climbed the stairs. He stopped in the open doorway.

"Oh no," he said. "Oh no."

# ~ 13 ~

# The Stolen Alleyway

The trap we had almost set off before had been sprung.

Crossbow bolts and arrows were stuck in the floor. Spiked balls made of metal had been flung into the walls from hidden mechanisms behind the shields that hung from the ceiling. The suits of armor had fallen like dominoes and now littered the floor.

Thin streaks of blood were everywhere.

The back door was standing open.

THE FOUR FRIENDS STOOD, UNABLE TO MOVE, STARING AT THE chaos in what had been a neat and orderly store shortly before.

"Where's Mr. Coates?" Clemency asked softly.

Finlay seemed to be searching for that answer as well. He darted over the threshold, squeezed between them, and began sniffing the wooden floor intently. He passed each of the blood trails after only a quick sniff, then followed his nose to the back door.

Then he gave a short bark and sat down.

Carefully, the four made their way through the mess and joined him.

The back door looked out on an alleyway behind the First Row, into the deeper parts of the Outer Market.

Like the image Ven had seen earlier in the morning when he had looked through his jack-rule, the world beyond the square of tents and kiosks was a gray one, with peeling paint and broken bricks. The neatly cobbled streets of the festival area gave way to a dirt pathway with only a few patches of bricks here and there. The farther in it seemed, the more shabby everything looked. And, as always, a slight mist hung in the air, even in the golden afternoon light, as if the place had something to hide, even from itself.

There was no sign of Mr. Coates.

"What do we do *now*, Ven?" Char asked. "Any bright ideas?"

"Saeli's out there somewhere, either in this part of the Outer Market or, the way my luck's been going, deep in the Inner Market," Ven replied in dismay. "For all I know, the Queen of Thieves herself has her."

"Queen of Thieves?" said Clemency. "What are you talking about?"

Ven sighed deeply. "Madame Sharra let me choose three dragon scales in my reading—that's how she sees the future. The second one, the one that was supposed to tell me what was coming, was the Queen of Thieves. As a fortune, it's supposed to warn that you are about to lose something important—that would be Saeli, no doubt. But she also said that the Thief Queen is a real person who lives deep in the Inner Market, and who rules the entire Gated City. She's supposed to be terribly evil, and terribly dangerous. She warned me to stay as far away from her as I could. So it just goes to figure that she's the one who took Saeli."

"If she did, what are we supposed to do about it?" Nick asked nervously. "Mr. Coates is a bloody *weaponsmaker*, and who knows what even happened to him? We only have a few hours at most to find her and get the heck out of this city. I don't see how that's possible."

"You're right," Ven said, staring at the misty streets behind the shop. "It isn't. So this is what I suggest—you three leave, get to the constable and ask his help. Even if he can't get inside here, he might have some ideas. Then go home and tell Mrs. Snodgrass what happened."

"I told you already, I'm not leaving," said Clemency firmly. "She's my responsibility. So Char and Nick can go, but I'm staying with you."

"Ya know, you really should know better'n that by now, Ven," said Char. "But it's important someone get the word to the inn—and get Ida home. She's prolly fleeced the whole city of Kingston by now, and they'll be lookin' to hang her in the morning."

"Nick, will you do that?" Ven asked, turning away from the dismal alleyway.

Nick sighed. "Sure, if that's what you want. I'll do my best to see if I can get someone back here before the Market closes. I'll try the constable first, and if he won't help, I'll get to the inn as fast as I can. And then I'll come back to town for Ida. She's not supposed to meet us for a while, so I can't take the time to look for her in Kingston."

"Thanks," Ven said. "Be careful on your way back across the floor, then head straight through the center of the town square until you get to the main gate. Don't stop for *anything*."

"Right. Stay together, you guys," Nick said. He clapped Ven on the shoulder, then inched his way back through the bloodstains and the fallen axes until he got to the door. Then he waved one more time and disappeared into the color and noise of the Thieves' Market.

The three remaining friends went down the back steps into the dreary part of the Outer Market past the First Row and onto the main street that ran north. Each of the side streets of this main road had signs—CUTPURSE ST., BURGLARS ROW, COIN RD., and the like. Even the alleyways were marked—FEVER LN., DARK A'WAY, PINCHER A'WAY.

As they walked, they passed many people, a few of whom had tokens around their necks. They were visiting shops and houses that were much seedier than anything in the bright market, their eyes darting around as if they wished not to be noticed. Children were more abundant here, running between the decaying buildings, playing hoop toss or tag, but none of them wore ribbons around their neck with the ticket out of the Gated City.

"Where do you even begin to look for a stolen person?" Clemency said aloud. "It would take us months, maybe even years, to look in every one of these places. She could be *anywhere*, Ven."

A tattered old woman passing by stopped in the street next to them.

"Sorry, dearies, did I hear ye say you'd had somethin' stolen?"

The children stopped. "Yes," Ven said, unsure of the wisdom of doing so.

"Well, then, ya might try lookin' in the Stolen Alleyway."

The three children followed her finger with their eyes. She was pointing past a large, open well in the middle of the road to a dark side alleyway off the main street, where a thin vapor of mist appeared stuck between the buildings. At the opening of the alleyway there was a sign.

STEAL A'WAY it read.

The old woman wiped her nose with the back of her tattered sleeve. "If yer looking fer somethin' that was stolen, ya best check there first, laddie," she said, her black teeth glistening in her mouth beside the holes where there were no teeth at all. "That's the place where stolen things are sold."

"Isn't everything in a Thieves' Market stolen?" Clemency asked.

The ragged woman drew herself up as tall as she could and snorted in contempt.

"That's a lie," she said angrily. "Not everyone in the Gated City's a thief. Some of us's just the kin o' thieves from long ago. Many honest folk works here in the Market." She seemed to reconsider her statement. "Well, maybe not *many*, but there's some here and there. Now, git." She shooed them away with her fingerless-gloved hands.

"I—I'm not sure about this," Char said nervously. "That place looks even creepier than the rest of this creepy city."

"Come on," said Ven impatiently, starting for the alley. "We don't have time to waste—if Saeli's in there, we have to get to her before she's sold. Let's go."

Clemency nodded and followed Ven, with Char catching up a moment later.

As soon as we stepped onto the sparse cobblestones of the Stolen Alleyway, I could understand why Char hesitated. It was almost impossible to see the buildings in the mist, but what I could see looked dark and abandoned, even in daylight. The street itself was winding, and curved off into the fog.

People were walking along the alleyway, stopping at the booths and tents that lined the street, just as they did in the circles in

*the square of Outer Market. But these shoppers were different.*
*Unlike the people wandering the brighter parts of the Gated City,*
*glancing at all the different wares, these people seemed as if they*
*were looking for something specific. They also seemed much more*
*nervous, much more desperate.*

*We understood how they felt.*

The booths of this alleyway were not so brightly colored as the
ones in the main streets. Instead of the carefully painted banners
and the carved boothplates there were simple signs above each
stall made from ragged gray cloth, each bearing the name of the
goods offered, printed on them in ink.

Char and Clemency stopped in the middle of the street as
Ven approached the first booth. He squinted to read the sign.

### KISSES

Ven's eyes moved down from the sign to the person sitting beneath it.

A white-haired woman, or what appeared to be a woman,
grinned back at him toothlessly, the wart on her chin sprouting
hairs as long as the ones on her head.

Ven backed away in alarm.

Clem grabbed his arm and led him deeper into the alleyway.

"Might want to avoid that one," she said.

"Er—yes." Ven coughed.

"This is the oddest place I've ever been, and I've been in
some doozies," Char muttered as they made their way past the
huddled shoppers, looking at the strange booths and the signs
above them.

"What can this possibly mean?" Clemency asked as she read more of the signs on the booths.

THOUGHTS

MOMENTS

GLANCES

"They're all things that can be stolen, just like actual stuff," said Ven, passing a gray rag banner reading DREAMS. "Stolen thoughts, stolen moments, stolen glances, stolen dreams—I've heard of all those things, but I never thought they could be resold."

"Well, if you ever had a kiss stolen, you can go back an' get it from her," Char said, pointing over his shoulder at the booth where the warty old woman had been. "But she can *have* the one Lucy Dockenbiggle took off 'a me when I was nine, thanks anyway. I can't believe anyone would buy that one—it was pretty awful."

"Who is Lucy Dockenbiggle?" Clemency asked.

"Keep moving," said Ven under his breath. "I don't think we want to linger long here."

They continued down the Stolen Alley, past signs for YOUTH, KNOWLEDGE, IDENTITY, and TIME. Some of the booths were empty, while others had a single person sitting within them, waiting for customers. Ven slowed down for a moment in front of one reading SHIRTS. Within the drapes of that stall they could see shirts of all sizes and colors hanging, flapping gently in the foggy breeze.

"This one doesn't make sense to me," he said, coming to a halt.

"Shirts? What is this doing in the Stolen Alleyway? Shouldn't it just be in the Outer Market with all the rest of the goods?"

"No," Char said, tugging at his arm. "Haven't ya never heard of someone losin' his shirt? It means he got taken for *everything* he had. I don't think we want to be near this booth especially."

"Yes, my guess is that the residents of this place could steal the shirts from our backs and we might not even notice," added Clemency. "Keep moving."

"I only see three more booths anyway, and no sign of Saeli," said Ven anxiously. "It was probably a mistake to come here."

They hurried down to the end of the alleyway, passing booths for stolen IDEAS and FUTURES, until they came to the last stall on the street. The ratty gray sign read

### CHILDHOOD

"Saeli!" Ven shouted, looking up and down the street. His word seemed to be almost instantly swallowed; it did not echo as it should have.

"Let's get out of here," said Clem, glancing around. "She must be somewhere else. I think we should look for a flower seller—that's the kind of person who might make use of a Gwadd."

"Yeah, let's go," Char urged. "I wanna go back to the normal part of the market, where everyone is just a thief looking to take your money. This place is givin' me hives."

Ven nodded, and turned to head back out the way they came. Just as he did, he and the other children heard a soft female voice behind them call out.

"Char!"

The three turned around in shock.

There was no one in the street looking their way, just the same shoppers with their heads down, their eyes averted, milling through the alleyway toward the booths they sought.

"Saeli?" Char called.

"Over here," replied the voice. It was coming from within the last booth, the one labeled CHILDHOOD.

"Saeli!" Ven shouted again, as the three ran toward the booth.

Just as they came to within a few feet of it, the drape in front was pulled back. Inside the booth was a young woman with dark eyes and hair, and a bright, warm smile. Her eyes never glanced at Clemency or Ven, but rather went directly to Char. Her smile widened.

"Char," she said. Her voice was soft and warm in Ven's ears.

Char's face was as white as snow.

"How—how do you know my name?" he stammered.

---

*I thought back to something McLean once told me when he called me by name even before being introduced to me. He said that once I had spoken my name in the inn it was on the wind, and could be heard by Storysingers and other people who know how to listen to what the wind hears.*

*The young woman in the booth might have been part Lirin, though she seemed very human. Perhaps she was a Singer, but my guess was that she was not. Singers take an oath to always tell the truth, and I had my doubts that anyone in this alleyway could have ever made good on that promise.*

---

The young woman looked for the first time at Ven, then at Clemency. Then she shook her head.

"No, I'm sorry, I have nothing for you two," she said briskly. "You must both have had happy childhoods—or acceptable ones." Her attention returned to Char. "But you, now—you were robbed of yours fairly early, weren't you, Char?"

Ven glanced at his friend. Char was trembling violently.

"Let's go," he said, taking him by the shoulder.

"Wait!" said the young woman quickly. "If you leave now, Char, you may never get the chance to find it again."

Char's eyes were focused straight ahead. He shrugged off Ven's hand and walked slowly up to the booth.

The woman within the stall smiled again. She reached under the counter and pulled out a tiny glass box with a purple oval stone set in the top.

"How—how much?" Char asked, his voice shaking.

"Char—don't," Ven said, but his words seemed to be swallowed again by the mist in the alley.

The woman's smile grew brighter, and her cheeks took on a rosy glow. "For the whole box—one thousand gold crowns," she said sweetly.

Char's face went slack. "I—I don't have that kind of money," he whispered. "I prolly won't see that much in my whole lifetime."

The woman nodded. "Some people are willing to spend everything they gain in a lifetime to recapture their lost childhoods," she said. Her voice was smooth as caramel candy. "That's a high price to pay. But for a single gold piece, I would be willing to let you see a moment of yours."

"I—I—"

"Leave him alone," said Ven angrily. "You're a cheat and a charlatan! Nobody can buy back childhood. Come on, Char, let's get out of this place."

"Shut up!" Char snapped; his eyes were glowing with interest and fear. He fumbled in his pockets and produced the single gold piece the moneychanger had given him, then held it out, his hand quivering, to the young woman.

Her hand shot out quickly, like all the other hands of the sellers in the market, and snagged the coin. Then she slid the box with the purple stone forward on the counter.

"Go ahead," she said. "Have a peek."

Slowly Char took hold of the top of the box and raised it.

Ven looked inside. There was nothing in it, just a velvet lined bottom the color of a cloudless sky.

"You tricked him," Clemency accused. "Give him back his gold piece."

The woman's smile grew brighter still. She looked at Char, who was staring into the box, his eyes glistening.

"Do you want your coin back, Char?" she asked, amused.

"No!" Char gasped, his voice harsh. "Shhhhhh."

*I have no idea what he was looking at. The box was empty; I could tell from Clem's expression that she was seeing it the same way I was. But Char continued to stare into it, his eyes gleaming, until the young woman slammed the top down. Then he looked as if he had been slapped across the face.*

"That's all one gold piece buys you, I'm afraid," she said to Char regretfully. "But you can take it if you want."

She opened the box again. Char reached in quickly, and pulled his hand back as she closed the top again, gently this time.

"I—I could work for it," Char said. Ven was alarmed by the intensity in his voice. "I can cook, an' I have experience as a deckhand—"

The woman nodded thoughtfully. "I suppose we could arrange something like that."

"No! Char, snap out of it!" Ven shouted, shaking his roommate by the arm. With Clem's help he dragged Char, struggling, away from the table, away from the woman with the warm, black eyes, down the street of the Stolen Alleyway, and back into the bright light of the late afternoon in the open air of the Outer Market.

Ven did not stop until he had reached the well in the center of the street. He pushed Char down onto the well's rim, then hauled up a bucket and splashed the water from it in his friend's face.

"What happened?" he asked as Char shook his head, spattering drops of water everywhere. "What did you see in that box?"

Char looked down at the cobblestones of the street.

"I can't explain," he said finally. "Happy times, the warm grass—maybe a picnic. Images of things in my memory that didn' make no sense at the time, and don't now. But they were *real*; she wasn't fakin' me. Especially this." He opened his hand.

In it was a red glass bead.

"I remember this," Char continued. "I'm not sure how, but I remember being held and playing with this. Maybe a whole string of 'em." He turned the bead over in his hand. "And the smell of lemon and roses. I remember that still, too. Whoever was holdin' me smelled like lemon and roses."

"Did you see anyone's face?" Clem asked.

Char shook his head.

In the distance, near the main gate, a bell clanged harshly.

All around them, the visitors to the Gated City looked up, checked the tokens around their necks, and began finishing up their shopping.

"That's the warning bell," said Clemency, looking nervous. "One hour, and the city closes for a whole week."

"We can't abandon Saeli here," said Ven. "She'll never get out on her own. We have to keep looking."

"There's no way Nick made it back to the inn already," added Char. "And even if he did, no one's gettin' back here before those bloody gates close."

"Where do you suppose the constable is?" Clem asked as a group of shoppers stopped for a drink at the well before heading to the gates.

"Feedin' whoever's in the jail supper about now," said Char. "He's not comin' in here. He's got no authority here, anyway."

"I hope he's not feeding Ida," said Clemency. "If she got arrested for stealing, that would just make our day perfect."

Ven ran his hand over his chin, stopping to rub the single whisker on it.

"She's not in jail," he said. "She only gets caught when she wants to." His head began to itch fiercely. "You know, maybe she *wasn't* lying. Maybe when she said she knew her way around the Gated City, she was telling the truth."

"Well, that would be a first," muttered Char. "You think a street kid with no money has been inside a market that costs ten gold crowns to get inside 'a bajillion times'?"

"Maybe not a bajillion," said Ven. "But maybe *once*. I don't know—it doesn't make sense, but there's no harm in trying at this point. For the next hour we need every pair of eyes that we can get."

"I'll go get her." Clem stood up and pulled Char up from the well's edge with her. "I can be back in fifteen minutes. I know all her favorite hunting grounds in Kingston." She held up Saeli's lost token. "I'll need to use this to get her in, so we may have some trouble getting everyone out. But we can jump off that bridge when we come to it. In the meantime, you two keep looking for Saeli. We'll meet by the soup pumpkin in the market square."

"Go," Ven agreed. His gaze wandered to the ladders that led to the streets in the air. "I think maybe we need to be looking at things from a new angle."

# - 14 -

# The Skywalk

We walked Clem as far as the center of the square in the bright Outer Market. We could see her get all the way to the gate from there, which made Char and me feel a little bit better. We had been told over and over again to stick together, and all we had done was split up. I wanted to make certain Clem at least got out, and didn't get stolen as well.

Now there were just the two of us, Char and me, alone in the Market.

**N**OW THAT THE WARNING BELL HAD RUNG, THE FESTIVAL NO longer looked the same as it had in the bright morning sun.

The shops and the kiosks had begun to close. The colorfully dressed street people looked sweaty and tired, their clothes soiled after a long day. Instead of the bright smiles they had worn that morning, their faces were grimly set as they worked to complete the breaking down of the festival. The streets were covered with litter.

The two boys passed the food merchants, who were putting away their wares. The appetizing smells from earlier in the day had given way to a sick, greasy stench of doused charcoal and bleach.

Two men were taking apart the soup pumpkin. What that morning had appeared to be an enormous shell of a real giant squash actually was nothing more than a big metal pot, like a tin bathtub, with molded paper around it to make it look as if it had been real.

Char sighed in disappointment.

"Well, the soup tasted good, anyway," he said. "Even if it really wasn't a magical soup pumpkin."

"When I first went to see him, the king said something about court magicians and the real magic in the world," Ven said as they hurried past barkers and street folk carrying away boxes and bins of sad-looking hats and toys. "It's hard when you realize that most of the 'magic' that you see is fake."

He thought back to the king's words as they sat alone in the Royal Puzzle Room.

*My father had a court full of magicians and conjurers, as did his father before him, and every other high king in history. I sent them all away when I became king, because I saw what they did as tricks, as amusement. I kept my Viziers—they are advisers who can see things that others can't. The chief Vizier, Graal, is very old, and very wise, and Galliard is his student, also very knowledgeable. But all the men in funny hats making snakes out of silk scarves that used to work in the palace are now out there among the people, entertaining children with their tricks. Because, as king, I only wanted to see the real magic in the world, so that I could learn from it, and preserve it.*

"It's pretty weird having a friend your age who goes and chats regular with the *king*," Char said grumpily. "Just about now, I'm kinda wonderin' how good a friend of yours that king really is, considerin' he sent us in here in the first place."

Ven stepped over a mound of soiled paper cones in the street that had once held fried apples.

"No, he didn't," he said, his eyes scanning the buildings at the harbor side of the square in the First Row. "I think I am beginning to see why he fired me, though. Maybe he could only suggest I come here as my friend, not as the king, because he couldn't be responsible for what might happen."

"Well, that's pretty *sick*," said Char. "If a king can't be responsible for somethin', who can be? Hey—where are we goin', anyway?"

Ven looked both ways before crossing the street to the side of the First Row that ran north along the harbor.

"Remember how I said we might need to look at things from a new angle?" he asked.

"Yeah?"

Ven stopped in front of a wooden ladder that went up to the elevated street he had seen earlier that morning. A sign next to it with an arrow pointing up read *SKYWALK*.

"How about a bird's-eye view? What do you say we take a look for Saeli from up here?"

Char's thin face brightened. "That's a *great* idea, mate!" he said. "We might actually see somethin' from above. Good thinkin'."

"Don't get too excited yet," Ven said. "One step at a time."

Quickly, like they were summiting the mast of the *Serelinda*, the two boys climbed the ladder up to the walkway above the street.

When they got to the top, they had to stop in amazement.

The rooftops of the Gated City seemed to hold a totally different world from the one that was visible from the streets. Past the beautifully carved arches at the front of the roofs that could be seen from below were gardens blooming with flowers, many with neat rows of vegetables and even small fruit trees. There were pathways between the housetops, all of which stood side by side with no alleyways between. Some of the children that had been listening to the Singer's tales were running between the house roofs, playing.

A fresh breeze blew here that was missing in the streets, free from the walls that surrounded the lower part of the city. In the distance he could see the top of the northernmost light tower of Kingston harbor, far away.

*How sad it must be to live so close to the sea, and yet be held prisoner within tall walls with archers*, he thought. The sea where he lived in Vaarn had always called to him, singing him songs of adventure, of lands beyond his hometown. He listened to it every night when he was falling asleep, dreaming of other lands, other places he wished to see. He wondered if the residents of the Gated City wished for that adventure as much as he had.

From above they could see the last of the Market Day visitors heading out of the city, while more and more workmen were taking the festival apart. He tried to look beyond the gates for a sign of Clemency or Ida, but could see nothing due to the presence of a very large guard tower near the Kingston end of the Skywalk.

Ven turned around and looked the other way, where the Skywalk led deeper in, north, toward the Inner Market.

The houses began to fade past the First Row, taking on the decaying gray look they had seen out behind Mr. Coates's shop and in the Stolen Alleyway.

"This way," he said to Char, who sighed and nodded.

The elevated wooden sidewalk had no handrails, no edges. It was as if a giant had ripped a pier out of the harbor and had placed it at the level of the roofs. The planking bounced and swayed beneath their feet as they walked, two floors above the street.

"It's a really good thing you started life as a sailor, Char, and that I grew up in a shipbuilding family," said Ven as he made his way down the Skywalk.

"Why's that?" Char asked, hurrying after him.

"Because we've both had a lot of experience climbing rope riggings and on moving decks," Ven said. "The Skywalk is clearly not intended for visitors. Regular people up here wouldn't have a chance—between the lack of a railing and the wind, they would fall to their deaths. This is meant to be a tool for the *thieves*, not the common folks from Kingston." He glanced around. "In fact, at this point it's probably a good idea to hide our Market Day tokens. By now everyone who lives here expects the visitors to be gone. We probably don't want to stand out if we don't have to." He took the ribbon from around his neck and stuffed it into his pocket.

"Right," Char mumbled as he did the same. "An' people are more likely to try an' steal 'em from us now."

They passed the east-to-west end of the First Row, where Mr. Coates's shop and the fabric store stood, then the alleyway behind it, where the streets began to fade to gray.

They stopped when they came to the area above the Stolen Alleyway. Ven could see the mist from a distance of about two streets away. Even from above, it clung to the buildings there, hiding whatever was within the alleyway from view.

At the edge of his vision he could see another wall like the one that surrounded the city, this one running east to west, inside, across the whole of the Market. It, too, had guard towers. The Skywalk seemed to end a few dozen feet before that inner wall, dropping off to the cobblestones below.

In the middle of the wall was a guarded gate.

Shaped like a keyhole.

Ven's blood ran cold.

"Oh boy," he whispered to Char. "That's it—that's the Inner Market."

"Well, maybe Saeli's still somewhere in this part of the Outer Market," Char suggested. "Take a look through the jack-rule and see if you can find any more of the flowers she was droppin' like bread crumbs."

Ven looked behind him to make sure they were still alone on this part of the Skywalk, then pulled the jack-rule from his pocket. He extended the telescoping lens.

He scanned around the broken road of the Outer Market until he found the second of the patches of Forget-Me-Nots that Finlay had sniffed out. From there he looked for, and located, the next patch, and kept following along until he was looking into the Inner Market.

Where a small mound of them grew in the center of the street beyond the gate.

Ven sighed. "She's past the gate somewhere. Now I have no idea what to do."

Whatever Char said was lost in the cry of a seabird overhead.

The boys looked up. High above, the albatross swooped in from the harbor side, flying smoothly over the wall and into the skies above the Gated City.

"There it is again." Ven crouched down on the boards of the Skywalk, gesturing for Char to do so as well.

"Why are you hiding from a bird?" Char whispered as they squatted down.

"Madame Sharra says it's a spy for someone who is watching me from far away," Ven replied anxiously. "I think it's a friendly someone, but I can't be sure. She said that person is either trying to protect me, or to keep me alive until he—or she—can kill me personally."

"Great," said Char. "Well, at least being your roommate is never boring."

The bird headed to the middle of the city, then began to fly in circles over and over again. Ven sighted the jack-rule lens on it, then moved it down to see what it was flying over.

The lens reflected an up-close view of the keyhole gate.

"Oh boy," he murmured. He looked closer.

Standing at the gate was a tall man, or what Ven assumed was a man, in a long gray hooded cloak. The garment covered him from his head all the way to the ground, strange clothing for the heat of early summer. His back was turned to Ven as he spoke with the gate's guard, a thin, swarthy man with long black hair. On the wall above, archers in ragged leather had their bows trained on him, as they did on each person who presented himself at the gate.

Ven strained to look closer.

The gate guard finally nodded, signaled to the archers and the two huge men standing at either side of the keyhole-shaped entrance, and opened the steel gate for the man to enter. As he did, Ven caught sight of a slightly hooked nose, or at least thought he did.

A harsh bird cry sounded. Ven looked up, out of the jack-rule's lens.

The albatross made one more circling pass, then flew out to sea again.

Behind it was a low-flying squadron of black birds, glinting blue in the late-afternoon sun. They flew as far as the harborside wall, then circled back and returned to the depths of the Inner Market.

"Did you recognize the man?" Char asked after Ven related what he had seen.

Ven shook his head. "It was just a nose—and many of the humans I've seen since I came here seem to have hooked noses. Lots of people in the Market do."

"Maurice Whiting has a hooked nose," said Char.

Ven stared at his friend. He had not thought about Mr. Whiting since they passed the White Fern Inn, but Char was right—one very prominent feature on his face was a great hooked nose.

Ven shuddered. He had hoped that he was finished with Mr. Whiting, ever since the man had accused him of terrible crimes and had had him arrested. The king had seen through Mr. Whiting's lies, but Whiting had warned Ven that their interactions were not finished as he left the Crossroads Inn for the last time.

*This isn't over, Polypheme.*

*It's never over with men like you until you die, Mr. Whiting,* Ven had replied. *Fortunately, as a* Nain, *I will outlive you by four times over.*

Whiting had stared at him intently for a long moment. *Perhaps,* he said finally. *Perhaps not.* Then he stalked up the steps and slammed the inn door behind him as he left.

"I hope that's not Mr. Whiting," he said. "That would make an impossible situation even worse. If that's possible."

"We should get back," Char said, glancing at the setting sun. "Clem's prolly back by now."

"You're right." Ven rose carefully and waited until Char was standing as well, then hurried off down the Skywalk, back into the center of the Outer Market.

Clemency and Ida were searching the alleyways of the Outer Market when they returned. The boys climbed down a different access ladder and ran to meet them.

"Don't bother looking there," Ven called to the girls. "She's inside the Inner Market, past the keyhole gate."

Clemency's face went slack. Ida just exhaled.

"Oh, no," Clem whispered. "You're sure? What are we going to do now?"

"I don't have any idea," Ven admitted. He looked at Ida, who was wearing Saeli's token around her neck. "Thanks for coming in to help look, Ida." The girl nodded curtly. "I think you both ought to get out of here while you can. Go back to Mouse Lodge, and make sure Nick got home."

A harsh clanging shattered the air. The children looked out of the alleyway toward the great town gate as it slowly closed, slamming shut with a terrifying *thud*.

"Bright idea, Ven Folly-scheme," Ida said. "Little too late, though, doncha think?"

"Well, that's it," said Char dismally. "Any chance we had of gettin' out of here just disappeared. I guess we should find somewhere to hide for the night an' start working on findin' her in the morning. I don't think we're safe in the dark in this place."

Ida chuckled sourly. "*You* wouldn't be safe in this place in broad daylight, surrounded by an army." She turned away and started up the main street toward the Inner Market.

"Ida, where are you goin'?" Char demanded, chasing after her. He grabbed for her wrist, but she twisted away, knocking him onto his backside with the movement of her arm. Ven and Clemency exchanged a glance, then followed her, Ven stopping long enough to pull Char from the ground.

She walked resolutely down the main central street, out of the festival square and into the gray, decaying part of the Outer Market, all the way up to the keyhole gate. The other children trailed behind, exchanging confused and terrified glances.

Ida stopped at the gate, directly in front of the swarthy man with long, greasy black hair. She stared at him for a moment, then took a deep breath.

"I want to see my mother."

# -- 15 --

# Beyond the Keyhole Gate

I did *not* want to hear those words.

I cannot tell you how much I did not want to hear those words.

Those were about the last words in the world I would ever want to hear.

Up until that moment I had believed Ida was an orphan, like Char and Cadwalder and most of the other kids in Hare Warren and Mouse Lodge.

But here she was, standing at the keyhole gate of the Inner Market of the Gated City, demanding to see her mother.

I wanted to believe that Ida's mother was a little ragged lady, like the one who had kindly pointed us to the Stolen Alleyway. I wanted to believe she was a colorless woman, as colorless as Ida's hair, who stared at you when you talked to her but was otherwise harmless.

But when I saw the swarthy man look at her in shock, then step back and open the gate without another word, I got a very bad feeling as to who Ida's mother was.

And to think I thought my day was miserable *yesterday*.

THE GATE GUARD MOTIONED FOR HER TO COME INSIDE. UP ON the wall, the archers lowered their weapons.

Ida turned to the others and gestured for them to come.

Ven, Char, and Clem looked at each other.

Ida exhaled in annoyance. "Excuse me a minute," she said to the huge men and the wiry guard with the greasy hair. She stalked back to the group of children.

"Maybe I should have made this clearer," she said in a low voice. "You've got no chance of gettin' out of the Market alive if you don't come with me. Now, decide. Live or die. I don't care what you choose, but you're makin' me look bad, and that's *very* unwise."

She turned and walked back to the keyhole gate.

The three exchanged another glance, then hurried after her.

They passed through the iron grating, wincing as it slammed securely shut behind them. Ida didn't seem to notice. She just continued walking down the middle of the dark street, the sun setting to her left, spilling bloody red light across the unevenly cobbled streets.

As the four walked deeper into the Inner Market, shadows began slinking out of dark alleyways and from around corners of buildings. Many of these people were gray, like the Market itself, and slowly appeared at the edges of their group, walking casually alongside them. The farther away from the keyhole gate they got, the larger the number of people in the group escorting them seemed to become. Ven, Char, and Clemency kept glancing sideways, their anxiety growing as the size of the crowd grew.

Ida just kept her sharp chin high and her focus directly in front of her. She didn't even glance to the side. And she said absolutely nothing.

A flash of black in the sky caught Ven's eye. He looked up. Above their heads a flock of birds was circling, moving deeper into the Market with them. Their shadows danced in the red light of the setting sun on the street.

By the time they arrived at a place where streets split off, the people crowd was beginning to murmur and laugh under their breath, a terrifying sound that blended with the raucous noise of the birds above. It was all Ven could do to keep from shaking as he walked. Clemency's back was rigid, and Char was as pale as Ven had ever seen him.

They turned left at an enormous public well in the center of a street that led toward the harbor. By now darkness had set in, the darkness of coming night adding to the darkness of the crumbling buildings and the mist that hung everywhere. The last light of day was leaving the sky, taking with it any hope Ven still had.

As they turned onto one last street, the crowd began to peel away, leaving only the ravens circling above them.

At the end of that street stood a building larger than any Ven had seen since entering the Market. Like the others inside the Gated City, it had an odor of decay about it, but it was grand in size and scale. Huge pillars of carved dark stone held up the roof, while the walls were formed of sculpted granite with no visible windows in the front. The building seemed to go back forever. A tall tower hovered above the roof in the center, around which more black birds than Ven had ever seen in his life put together were roosting.

Out in front of the building were rich gardens blooming with beautiful flowers, mostly in purple and white, some red, carefully tended. A neat pathway led through the gardens up to the heavy brass door in the center of the windowless wall. In the center of the door was a brass knocker shaped like a raven, its feet clutching a brass necklace set with brass gems. Ven suspected that while this door might be usable, most of the people who entered this establishment did so from other hidden entrances.

"The Raven's Nest?" he murmured quietly to Ida.

Ida nodded ever-so-slightly in return.

*Wonderful*, Ven thought.

Ida marched up the path, the other three close behind, seized the knocker, and banged loudly on the door.

It opened very quickly, as if she was expected.

A thin man with very thin, white hair, an oversized skull and deep-set eyes, was standing in the doorway.

"Miss Ida," he said in a brittle, thin voice. "So nice to see you back home again. We've missed you."

Ida's face did not change. "Take me to my mother."

The thin man smiled unpleasantly. "As you wish." He held the door open wider so that all of them could enter, then closed it quickly behind them.

It was very dark within the foyer of the Raven's Nest. A single lantern burned near the doorway, casting light down a long, dark hallway ahead.

The thin man walked over to a wall to the right of the hallway where many long-handled levers jutted. He took hold of two of them and pulled, then moved farther along the wall and pulled a few more.

Horrible grinding noises could be heard down the dark hallway.

Suddenly a wall slid out of the left side of the hall, blocking it off and revealing a different passageway, this one running in the opposite direction.

"They change the entrances and exits bunches of times a day," Ida muttered under her breath. "Don't bother to memorize where you are. It'll be different in a few minutes."

All three of the others sighed in unison.

The thin man led them down several twisting corridors, all of them without light. Ven could hear Clemency and Char stumble on occasion, but his Nain eyes had little trouble adjusting to the darkness.

After what seemed like forever wandering through hallways that circled back on themselves, they finally came to a place where the corridor ended.

Directly across from them was a wall of rough bricks and stones, mostly dark, on which had been sculpted a huge three-dimensional dragon, cruel-looking and sinister. It had obviously been carved from the stone of the wall, but it was so real-looking that Ven could have sworn he saw its narrow, glinting eyes move. A second later he thought he saw it breathe.

The stone dragon was draped over the top of what appeared to be a keyhole-shaped doorway. Its top claws clutched the lintel above the door, while its lower body hung down the side and curled around the bottom, so that someone would have to step over its tail to enter the doorway.

Instead of empty space, the doorway opening appeared to be made of stone as well. In the center of it was a jumbled pattern of stone puzzle pieces that looked like they formed a key when correctly assembled.

The thin man stepped aside and gestured at the doorway.

"Would you like to open the dragon trap again, Miss Ida?" he asked politely. "It's always such a thrill to watch you do it, a true artist at work."

Ida's stoic expression relaxed into her usual smirk.

"I dunno," she said. "Are you gettin' rusty? It would be so much more fun to watch you burn to cinders."

Ven looked down. On the floor and walls around him were scorch marks, signs of fire and soot. Dust and ash clung to the cracks in the floor.

The thin man smirked in return, then went over to the wall. He stared at the puzzle pieces for a moment, then reached out and carefully slid one into place.

The picture on it disappeared, leaving the stone piece blank.

The children blinked, all but Ida, who was watching intently.

The thief studied the wall again, then selected another puzzle piece. He moved that one lower down, below where the now-blank first piece had been.

The second picture disappeared.

"Oh man," Char whispered to Ven and Clemency. "That's *murder*—you have to *remember* what each piece looked like? Who could do a puzzle like that?"

"I bet Ida can," Clemency said quietly in return. "But I sure wouldn't want to try."

The thief moved a third, then a fourth piece into place.

In a flash, the eyes of the dragon shifted. Its gaze was now locked on the white-haired man.

Ida looked over her shoulder at the other children. "You guys may wanna step back," she said.

The thin man looked up. He glanced at Ida, then up at the dragon above him. Beads of sweat popped out on his pale, over-sized forehead.

"I hear it's painful," Ida added helpfully. "Gettin' crisped."

The expression on the thief's face hardened. He returned to the puzzle, slowly sliding the remaining pieces into place, as steam began to leak from the dragon's nostrils. Char and Ven exchanged a glance, and then slowly inched back and away from where the man was standing.

Without turning around, the thief whipped a dagger from his sleeve and heaved it at the floor half a step away from Char's toes. The knife landed, point stuck into the cracks of the stones, with a metallic *thunk*.

The boys froze in place.

The man returned to his work. Finally, when the last piece of the puzzle was in place, a puff of smoke, but no fire, emerged from the dragon's nose. The wall within the keyhole doorway separated into many jagged pieces and slid out of the way, leaving an entrance that led down another long hallway, this one so bright that their eyes stung.

The thief let out the breath he had been holding, then turned and smiled at them.

"This way," he said, gesturing through the doorway.

Ida stepped over the dragon's tail and into the long corridor beyond, followed by the others. When it ended, the thief opened a door and led them into a bright room with a glass ceiling. The room was filled with even more plants than grew in the gardens out front, most of them fragrant and bursting with flowers.

"Try not to breathe too much in here," Ida said quietly.

Clemency nodded as she looked around. "Datura, belladonna, white cedar, oleander. These are all very poisonous. The Spice Folk at the inn won't even speak to the fairies who take care of these plants—they consider them evil."

"Imagine that," said Char. "Evil plants in this place. Shockin'."

At the other end of the garden was a door that opened into a room where a fire was burning on a large hearth. Huge mirrors hung on every wall, reflecting the light of the fire, making the room full of shadows. They followed Ida inside.

That room was also full of glorious plants, tall, twisting vines with trumpet-shaped flowers dangling from them. Mist hung in the air, which was heavy and hard to breathe. On the floor, lazing in the shadows, were many black cats. They watched the children as they entered the room with yellow eyes that glowed eerily in the dark.

The door to the large room closed quietly behind them.

"Well, well. Look what the cat dragged back into the Market."

The voice was low and musical, almost sweet to Ven's ear. He followed the sound of it to a corner of the room partially hidden in shadow and flowers.

A beautiful woman sat on a gigantic chair of heavily carved dark wood. She had pale skin, long blond hair looped in what looked like nooses, and eyes so black and deep that Ven felt like he was drowning in them when they came to rest on him. A thin silver knife was in her hands, which she was using to clean beneath long neatly manicured red nails, nothing like the black talons on the scale in Madame Sharra's deck. In fact, if she had not been stretched across a throne in this room of shadows, Ven would have believed she was nothing more than a pretty sailor's wife, a teacher, or any other normal person.

The beautiful woman sat up straighter in her chair.

"It's been quite a while, now, hasn't it, Ida? Come give Mummy a kiss."

"Kiss mine," Ida retorted.

The black eyes narrowed into slits, though the woman's smile remained bright.

"Now, now, there's no need to be unpleasant, especially in front of your friends. Mummy is very displeased with you, dear."

"I'm cryin' about that," said Ida.

The woman exhaled. "Impudent as always. I'm glad to see nothing's changed." She turned to the other children. "Since my daughter has not seen fit to introduce me, allow me to do so. I am Felonia. You may refer to me as Your Majesty. Your names don't matter—you won't be here very long. I suppose Ida has told you all about me."

"Actually, no," said Char. "Ida doesn't say much about anythin'."

The Queen of Thieves nodded. "Good. I guess some of her training stuck, then."

She turned back to Ida. "So to what do I owe the exceeding displeasure of your company, Ida? Why did you come back? I assume it wasn't because I ordered you to."

"Heck no," Ida said bluntly. "Someone stole my Gwadd and I want it back."

The Queen leaned back in her throne.

"Really," she said, her voice thick with interest. "A Gwadd? You don't say. Those bring a high price. I'm surprised no one told me that one was available. Well, I suppose I can arrange to find out who has it, and have it brought here. As a wedding present, perhaps."

The only sound in the room was the crackle of the flames on the hearth.

"Er—wedding present?" Ven asked finally, unable to resist.

The Thief Queen turned, as if surprised to hear him speak.

"Well, yes," she said. "You didn't know that Ida is engaged?"

"I hope you're joking," Clemency said.

"Not at all. I believe that's why she ran away this last time—it's not unusual for brides to get cold feet. She is betrothed to a very lovely man, a very important and powerful man, no more than sixty years old, I'm sure. He took a fancy to her years ago, and has wanted to marry her ever since."

"*Her?*" Char demanded in disbelief.

Felonia shrugged. "So he has questionable taste," she said offhandedly. "I learned a long time ago that people desire strange things for strange reasons. I don't question those desires; I just use them to my advantage. This gentleman wants her. His cooperation will expand my business a hundred times over. A small price to pay to keep such an important contact happy." Her eyes looked over Ida from head to toe. "Fortunately, it will take six weeks to get word to him, and for him to travel back here for the wedding. We will have to bathe you every day until then just to get the top layers of dirt off."

"Ida bathes once a week at least," Clemency said indignantly. "I'm her steward, and I make certain of it." She glanced over at Ida. "At least when she's out of jail."

The Queen of Thieves nodded. "Her husband-to-be is a very particular gentleman, and an important ally," she said, running the blade of her knife under the edges of her long fingernails.

"He is very picky about cleanliness. I may have to have her boiled to make her presentable. But her hygiene, or lack of it, is no longer your affair, steward."

"Surely Ida is too young to get married," Ven protested.

Felonia rolled her eyes. "Oh, come now, that's nonsense," she said in Ida's general direction. "You're how old now? Thirteen? Or at least twelve, aren't you?"

Ida shrugged. "I dunno. You were there when I was born, supposedly, and I wasn't payin' attention at the time. If you don't remember, how am I supposed to?"

The thin man with the thin hair coughed politely from the corner of the room.

"Ida is eleven, mistress."

Felonia waved her hand dismissively. "More than old enough."

"That's *sick*!" Char shouted before Ven could stop him. "A *snake's* a better mother than you."

The Queen of Thieves sat up straight, as if she had been slapped across the face. Her black eyes opened wide in shock, then narrowed as they came to rest on the trembling cook's mate.

"What did you say?" she asked softly. Her voice was as silky as the black satin Clemency had admired in the Market, but with a knife's sharpness hidden in it.

Even Ida, who had been maintaining an expression of insolence since entering Felonia's chambers, looked alarmed for a moment. Then her face settled back into its customary smirk.

"Never mind him," she said to her mother. "I want the Gwadd, or I'm not gettin' married. And that's final. Make the arrangements. I want my wedding gown to be pink. With purple lace. An' a big white bow on the butt—I've always wanted one of those."

The Thief Queen stared at Char for a moment longer, then returned her gaze to Ida.

"You're planning to run off again, aren't you?" Her voice was deadly.

"Neh," said Ida.

"Well, while I admire your ability to lie without hesitation, even to me, I will make certain that you are unable to get outside the gates again." Felonia turned to the thin thief. "Climb the tower and set the Screaming Ravens free."

The man inhaled deeply, then bowed and hurried from the room.

The Queen of Thieves smiled at the children.

"The release of those birds is a signal to the constable of Kingston and all of his guards that a particularly dangerous and violent criminal is loose in the Gated City, attempting to escape. Such a warning is an extreme measure, and it terrifies the citizens of Kingston. They will shut down every possible exit, and man the top of the wall with archers, shooting anyone who attempts to leave. It frightens those who live in the Market as well; all the secret exits will be closed, too. Let's all just wait here until that alarm has been sounded, shall we?"

Ven, Char, and Clem stared at each other nervously. Only Ida met Felonia's eye defiantly, even as the hideous screeching began in the tower above them, then spread quickly across the city.

*The sound was the highest pitched, most horrible noise I had ever heard, like the dragging of fingernails across a chalkboard slate inside my ears. It vibrated through my skull, and the skulls of Char and Clem. I could tell because their faces twisted into the same masks of pain I felt mine contort into.*

*The cry of the Screaming Ravens filled the streets, echoing against the cobblestones and alleyways, until it was one great wail of alarm, vibrating through the ground and the air. Even knowing it was coming, the noise scared me absolutely witless.*

In the distance they heard Kingston's guardian bells ringing wildly in answer.

All across the Gated City, doors began slamming amid shouts of alarm and the sound of running feet as the people of the Market of Thieves scurried into whatever shelter they could find.

The Thief Queen listened until the shrieking sound had died away.

"All right, then, Ida, go and have your bath. I will send for your groom, as well as for the Gwadd. And if you have any notion of escaping the city, forget it. You've just cost this Market a great deal of business and worry. They will not appreciate it, believe me. No one is going to help you." She eyed Ven, Char, and Clem. "If you are her friends, you will help convince her of this. And if you have any of your own thoughts of escaping, please reconsider, for Ida's sake. It is always unfortunate when one's wedding guests die before the ceremony. It means fewer gifts."

She signaled for the door to be opened. Two guards stood there, waiting, armed to the teeth. One was muscle-bound and as wide as he was tall.

The other had brown hair—and a hooked nose.

Felonia signaled impatiently. The guards bowed, then opened the door wider.

The children followed the guards out of her chamber.

Once in the hallway, the thief with the hooked nose took Ida by the arm. He nodded to the other guard, pointing in the other direction.

"I can't believe you agreed to this, Ida," Clem said as the second guard motioned for her and the boys to follow him. Ida just shrugged and walked away with the hook-nosed thief.

"You understand why she did, don't you?" Ven asked when she was out of sight.

"She's tryin' to save Saeli," said Char glumly.

"Yes," Ven said as they fell in line behind the second guard. "And *you*—if she hadn't spoken when she did, you would have been nothing more than a stain on the floor and a memory at this moment. Try to avoid insulting the Queen of Thieves again, Char, if you please—at least while I'm standing next to you. Just in case she misses with her knife."

"She never misses," said Clemency. "I'm sure of it."

The guard jangled his keys in their direction.

"Just out of curiosity, Ven," said Clemency, "Does everyone who spends time with you end up under lock and key?"

"It does seem that way, doesn't it?" Ven replied. "Sorry about that."

The guard gestured impatiently, and led them off down a dark passageway into the belly of the guildhall.

## - 16 -

# Under Lock and Key—Again

I have passed some awful nights in my life.

When I was a very small lad of twenty-four, I got the Brown Flu. One does not discuss the symptoms of the Brown Flu in polite company, but let me just say this—everything that was put into my body came immediately right back out by way of random exits. I try not to think about that night if I can help it.

The nights I spent in the middle of the sea on my back on a piece of floating wreckage were pretty miserable as well. I actually remember very little about it, except for the shivering cold and the sting of the salty sea in my eyes. I was shivering so much that I couldn't make myself be still. What I remember most was that Amariel was with me the whole time. She never left, but stayed by my side, telling me merrow tales and singing me songs in her haunting, beautiful voice. So even though I thought I was going to die, and I was so cold at times dying seemed like a good thing, at least I had a friend to keep me going.

Even after I was rescued, I had some pretty awful nights on the *Serelinda*. I was exhausted, feeling guilty, missing my family, all of which would have been tolerable except for the snoring of the sailors in the hammocks around me. Lying in a swinging rope bed on a pitching ship with the people around you sounding like they are strangling or boiling small animals alive is not a great way to get a night's sleep.

As Clemency had pointed out, I seem to have a tendency to get locked up. My nights in the castle dungeon, waiting for the king to return and pass judgment on me, were also pretty terrible ones, lonely and scary.

All those nights put together were one big walk in the park compared to the time we were locked up in the belly of the Raven's Nest.

T HE MUSCLE-BOUND THIEF LED THEM DOWN A VERY DARK HALLway to a small curved door with a grated window that was bound in steel. He took a long, thin tool from his pocket and jiggled it expertly inside the door's lock. Ven heard a *click*; then the guard swung the door opened and gestured for them to go inside.

"Er, I need to use the head," said Char to the thief.

The big man seized him by the shoulder and pushed him through the door. "There's one in there," he called after Char. Then he turned to Ven and Clem.

"Right," Ven said, putting his hands up. "Thanks." He went over to the door.

"Watch yer step," the guard said.

The warning came a moment too late. Ven stepped into the blackness, tripped, and fell about two feet down to a dirt floor where Char was already sitting, dazed. He landed with a solid *whump*.

In the dim light of the hallway they saw Clem's shadow come into the doorway; then she was on the floor beside them, too. The door slammed shut, leaving them in total darkness.

"Well, this is just lovely," Char said. Ven could feel his friend beside him, but the room was so dark that he could not even make out his shape. "Where do you suppose the privy is?"

"I hope it's separate from the rest of the floor," Clemency said from the other side of Ven, "but the way this place smells, I'm kinda doubting it."

"Ugh," said Char. "I guess I'll hold it. How long ya think she'll keep us in here?"

"I hope you can hold it for six weeks," Ven said. "I doubt she's going to release us before Ida's wedding."

"That's *so* disgusting," Char said. "It makes me sick to even think about it."

"Poor Ida," Clemency said. "I guess this all explains why she's the way she is."

"Well, it certainly explains why she's so talented," Char agreed. "She's the bloody Thief Queen's *daughter*. No wonder she can work impossible puzzle boxes an' clean your pockets out from across the room an' all the other things she can do."

"And how she could be telling the truth when she said she has been in the Market a bajillion times," Ven said pointedly. "You called her a liar, Char. You owe her an apology."

"Guess so," Char muttered. "I'll work on that after I find a privy."

Ven reached into his pocket and took out the king's stone. The glow filled the dank little room, shining to all the corners, making the three of them wince until their eyes became accustomed to the light.

"Look around," he said. "Maybe there's a chamber pot or something like it. That's what I had in the dungeon of the castle. That was a *much* nicer place than this, by the way."

"Glad we have an experienced prisoner with us, anyway," said Char darkly. He rose, sore from his fall, and walked gingerly around the small dirty room, until he came to the farthest corner. "Eeeuuuuw," he said. "It's just a Johnny-hole an' a ditch. Never mind. I'll wait awhile."

"Now what do we do, Ven?" Clemency asked.

Ven set the light down on his lap.

"I guess we just wait Char's 'while,' however long that is," he said.

*I'm not sure how long that "while" turned out to be. To keep from panicking we talked. We told all the stories we knew. Char knows some especially good ones, being a sailor. And Clem has been listening to McLean talking to the Spice Folk for a long time, telling them tales, so she had a lot to share as well.*

*All I could tell was the jokes and tales I had heard from my family. But that was not as helpful as it might have been. Every time I started one, I remembered the brother or sister who told it, or the look on my mother's face if the joke was too crude. My father is the best storyteller of the entire family. Whenever I started one of his, my voice broke and I couldn't finish it.*

*So finally we were silent, in the glowing dark pit. We tried to sleep to keep from concentrating on how hungry we were.*

*And how much trouble we were in.*

*"They will feed us sooner or later, won' they?" Char had said hopefully. "If they want us to stay alive for the weddin' an' all."*

*But no food ever came. In fact, no one came for any reason at all.*

*After that we lost all track of time. It seemed like we were in the black smelly hole forever.*

Finally they heard the sound of footsteps approaching.

Ven rose wearily to his feet. Weak from hunger, he snatched the king's stone from the dirt floor and tucked it back into his pocket, dousing the light.

They heard the sound of the lock being picked. Then the door swung open.

The children flinched as the dim light stabbed their eyes.

A long hooked stick was lowered into the room. The dark shadow on the other end swung it toward Char, who took a few steps back. He tried to dodge, but was so weak and blind that he stepped into the path of the big hook. Caught around the waist, he barely struggled as he was lifted like a fish out of the room.

"Just lower the pole down, and we'll grab on," Ven called up as the shadow moved back into the doorway. "Believe me, we *want* to get out of here."

"No funny stuff, now," a gruff voice called back. The pole came straight down to where Ven and Clem were standing.

"You want next, or last?" Ven asked Clemency.

Clem just exhaled and took hold of the pole. With a lurch, she was pulled from the room and out of sight.

The door swung shut, taking the light with it.

"Hold on!" Ven shouted desperately. "Don't leave me down here!"

He could hear the muffled protests of his friends beyond the door. It swung open again.

"Aw, quit yer yapping," the guard called down to him. "The Queen just said ta bring the kids. She won't miss one less beggar."

"Drag 'im up," another voice ordered. "Ya never know."

"Awright," the first voice said grudgingly. The pole was lowered again, and Ven took hold quickly, before the thieves changed their minds.

"Oh, man," groaned one of them as they lifted him out of the hole. "This one's a monster. Get movin', ya fat thing." He poked Ven in the back with the pole.

The three friends started down the hallway.

They were herded through many twists and turns, just like before, until they finally came to the deadly garden outside the throne room of the Raven's Nest.

"Get in there," the guard growled behind them.

*The room had been transformed since we were last in there. The fire was no longer burning. Now there were round globes with candle flames inside them burning all around the room on the walls, making it bright as day. There were still a few shadows clinging to the corners and to the giant collection of plants, but the rest of the room was easily seen.*

In the center of the room were two enormous cages with metal bars, each as thick as the pole they had been pulled out of the hole with. In the middle of one of them sat Ida, her legs crossed, her elbows on her knees, her chin resting on her hands.

In the other cage, looking terrified, was a tiny Gwadd girl.

"Saeli!" the three shouted, running to the cage and looking in.

"Saeli, are you all right?" Clemency asked, her voice breaking. Ven and Char's words fell over hers as they all greeted their tiny friend at the same time.

Saeli nodded, still looking terrified.

Ven glanced over his shoulder while Char and Clem talked in excitement to Saeli. Ida had not moved, and her expression had not changed, but he thought he saw a look in her eye that made his heart sick.

"Ida—you all right?" he called across the room. "Are they—uummph!"

A pole hit him squarely in the back.

One of the guards opened Saeli's cage. "Get in 'ere," he ordered.

Clemency scurried inside, followed by Char, who ducked to keep out of reach of the pole. Ven waited until last, watching Ida, but she didn't respond.

The guard raised the pole again, and Ven stepped into the cage, still looking over to Ida as the door slammed shut.

"Well, good afternoon, my sweet little girl," came a familiar silky voice from the garden. Felonia entered the brightly lit room, a bowl of purple grapes in her hand. "I've brought you a lovely snack."

Ida leaned back and rolled her eyes. "Spare me."

The Thief Queen looked at her disdainfully.

"I wasn't talking to *you*," she said. "You've caused nothing but trouble ever since you've been back. Escaping three times, *really* now. I hope you like your new cage, Ida." She came over to the cage where the others hovered near the door, and bent down in front of Saeli. The little Gwadd girl shrank away.

"Here you go, sweetie," Felonia coaxed. "Have some grapes—I hear they are a favorite among the Gwadd."

Saeli looked to her left, and saw the hollow looks of hunger on Char's and Clem's faces. She looked to the right, and saw a similar one on Ven's. Reluctantly she reached through the bars and took the bunch of grapes that the Thief Queen was offering. She pulled several loose, then reached out to Char with them.

Like a snake striking, the Thief Queen's hand shot into the cage and blocked Saeli's reach. "Ah, ah, not him," she said sweetly, but there was a hard edge under her tone. "Just you. No need to waste food on guests who, hmmm, who won't be staying long. Eat, dear."

Saeli's eyes narrowed. She handed the bunch of grapes back and shook her head resolutely.

Felonia crouched down until she was closer to Saeli's height.

"Are you sure?" she asked. Her tone was deadly.

Saeli nodded.

The Thief Queen exhaled. "All right, then," she said, taking the grapes back. She stood and walked back to her throne where the lush array of plants stood. "Deebuld, shoot the skinny one."

Char's eyebrows shot up, and his face went pale, as did each of the other children's faces.

Quickly Saeli reached through the bars of the cage again.

The Thief Queen smiled broadly. She came back to the cage, crouched down again, and handed the grapes to the little Gwadd

girl. Then she glared at the other three, who shrank quickly back against the far wall of the cage.

"Eat them now," she said seriously, "so I can watch."

Tears rolled down Saeli's cheeks. She took one grape, put it slowly in her mouth and tried to chew, gagging slightly as she tried to swallow.

Felonia smiled brightly. "That's it," she said, pleased. "Keep at it, now."

From the cage across the room there came a deep, disgusted sigh.

"It's all right, Saeli," Char said encouragingly. "We had tons to eat before we got in here."

"He's a liar," said Felonia. Her expression turned smug. "But you knew that, didn't you? You must eat to keep your strength up, little one. You alone have value to me in this room—you can be of great assistance with my darling plants."

There was something about the way the Queen looked at the flowering vines and bushes growing all around her that rang a bell in my head. *What entranced her?* the Singer in the Market had asked about Saeli. He was helping us find something so interesting, so meaningful to Saeli that she would forget to be careful in a place where being careless could cost her life.

Maybe this was the Thief Queen's one weakness.

If she had any at all.

"Your plants *are* lovely," Ven admitted. He leaned against the side of the cage so he could see them better. "Now that it's light in here, I can really see how beautiful they are."

The Thief Queen looked surprised, then pleased.

"They are, aren't they?" she said admiringly. "And useful, too—the passionflowers are a wonderful sleep aid, and the aroma of the Stuff-of-Dreams can give lovely night visions. Citronella keeps mosquitoes away. The catnip makes my kitties happy, and the belladonna can be used as a tonic for illnesses of the eyes. But, of course, that's not why I keep any of them."

"Why *do* you keep them, then?" asked Clemency. She glanced at Ven, who nodded. Felonia shot her a suspicious look. "If I may be so bold as to ask, Your Majesty. It seems like a person as busy as yourself would have a hard time keeping up with their care."

The Thief Queen stared at her a moment longer, then turned and went back to her small forest, where the cats drowsed beneath the plants she had pointed out as catnip.

"Lovely and innocent as these precious plants appear, any of them in a strong enough concentration will kill just about anyone or anything," Felonia said. "I have a fascination with things that are both beautiful and deadly."

"I wonder why," Char muttered under his breath. Clemency elbowed him in the ribs.

"These are Deadly Nightshade—aren't they splendid?" the Thief Queen mused, running her long-taloned index finger over the huge, starlike blossoms of white and purple. She ran her hand up a tall, treelike vine of innocent-looking red berries. "This one's my favorite, aren't you, boy?" She patted the tree lovingly. "This is Waylon. He's my prize possession, my baby."

*My mother is not the easiest mother in the world to have.*

*She has raised thirteen children, twelve boys who like to argue and bounce each other into the harbor when they aren't* winning those arguments, and the most pig-headed daughter in all of the city of Vaarn. We are Nain in a city of humans, and so that meant, at least before my brother Luther was born, that her children got picked on a lot. That couldn't have been easy for her. By the time I came along, no one was bothering the Polypheme kids anymore, because Luther, brother number three, had already earned his reputation as Scariest Person in Town.

Luther bites. When he bites, people lose fingers and toes.

My mother takes the shipbuilding factory in which we all work as seriously as my father does. They both think manufacturing is a mission. He manufactures the ships. She manufactures the workers who build the ships. We are the machines that make the business run. So we all are very well looked after, from our lessons to our clothing to our food to our manners. She is particularly fussy about our health and manners. Being late is something she does not tolerate well at all, especially being late for tea. She is not especially cuddly, and sometimes can be quite gruff. My mother is a serious person, just like the Queen of Thieves.

But, even for all her strictness, there has never been a single moment in my life that I did not know how much my mother loves me, and how important I am to her. Every one of my siblings has said the same thing to me at one time or another.

I remembered how mad I was at her letter this morning. Then I glanced over at Ida's face. I felt like I had been kicked in the gut, hearing her mother talk to her as if she were talking to garbage, then turn around and speak so sweetly to a stupid poisonous plant, the same way she had to Saeli. If I was feeling that way, I can't imagine how Ida must be feeling.

But Ida didn't flinch. Her expression didn't change at all.

There was a polite knock at the throne room door.

"Enter," said the Queen idly, caressing Waylon's leaves.

The muscle-bound thief popped his head into the room.

"Your guest is here, Mistress," he said.

Felonia sighed. She came back to the cage and took what remained of the grapes from Saeli's hands, leaving her with but one. Then she headed to the door.

"Ta ta, Ida, darling," she said, not even looking at her daughter. "I have someone actually *important* to attend to." As she passed the guard, she looked back at the cages. "Ida can pick that lock in her sleep. To discourage her from doing so, please station four archers in here right now. If she comes within two feet of her cage door, shoot one of her friends. Start with the skinny one. Leave the Gwadd for last. In fact, if you have to choose between them, just shoot Ida."

She finally looked over at her daughter's cage. "I'll be leaving on a little trip in a few days, once the Screaming Raven alarm has settled down—is there anything you would like Mummy to bring back for you?"

"Orphanhood?" Ida suggested.

"Uh—" Char interrupted as the Thief Queen's expression grew frighteningly cold. "Your Majesty, could I please ask a question before you go? I'll never get to tell anyone the answer, since Ida will no doubt try to escape at least once. She doesn't like me all that much, so choosin' me to get shot first is actually doin' her a favor."

Felonia continued to stare at Ida for a moment longer, then looked his way.

"What's your question?"

"How do you get out of the Market? I mean, don't you sorta need a token?"

The Thief Queen's expression melted into one of amusement. She strode over to one of the corners in the room and dragged out an enormous chest, then flipped the lid open.

It was crammed full to the top of ribbons with Market Day tokens. Tokens spilled out over the sides to the floor.

"You mean like this?" she asked innocently. She tried to contain her merriment at the expressions of total shock on the children's faces, but couldn't. Felonia threw her head back and began to laugh. She picked up a lazing cat that was sprawling near the chest at her feet, slung it over her shoulder, and left the room, still laughing.

# - 17 -

# In the Thief
# Queen's Chambers

THIS IS GOING WELL," SAID CHAR GLOOMILY AS FOUR ARCHERS took their places across the room near Felonia's throne. "At least the Thief Queen thinks I'm important enough to kill first. Woo hoo."

"I don't believe the Thief Queen thinks any of us is important in any way except Saeli," said Clemency, looking across the room to the other cage. "Especially Ida. I want to be sick every time she speaks to her."

Suddenly Char sat up as a happy thought occurred to him. "Hey!—whatever happened to those dusty pretzels Nick had ta buy off that guy with the pole? Did he give them to you, Clem?"

Clemency shook her head.

"If he did, don't you think we would have eaten them in the hole?" she asked. "Your hunger is starting to get to you, Char. Try to stay focused. We have to think of a way to get out of here, or we're all going to die."

Ven was watching Saeli. She was staring at the single grape in her hand, then at the three of them, trying to decide what to do with it. Finally, she inserted a tiny fingernail, tore the grape in half, and offered one half of it to Char.

"Take it and say thank you," Clemency said quickly, interrupting Char's protests. "She's right. You need it more than Ven and I do. Eat."

Reluctantly Char took the grape half, mumbled his thanks, then popped it into his mouth.

Saeli reached behind her head to the base of her neck where her long caramel-colored braid began and popped the other half into her hair.

The other children looked at her in astonishment.

Char walked slowly behind her, trying not to catch the notice of the guards.

"Er, Saeli," he said in a low voice, "your hair is moving."

Saeli nodded casually, then turned so that her back was facing the other three.

A tiny face peeked out from between the strands of her braid, a partially eaten grape half in its little hands.

Ven's eyes opened in amazement.

*It was the puffy little monkey creature from the kiosk of animals. It had huge eyes and a small black face, with miniature hands that were expertly turning the remains of the grape to get all the juicy parts near its mouth.*

*I heard the Singer's words again in my head: What entranced her? I guess there are just some things in this world that are so fascinating, so hard to resist, that you will do anything, even risk your life and your freedom, to have them.*

*Or to help them. Apparently Saeli felt that way about this little monkeylike thing.*

*I understand. I feel that way about the Ultimate Adventure.
It's sort of embarrassing to admit, but in my heart I believe
that somewhere out there is something so exciting, so amazing,
so entrancing, that when I finally come across it, it will
satisfy my curiosity at last. The itch will go away, and I'll
be happy to stay wherever I am, and look no farther for
adventure.*

*If I live long enough to find it.*

*I could be wrong, but I think that may be how the Thief
Queen feels about her plants.*

The creature disappeared back into the depths of Saeli's hair.
In the cage across the room, Ida stood up and stretched.

Instantly the four archers aimed their weapons at Char.

Ida rolled her eyes. "Oh, keep your pants on," she said to the
guards.

"Yeah," Char said. "I don' even care if ya want ta take 'em
off—just put down the bows, please."

"I can see this is going to be another *lovely* day," Clemency
said, sitting down on the cage floor.

Ven sighed. He looked over at Ida again, who was pacing
around her own cage.

"Are you all right, Ida?" he asked again. "Did you get hurt
while we were separated?"

Ida didn't look at him, but just shook her head and continued
to pace.

The thief guards looked from cage to cage, watching Ida,
then Char, then Ida, then back at Char again. Finally the leader
of them signaled in disgust for two of them to put down their
bows, and kept his eye on the Thief Queen's daughter.

Ven was watching the leader when his eye caught a slight movement over the man's head.

A beautiful spray of waxy blooms with fringy purple centers that Felonia had referred to as passionflowers stretched, then glistened. Ven couldn't be certain, but he thought they might have been slightly larger than they had been a moment before.

He glanced over at Saeli, who was concentrating intently. Then she turned and smiled at him.

He looked back. The flowers Felonia had pointed out as the Stuff-of-Dreams were opening wider, liquid shimmering on their silky petals.

Saeli stretched her arms over her head in an exaggerated yawn, then lay down on the cage floor and curled up in a sleeping pose, her nose buried in her arms.

Ven looked back at the glorious flowers. They were all vibrating slightly, especially the Stuff-of-Dreams.

He caught Clemency's eye, and nodded toward Saeli. Clem's brows drew together, but when she followed Ven's glance back to the bower of poisonous plants, she caught the message and slowly began to make sleepy sounds as well.

Ven went back to the bars of the cage and tried to get Ida's attention.

"Did you get any sleep at all, Ida?" he asked, trying to sound sleepy himself.

"Stow it, Polywog," Ida shot back crossly.

Ven saw the recognition take hold on Char's face.

"I'm pretty spent myself," the cook's mate said, stretching. "Got none in that black, filthy hole." He turned and addressed the guards. "I'll try to sleep wi' my back to you gents so that you have a clear shot if Ida tries to get out." Then he lay down on the floor.

Only Ven continued to stand, trying to get Ida's attention, for a few moments longer. Then he sat down, leaning up against the cage bars, and pretended to go to sleep, his nose covered by the collar of his shirt.

Out of the corner of his eye he could see the passionflowers swelling, growing, filling the air with vapor. The beautiful pink-and-white blooms of the Stuff-of-Dreams were gently expanding and contracting, releasing tiny puffs of dustlike powder each time they did. Even across the room as he was, Ven could smell the scent growing heavier.

He remained there with his head down until a tiny hand gripped his shoulder and shook him.

He shook off his drowsiness to see Saeli's heart-shaped face smiling down at him. Ven looked up, then around.

The four guards were slumped on the floor, snoring. Two of them had silly grins on their faces, while a third was hugging his bow, planting kisses on it every now and then. The abundant blossoms of passionflowers and Stuff-of-Dreams, which had more than tripled in number and size, were hanging above them, dripping nectar and puffing pollen over their heads. The vine plants in Felonia's collection were slowly winding around the men's feet.

Ven struggled to his own.

"Good work, Saeli," he whispered. He nodded at Clemency, who was shaking Char awake, then went to the door of the cage and looked across the room.

Ida was sitting as she had been when they came into the room, her elbows on her knees, her chin in her hands.

Sound asleep.

"Ida," Ven whispered. There was no response. "*Ida*," he whispered a little louder, "wake up! You've got to get us out of here!"

"Mmzzzverdmple," Ida muttered.

Char, now awake, joined him at the cage door.

"Come on, Ida," he said. "Wake up."

Ida's head swung from side to side, but still she did not awaken.

Ven searched in his pockets for something to throw at her, finally deciding on his Market Day token.

"I'm surprised the Thief Queen didn't strip us of everything we had," he said as he wrapped the ribbon around the token in a wad.

"We can probably thank Mr. Coates for that," Clemency said. "The marks of worthlessness are still on our backs. Everyone in the Market believed we have nothing worth stealing, even Felonia."

"Yeah, I hope he's all right," Char said nervously.

"I bet he is," Ven said, reaching through the cage bars as far as he could. "The people in this place seem to know how to survive. That's probably why the back door was open—his trap went off, and he got out in time."

"Let's hope so," said Clem.

Ven held his breath, then tossed the ribbon-wrapped token across the room at Ida. It sailed in a slow underhand arc through the bars of her cage, hit the top, and landed on the floor in front of her.

Ida stirred, then blinked.

"Hizzzump?" she said woozily.

"Ida, *wake up*," Ven said as loudly as he dared. "Open your cage, and ours!"

Ida rose shakily to a stand.

"Just how do ya want me to do *that*, Polywog?" she demanded. "They cleaned me out from head ta toe the first night here. What do you want me to pick the lock with, my *teeth*?"

Ven was taken aback. "Well, what do you need?"

"A tool of some sort would be nice. Anything."

Ven, Char, Clem, and Saeli searched their pockets. Other than Char's Market Day token and a few remaining copper coins, they had nothing.

Except Mr. Coates's gauntlet, which was too wide to fit between the bars.

And Ven's jack-rule.

*Desperate as our situation was, my heart sank into my stomach at the thought of anyone, especially Ida, handling my great-grandfather's jack-rule. It was my father's pride and joy, something he used, and then polished, every day. When he gave it to me on my birthday, we both knew that there was no gift in the world I would rather have had.*

*It was hard enough to hand it over to Mr. Coates, who was respectful of it. Now, the thought of giving it to someone who had stolen it from me before and used it to trim her toenails was enough to make me want to upchuck the last thing I had eaten, however long ago that was.*

Ven stared at the jack-rule a moment longer, then sighed. He crouched down and reached out of the bars, then with a firm push, sent the beloved tool skimming across the floor until it stopped with a clatter against Ida's cage.

"*ZZZZZZppp?*" one of the guards muttered at the sound.

Saeli folded her hands and concentrated again. A large trumpet of Stuff-of-Dreams expanded, dripping a glistening drop into his open mouth. The man sighed and returned to snoring.

"Will that do?" Ven asked anxiously.

Ida nodded as if she had a headache. She bent down, retrieved the jack-rule, pried open the knife, and stuck it expertly into the lock of her own cage. A few twists and turns later, the lock let out a loud *clank*. Ida opened the gated door and slipped out of the cage, then carefully closed the door behind her.

She took a step toward the sleeping guards, the knife open in the jack-rule.

"Ida?" Clemency asked. "What are you doing?"

Ida glanced back over her shoulder but said nothing.

"Please, Ida, let us out of here," Ven said quickly. "Felonia or that thin-haired thief may be back any time."

"Neh," Ida responded, rubbing the blade of the knife against her trousers and taking a few steps closer. "She's off with her guest, whoever that is, and he's mindin' the store. This will just take a minute." Her hand gripped the knife tighter.

"Ida, I know you're angry," Ven said carefully, watching the blade of his great-grandfather's heirloom jack-rule gleaming in the light of the candle globes as Ida approached the sleeping thieves. "But if you cut their throats, you will never be able to live with yourself."

Ida looked back over her shoulder and stared at him.

"You have no idea what you're talkin' about, Polywog," she said scornfully. "You have no idea what it takes to survive in this place, as you already proved. So stuff your advice, and shut up."

She turned around and walked resolutely over to where the guards lay, helpless in the poison stupor of passionflower juice and Stuff-of-Dreams pollen. She bent down next to the one who was cuddling his bow, and held the knife down near his neck.

"Ida!" Clemency gasped.

Ida flinched, then looked back, annoyed.

"Shut up!" she hissed. She bent over again with the knife, grabbed hold of one of the plants growing on the floor nearby, and neatly severed a stem of leaves. Then she stepped back and returned to the cage.

She tossed the greens to Ven, then thrust the knife into the lock and turned it. *Clank.* The cage door swung open.

"Er—what's this?" Ven asked, staring down at the leaves in his hands.

"Catnip, you idiot," Ida said as Saeli ran to her and hugged her. "You owe Murphy a treat, don' you?" She folded the knife back into the jack-rule and handed it back to Ven.

Clemency grinned as Ven and Char exhaled. Ida gestured impatiently.

"You comin' or not?" she asked.

Without another word, the children followed her out of their cage to the room's door. Ida looked back at the sleeping guards one more time, then silently opened the door and stepped out into the dim hallway.

"Follow close," she said. "I'm not waitin' for ya."

They ran down the hallway into darkness. Only the slightest light was visible from lanterns in corners or torches burning in wall sconces. The corridors twisted and turned, stopping for no reason and turning quickly at strange angles.

Just as they rounded a corner, a terrible grinding sound was heard in the walls to their right.

"They're changing the exits and entrances," said Ida. "Watch out."

Right in front of them a wall appeared from the ceiling and lowered into place, blocking the hallway. Beside them to the right, where the grinding noise had come from, another one opened up, revealing an entirely different route.

"Come on," Ida said, stepping into the new passageway.

They dodged moving walls and floors, hurrying through the maze of changing passageways, past doors behind which terrifying laughter or ominous noises could be heard.

Finally, at the end of a long, twisting hallway, Ida stopped in front of a sleek black door with a golden raven painted on it.

"Man, oh, man—we found it!" she said excitedly. "Polywog—gimme that knife thing again."

Char glanced nervously over his shoulder as Ven took out the jack-rule and handed it to Ida.

"Why don't I have a good feelin' about this?" he asked.

Ida sprang the lock and opened the door. The room beyond was magnificently messy and draped in black silk and shadows. "Maybe because this is Felonia's bedroom?"

"Yeah, that might be the reason," Char agreed. "What are you *thinkin'*?"

Ida pushed him inside, and the others followed quickly. She closed the door.

"I'm thinkin' there's a hidden passage in here somewhere—I heard her say so once, a long time ago. That's about the only way we're gettin' out of this place once they discover we're gone."

"We had better start looking," Ven said, starting into the room. Ida seized him by the shoulder.

"You might want to let me go first," she said. "All those

clothes on the floor, all the stuff lying around? She may be the embodiment of evil, but she's not a slob. Those are traps. Can't you smell the poison in this room?"

Ven sniffed the air, then shook his head.

"No," he said.

Ida rolled her eyes. "Pathetic," she murmured. "Walk this way."

She led them through the Thief Queen's outer chamber, which was a dressing room of sorts, past piles of what appeared to be discarded clothing, silken robes lying on the floor, shirts and trousers draped over chairs, and underwear tossed on a writing desk, which made everyone but Ida blush. Ven noticed that the letters on that desk were written in the same strange code that was inside the box that had held the king's stone. Thieves' Cant, Vandemere had called the language. His beliefs seemed to be borne out.

All along the way Ida stopped from time to time, removing a poison needle from the carpet, or undoing a trap of alarm bells hidden in a pile of trash. *I wonder what would have happened if she hadn't agreed to come back into the Market*, Ven thought as he saw her at work, taking apart her mother's carefully rigged snares. *Actually, I don't really have to wonder—and I'd rather not think about it.*

At the far end of the room was a door. Ida opened it.

The inner chamber was the bedroom. Unlike the outer chamber, it was tidy as a poisoned pin. A big, beautiful bed was neatly outfitted with black silk sheets and matching bedcurtains that draped down from a golden ring hanging from the ceiling that looked exactly like the Raven doorknocker. Its headboard and footboard were carved out of dark walnut wood, with the guild's symbol proudly carved in the center of the headboard.

"I don't think there are any traps in here," Ida said after looking around. "She doesn't expect anyone to make it all the way through the dressin' room unless they're supposed to be in here."

Ven looked around. "Did you see any sign of a hidden passageway?"

Ida shook her head. "I'm gonna check her closet," she said, closing the bedroom door and crossing to another one in the bedchamber. "This is gonna take a while—she has more clothes than are available in the rest of the Market."

"I'll help you," Clemency offered, as Saeli nodded. They followed Ida into the closet.

Ven and Char began looking gingerly around the base of the dresser and night tables. "Can I just say, in the very real possibility that we don't make it out of here, that life as your friend is never borin' at least?" Char said as he crawled beneath the chest of drawers, looking for something to open a passageway.

Ven sighed. "I'd settle for boring at this point. I haven't gotten the curiosity itch since we came through the keyhole gate."

His eyes wandered to the huge bed and the beautifully carved headboard. The bedposts were pointed like spear tips, making for an unfriendly appearance.

There was something familiar about them, however.

Ven walked over to examine them more closely. He touched the right bedpost, and as he did, his last odd job at the inn came rushing back to him.

*The inn's safe is down below here. It's triggered by a mechanism here in the bedpost.*

His hands shaking with excitement, Ven took hold of the spearlike spindle at the top of the bedpost on the right of the headboard and twisted it three times clockwise, two times counterclockwise, and once more clockwise.

A clicking sound was heard in the floor.

Smoothly, the bed turned in a circular arc. The bedcurtains were raised out of the way.

And a hole in the floor was revealed.

Char's eyes almost popped out of his head.

"Gah!" he choked. "How in blazes did you do *that*?"

"Lucky guess," Ven said, still somewhat in shock. "Go get the girls."

Clem, Saeli, and Ida had just returned from the closet, wearing expressions of relief, when they heard the door in the outer chamber open.

And the Thief Queen's voice.

## - 18 -

# Down the First of Many
# Dark Holes

"You really are taking a quite a risk coming here again," Felonia said over the creak of the door. "In broad daylight, no less. Why is that, I wonder?"

A man's voice in the distance retorted angrily. "What alternative do you suggest?" he said nastily. "If I don't come in person, I only get the information you choose to send me."

They could hear the outer chamber door close.

"Quick, get in the hole!" Ven whispered urgently.

Like lightning, Ida scrambled to the hidden passageway in the floor and dropped down inside it. Clem went after her, followed by Saeli, then Char, who turned around as he was descending.

"Er—Ven?"

"*What?*"

"Who's gonna close the bed?"

Ven looked back at the bedpost, then down at the hole.

"Oh man," he muttered in dismay.

Saeli's head appeared next to Char's legs, halfway down the hole.

"Keekee!" she said in her strange, gravelly voice.

"What?" Ven asked, trying not to panic.

The Gwadd girl reached into her hair, and pulled out the puffy monkey-creature.

"Keekee," she said again. She pointed at the bedpost. The small creature leapt from her hand, almost as if it were flying, then scrambled across the black sheets, up the headboard, and seized the spindle of the bedpost between its arms.

A clicking sound could be heard, as the voices in the outer chamber grew closer.

"Ven, get down!" Clemency urged. Ven complied, just as the bed began to rotate on its turntable in the floor.

The keekee turned and scampered across the bedcurtains, then dived in a lunge into the hole. Ven caught it just as the turntable closed, sliding the bed completely back in place.

Plunging them into blackness.

In the hollow silence of the dark passageway, they could hear the muffled sound of the door to Felonia's inner chamber opening. Ven passed the little creature back to Saeli and moved as close as he could to the passageway's cover to hear what was being said.

"That noise you are hearing is the birds on the roof," Felonia was saying as she came within earshot. "There's an unkindness of ravens that roosts on top of the guild. Their numbers are growing by the day. Aren't they spectacular?"

"An unkindness of ravens?" the man's voice asked.

"That's what a group of ravens is called," Felonia replied. Her voice was louder now, but still muffled. "Ravens are ever so much more interesting birds than crows—a group of those is called a *murder*. But a murder of crows is no match for an unkindness of ravens. Ravens are much smarter, much more cunning. Much more dangerous."

"Much more distracted by pretty, shiny things," said the man.

His voice was full of disdain. "Is that the problem with the Raven's Guild, Felonia? Have you been distracted from your assignments? I've had no reports for weeks."

"Everything is coming into place just as we had hoped," the Queen of Thieves could be heard saying. A soft creaking of wood and metal above them seemed to indicate she had sat down on her bed. "But these things take time. You have to be patient."

"I do not know that we *have* time," came the reply.

There was something vaguely familiar about the man's voice, Ven noted. He looked over at Char, but all he could see in the dark were Char's eyes, which were round as the moon. He had no idea if Char recognized the voice or if he was just terrified.

Even through the floor he could hear the Queen of Thieves chuckle.

"Perhaps you should move within the walls of the Gated City, then." Her voice sounded like it was wrapped in wool. "We have nothing but time here."

"I have been unpleasantly surprised each of the few times I have come," the man's voice said. "To find you so behind on your promises now being just the most recent disappointment."

"Perhaps you should come around more than every ten years or so," Felonia replied. "You could have met your daughter."

There was not much air in the stuffy passageway below the Thief Queen's bedroom. Whatever had been there a moment before was suddenly sucked away by Ida's gasp. I could hear her, farther away in the dark, moving forward, as if to hear better. I wasn't sure she was going to like what she was about to hear, but I couldn't very well stop her.

I was in shock myself.

"You really need to stop trying to use that against me," the man's voice answered. "You said she ran away from the Market years ago."

Ven could almost hear Felonia smile by the sound of her answer.

"She did—she does, from time to time. But she returned recently, so I'm about to send word to Northland that it's time for our alliance to be sealed. The wedding will be in six weeks, as long as everyone there agrees."

The man's voice grew harsh.

"I want to see her. Now."

Clemency looked at Ida, then at Ven. He could tell by the outline of her shadow moving in the dark.

"In good time," the Thief Queen replied. "She's really quite disappointing-looking when she's clean. In her current state, she's utterly embarrassing. Do yourself the favor of waiting until I've had her properly scrubbed down."

"I want to see her anyway," the man insisted. "She's my daughter, and it's my right to meet her. I have never even seen a painting of her—"

Felonia burst into laugher. "A *painting*? As if Ida would sit still for a painting. That's rich. And even if she would, I would never waste the time or the paint on such an undertaking. Ida is ugly. It's almost impossible to believe that child is related in any way to me."

"We agree on *something*, at least," Ida muttered under her breath.

"I had to give her an ugly nickname to match her ugly face. She must get her looks from you—she doesn't live up to the beautiful name she was given at birth. She's also stupid—her favorite phrase is 'I dunno,' so that's where she gets the name she carries. Again, must be from your side."

"You shouldn't press your luck with me, Felonia." The man's voice had an edge as sharp as the Thief Queen's knife.

The bed squeaked again, possibly indicating that she had stood up.

"It is *you* who do not wish to press your luck," Felonia answered, her voice even more deadly. "You may be an influential man outside the gates, but within this city you are less than nothing without my protection. And one on one, you certainly don't want to make me angry. If you cross me, you will not live to see your next breath."

"If you dislike her so intensely, give her to me," the man said. "Let that fat old fool in Northland find another bride."

Felonia chuckled loud enough to be heard through the floor.

"No, no," she said. "You do not understand the ways of the Raven's Guild. There never is much of a bond between the queen and her daughter-heir, because of what needs to be done to her to make her into a worthy successor. If I had feelings for her—I have feelings for no one, so that's not an issue—but if I did, I could never put her through the training that will make her a successful queen when I am gone. Consider this a kind of grooming—especially funny, since she has so little of it right now. One day, when she returns to the Market after her husband's untimely passing, she will be worthy to head the guild."

"You are going to kill her husband early, then?"

Felonia laughed again. "No, no. *She* will. It's all part of the training program." Her voice became deadly again. "The only part of mine that I ever failed was letting *you* live."

Far away the children heard a pounding on the outer chamber door.

"Enter," Felonia called harshly.

A moment later they heard a muffled voice, unmistakably terrified.

"Your Majesty, the, er, Miss Ida, and the others—"

"You had best not be telling me they are gone," said Felonia. Even below the ground, the five companions shivered at the tone in her voice.

There was no reply except for the sounds of footsteps walking rapidly away and the slamming of the bedchamber door.

Ven reached into his pocket and pulled out the king's stone.

Cold light flooded the little passageway, making everyone blink. They looked around.

The tunnel was dug in nothing more than earth, with no bricks or supports holding up the walls. It led off into darkness that even the light from the stone could not pierce.

"Let's go," Ven said. "We can't very well go back up, and, depending on where this leads, it's going to be a race."

"You go first," Clemency said. "You've got the light."

"All right." Ven slid past Clem, Char, and Ida to the front of the line, then started down the tunnel.

The wet odor of earth mixed with the sharp sting of mold was at first unpleasant to Ven's nose. The deeper he went in, however, the more the ground around him seemed welcoming, or at least familiar. He found that he could move very fast through the earthen tunnel along the dirt floor.

"For goodness' sake, Ven, wait up," Clemency called crossly when he got too far out of sight. "Not all of us are Nain like you. Slow down."

"Sorry," Ven called, coming to a stop at a place where the

tunnel branched off. He held the light above his head as he waited for his friends to catch up.

The tunnel itself continued forward, but a second, smaller branch led off on an angle. Ven looked around. To his right was a wall that appeared newer and more unsettled than the rest, as if it had been sealed off some time back. The wall there was less solid, like a pile of old dirt that had hardened over time.

"I think we should go through here," he said when the others arrived. "Felonia must know this exit is blocked."

"Uh, it *is* blocked, Ven," Char said.

"For the moment," Ven replied. He thought back to what the king had said about the building of the secret vault.

*I asked the lead stonemason to build this place in secret for me. He sent the bricklayers away and set the walls himself. He let me help so that I would be able to find it again. We did it in a single night— mostly because the stone almost seemed to move into place by itself when he touched it. Your race has an almost magical knack with stone and earth.*

Ven handed the king's stone to Char, then put his hand against the wall. It was solid beneath his touch. He pushed on it, but nothing happened.

Then he closed his eyes and concentrated.

*Please*, he thought. *Please move.*

In his head he thought he saw, or maybe felt, a fissure in the dirt mound, a place near the base of the floor where air had been trapped when the dirt was packed in. He moved his hands closer to it. Then he scraped at the wall with his fingers.

The dirt, long solid, came away in his hands like sand from a giant dune.

Excited, Ven kept digging. More and more dirt fell away.

"Back away an' let him go," Char said to the others, moving

Saeli away from the wall and holding up the light. "He did this once before, when he was buryin' the Rover's box at the cross-roads, remember?"

"Careful, Ven," Clemency cautioned. "That time you were taking dirt out of the ground. This time you might collapse the roof over our heads."

"I'll be careful," Ven promised, digging away. "This is really not a solid wall—it's just a pile of hard dirt that was filled in here. You could do this, too, Clem—there's nothing magical. I just can tell where the best places to dig are."

He dug until he had made a small tunnel near the floor. He shoved the dirt he had dug away out of the tunnel, then crawled inside and continued to dig, passing the loose dirt back to the others. He kept digging, humming the chants his family had sung when working in the factory, his mind racing, until a blast of cool air hit him in the face.

Ven blinked. He poked his head out of the tunnel and looked around. Then he crawled back inside.

"Good news—the tunnel opens to an alleyway of a sort," he said to his eager friends. "Bad news—it also opens into a garbage dump. Felonia probably had it sealed because the smell was seeping up into her bedroom."

"Who cares?" said Char. "We gotta get out of here. Let's go."

"Right," Ven said. He got back on his belly and crawled out the newly dug tunnel until he had emerged into a sea of fish heads, chicken bones, shredded cloth, smelly eggshells, and a host of other disgusting things all rotting in a huge pile in the al-ley outside the Raven's Guild wall. He scrambled out of the pile, holding his breath as long as he could to keep from breathing the putrid smell.

A moment later Clemency came crawling out, followed by Saeli and Ida. Char brought up the rear, still holding the light.

"Don' think the king's gonna want this thing back, mate," he said, tossing the stone to Ven and brushing the filth from his shoulders. Clemency took a potato peel from Ida's hair, while Saeli checked the keekee to make sure it hadn't been lost in the garbage pile.

The street was utterly dark. They had lost all track of time inside the windowless building, and so Ven was surprised to find that it was nighttime again. He had no idea what day it was, but he was glad they had come out of the tunnel in the dark, at a time when the ravens on the roost above were sleeping.

As if to scoff at the thought, a hideous shrieking filled the air, and a flutter of wings could be heard from the rooftops above them. Felonia was obviously angry that they hadn't been caught yet, and had sent up another alarm with the Screaming Ravens.

All over town they heard doors and windows banging shut.

Ven stuck the king's stone in his pocket. "Cover your ears and follow me," he said to the others.

# ~ 19 ~

# Out of the Frying Pan, Into the Fire

THEY HURRIED UP THE SPARSELY COBBLED STREET, PAST SEEDY buildings and houses that were falling down.

From around the corner they could hear the sounds of running footsteps, of shouts and curses. Some of Felonia's thugs had abandoned searching the Raven's Nest and had taken to the streets to find them. Ven could hear them growing closer all the time as they ran through the deserted alleyways.

There seemed to be a million of them.

"Hurry!" he urged. He could see that Ida was falling behind. They came around another corner and found themselves in the street they had walked down on the way to the Raven's Guild in the first place.

In the middle of the street was an enormous public well that took up a good deal of the roadway, deserted in the dark. It had a circular wall of about knee height around it, with buckets attached to ropes all around its edge.

"Clem, can you swim?" Ven asked as they ran.

"Yes," Clem puffed. "Why?"

"And you, Saeli—can you swim? Or at least float?"

The little girl shook her head, terrified, and kept running.

"I don't like where—this is goin'," Char said, struggling to catch up.

"I don't see that we have a choice," Ven said, his voice all but drowned out in the screams of the ravens and the shouts of the nearing thieves. "It can't be that deep—and they won't think to look in there. We can't outrun them for long."

As if to prove his words true, in the distance voices could be heard approaching the turn in the street.

Ven grabbed a bucket as he reached the well. He held it out to Saeli.

"Get in, and I'll lower you down." He glanced over the side. In the dark, it was impossible to see the water, but he could hear it splashing down in the depths of the well.

Clemency was staring behind her in panic.

"The first thing they teach you where I live is never, ever to fall down a well," she said nervously.

"You aren't falling, exactly," said Ven, watching the same place. "You're jumping. And if you don't, you're going to be caught again. Go for it, Clem—there's no other choice."

Ida shoved past her, stepped over the knee-wall, and jumped. A splash echoed up the well from below.

"You all right down there, Ida?" Ven called.

"Ducky," came the disgusted voice. "Just ducky. It's cold as a witch's—"

"I'm lowering Saeli down to you," Ven interrupted. "Catch the bucket and try to stay quiet. Clem, you're next. Now or never."

The curate-in-training sucked in her breath. "Very well." She climbed over the edge, then struggled to let go, finally doing so and shrieking a bit until she splashed.

"Try and keep to the edge, so as not to swamp the girls, but don't hit the sides with your head," Ven said to Char.

Char nodded. "Now for it, I guess."

At the end of the street, they could hear the first of the thieves round the corner in the darkness.

Ven nodded in return, and the two boys climbed over the wall and dropped into the water at the base of the well.

*Even though I had warned Char not to hit the edge, I did it myself, bruising my hand. It probably would have been worse, but the water was so cold that I couldn't feel it anyway. It closed over my head, shocking me, until I bobbed to the surface.*

*Everyone else seemed to be floating, Clem clinging to Saeli's bucket. I couldn't see anything but their outlines, but I could tell from their ragged breathing and the chattering of their teeth that they wouldn't survive long here in the freezing water.*

*Nor would I.*

"Move to the sides if you can," Ven said, his jaw shivering as he spoke. "Stay up against the edges of—the well and out of the center. If they look, they will—be—less likely to—see you."

The shouts of the members of the Raven's Guild were growing closer now. It seemed like the entire Inner Market had emptied out into the streets. Even down in the well Ven could see the shine of torchlight as the thieves combed the alleyways, turning over carts and crates and piles of trash looking for them.

He clung to the wall, trying to keep track of the others. The street was filled with traveling lights now, casting shadows all around above them.

As he was looking up, one flash of firelight fell inside the well for just an instant. In that instant, Ven caught sight of something strange.

About halfway up the well's wall there was an opening with a thin ledge, like a tunnel built just above the highest place where the water reached. Ven could see the watermark on the well shaft, ten or more feet above them. *I wonder if that's a drain of some sort*, he thought, *for use when the water table gets high in the spring*. Then the person carrying the torch moved down the street, and the light was gone.

He reached over in the dark and grabbed for Char's shoulder. His friend was shaking with cold, treading water and trying to help Ida keep afloat. He pointed to the opening, now little more than a dark archway.

"Whaddaya think, Char?" he whispered, trying to keep his voice from echoing up the well. "Can we get up there?"

The cook's mate followed his finger, then shook his head.

"There's no handholds in the wall," he said. His voice was filled with despair. "I don't know how we're gonna get out o' here, Ven. We may have done ourselves in by jumpin' down here."

"We can haul ourselves up the rope on Saeli's bucket," Ven said, but even as the words came out, he knew they were unrealistic.

"That's barely looped around a spike in the knee-wall," Char answered quietly. "It would never hold anyone's weight but maybe hers."

Ven's stomach tightened at his friend's words. He looked around for a hole in the well shaft, but the well had been lined with brick, and the mortar was solid. He couldn't find even the smallest hole in which to grab a hold.

A cold chill that came from within him, colder than the water around him, took hold. He was beginning to realize that he may have just been responsible for killing his friends. There was no way out of the well; even getting to the opening with the ledge was only halfway as far as they needed to go. Sooner or later the thieves would find them, either in the next few moments, or in the morning when people came to the well to draw water.

And by that time, he didn't think any of them would still be alive.

He looked down at the palm of his hand. Gleaming there was the circular stain that had been in his skin since he had drawn the Time Scissors scale.

*I wonder if now is the time to use this,* he thought. *I could wish to undo Time back to the point where I suggested that we jump into the well, and none of us would be here.*

He took a deep breath, considering the weight of the action. *But then, where would we be? Maybe using this power would land us all back in Felonia's cage—or worse. She would probably shoot Char as soon as she saw him.* He looked over at his friend.

Char was rustling around in the frigid water.

"What are you—doing?" Ven whispered. His body was shaking now.

"Shhh," Char replied. He was unwrapping the bundle over his shoulder. After a few agonizing moments, he held up what he had been struggling with.

Mr. Coates's gauntlet.

"What are you doing?" Ven repeated.

Char did not answer. Instead, he slipped the heavy metal glove on his arm, then flexed his fingers and made a fist.

A pair of metal spikes emerged from the knuckles.

A sense of excitement flooded through Ven, warming his freezing toes.

"I had forgotten about that!" he whispered again.

Char nodded, feeling around in the wall for the place where the bricks were sealed with mortar.

"Get—Saeli's bucket over here, so I can—use the rope to balance," Char said. He reached back as far as he could, and punched the wall just above him with his armored knuckles.

The double-pronged spike buried into the mortar, sticking his hand to the wall.

Ven swam over to where Clemency, Ida, and Saeli were floating in the water. "Hang on," he said to the girls, then steered Saeli and her bucket back over to where Char was hanging half out of the water. He positioned the rope near his friend's left hand, holding the bucket in place.

Char took hold of the rope with his left hand and heaved himself out of the water. He pulled the gauntlet from the wall with a tug that sent crumbs of dried mortar raining down on Ven and the girls and into the water below him.

Char spun as he clung to the rope, twisting with it as it turned in the air. Saeli, whose bucket was attached to that rope, spun on the surface of the water, looking terrified in the dark. She covered her head as Char punched the wall a little farther up and hoisted himself between the rope and the gauntlet, climbing hand over hand, his feet sliding on the slippery sides of the well.

After several agonizing minutes and as many showers of mortar grit, he was able to reach the ledge. He lunged into the opening on his belly, then scrambled inside. Then he turned around and hoisted Saeli's bucket out of the water and up to the ledge with him.

"I'm out!" he called quietly down the well. Ven saw him lean out of the opening and look above, where the flashes of torchlight were still dancing. Saeli climbed out of the bucket, and Char lowered it back down.

"Hang on to this, put your feet on the wall, and I'll pull you up," he called down.

"You first, Ida," Ven said, treading water over to the girls. Ida had said nothing since jumping in, and Ven suspected she was suffering even more than he and Clemency were, being thin as she was. "Once you get up there, help Char with the rope."

Ida nodded. Ven wrapped the rope around her waist.

"All right, Char, heave her up," he called up to the ledge.

With a series of tugs, Ida lurched up the side of the well, her feet slipping helplessly on the sides. Char was cold, but he was strong, and he had the gauntlet, so a few moments later she was over the ledge and into the opening.

The bucket splashed down in the water again.

"Up, Clem," Ven whispered. "It's going to take all of you to lift me."

The voices in the street were beginning to gather around the well. Without a word, Clemency took hold of the rope and followed Ida, scrambling with much less grace than the Thief Queen's daughter had.

At last the bucket splashed down again.

"We're ready," Char said, his voice low. "Hang on."

As he was raised out of the icy water, Ven could hear Char quietly calling out a short-drag cadence, a sea-chantey the sailors had sung to make the raising of sails or to haul longboats aboard the *Serelinda*. He had just reached the ledge and was being pulled over when a bright light splashed down the well from above.

"What'erya doin', Vince?" a voice called from the street as the shadow of a head appeared at the well rim, a torch in a raised hand.

"Thought I heard somethin' down here," the dark shadow replied. He thrust the torch into the well, lighting the sides brightly.

Ven and the others pressed themselves against the walls of the alcove, holding their breath.

The man spun the torch around inside the well again.

"Prob'ly rats," the man behind him said. "Come on, gotta find them brats."

The man called Vince waited a few moments longer, then pulled the torch from the well. The light danced away, then disappeared.

The children remained pressed against the wall of the drain, or whatever the opening was, until the last of the voices and torchlight had moved on. Then they all let out their breath at the same time.

"That's another one we owe Mr. Coates," said Clemency, still shivering. "Good work, Char."

"Yeah, this really is a handy thing," Char said, holding up the gauntlet admiringly. He turned his hand over as Mr. Coates had done, in his shop, what seemed like a million years before. The double spike popped back into the armored glove. Then he flicked the thumb, and the flint and steel ignited. A tiny flame burned from the thumb.

Ven laughed. Clemency and Saeli giggled in relief. Char smiled. Only Ida was silent.

"Ven—did you know that your eyes glow in the dark when light hits 'em, like an animal's?" Char said, settling back against the wall of the drain.

Ven blinked in surprise. "Don't everyone's?"

"Uh—no."

"Maybe it's just Nain, then," Ven said. "All my family's eyes do."

"Hmmm," Char said, leaning his head back. "That's odd."

"Nain live inside the earth," Clemency said, squeezing the water out of her hair. "If they couldn't see in the dark, that would be a problem."

"Is the keekee all right?" Ven asked Saeli, who was cuddling the little creature to warm it up. Saeli nodded.

As she did, Ven saw movement behind her.

The flame from the gauntlet cast long shadows down the drain tunnel behind them. In those shadows stood three more shadows.

Only these looked human.

Each of those shadows was thin, though one was especially so. He was crouched on the floor of the drain, watching them with glittering eyes, eyes that glowed like Ven's own. A taller, broader man was leaning up against the drain wall, while another even taller shadow loomed behind him. The tall man spoke, and his voice had the ring of dark amusement to it.

"Well, lookee here, Percy. What does that look like ta you?"

The shadow of the thin man seemed to lean forward out of the dark, and the children could hear the sound of sniffing.

The thin man settled back on his feet and grinned broadly, his teeth catching the light of the glowing stone. When he spoke, his voice came out in a terrifying hiss.

"Fresh meat," he whispered.

# - 20 -

# The Downworlders

Aw, NOW, PERCY, THAT WASN' NICE," THE FIRST MAN SCOLDED. "Downright unfriendly, in fact. No point in frightenin' the little blighters. Yer great-grandmum was a runaway just like that once."

*The words "fresh meat" had made my brain stop working. I was terrified, but not as bad as Char. I could tell how scared he was by how much the gauntlet was shaking. The shuddering flame in the thumb was throwing flashes of light all around the dark tunnel.*

The taller man squeezed past Percy in the tunnel.

"You little blokes musta really had it rough to get to this place through the well," he said.

When Char's shaking light hit him, Ven could see that he was a pale man with colorless hair, a little like Ida's, and light blue eyes that gleamed in the dark. He was missing a good many teeth, as all the men seemed to be. "Well, sorry ta tell you this, kids, but no matter how hard yer life was up ta now, it'll be harder from here on out."

Char's little flame burned out with a whisper.

Leaving them in darkness.

"Come with us," the tall man's voice said.

The friends spun around, looking for an escape. Behind them the tunnel opened back into the well shaft. All else was dark.

"What do we do?" Clemency choked.

A metallic clink came from over Ven's shoulder. He turned around.

With his Nain eyes he could see Char standing there, trembling, the gauntlet outstretched.

The dagger extended.

"We're not goin' anywhere with you," Char said. It was a brave statement, but his voice cracked as he said it.

The men at the other end of the tunnel broke into raucous laughter.

"Is that so?" said the one called Percy.

In his head Ven could hear the words Mr. Coates had spoken.

*You don't want to be carrying a weapon, visible or otherwise, in this place. Even the youngest infant who lives within these walls is better with any weapon than you would be. You should never look more ready for a fight than you are, young'uns. It's the best way to get yourselves killed.*

He thought back to the most dangerous situation he had ever been in before this. He was just beyond the harbor of Vaarn, inspecting a new ship his father had built, when Fire Pirates attacked. The only thing that was ever known for certain about Fire Pirates was that they never left any of their victims alive. He remembered what he had said to the first mate on that ship as they were gathering weapons to fight, even though they were outnumbered ten to one.

*If we don't fight, we're all done for.*

The first mate had looked at him sadly.

*We're all done for anyway, lad.*

*I don't want to fight, but I don't really think we have any choice*, he thought miserably now. *What other option do we have?* He pulled the jack-rule from his pocket and flipped open the knife.

"Leave us alone," he said, trying to sound menacing. "We're armed."

"Sure ye are," came the reply. "Come along, now."

With the other hand, Ven reached into his pocket and pulled out the king's stone. He raised it high above his head, trying to make the shadow of Char's weapon and his own seem longer.

"*Leave us alone!*" he shouted.

The men at the end of the tunnel shied away from the light, squinting. Then they blinked. Their mouths fell open and their faces went slack in surprise.

"The Lightstone," Percy whispered. "They got the Lightstone."

The friends looked at each other in shock. When they looked back, the men were gone.

"What—was that?" Clemency asked in amazement. "What just happened?"

Ven looked down at the glowing stone in his hand. It was radiating a cool blue light, as it had before, but at the center there was a hint of gold, much in the same way there had been when it was in the hand of King Vandemere. The internal cracks and squiggles were clearer now than they had been when the king had given it to him. In the middle, one long, straight vertical crack had a number of lines and squiggles branching off it. On one of those branches was the large starburst-shaped flaw Ven had seen the first day.

The golden glow was coming from there.

"I've no idea," he murmured. "They called it the Lightstone—they must know what it is." The burning curiosity that had been absent since Saeli's disappearance began to take root again. "And maybe that means they know who sent it to the king—and why."

"Or maybe *they* did," Char noted.

The others looked at him in silence.

Ven stared deeper at the cracks in the translucent stone. A small vertical crack seemed to pulse when his hand was closer to the opening of the drain where they had come in. He stepped back to the edge and looked up the well shaft.

The vertical line glowed bright blue.

Ven's eyes opened as wide as those of the men in the tunnel.

"Of course," he said as excitement rushed through him, making him hot inside. "Of course—it's a *map*! These are the tunnels I saw when I looked at the Lightstone with the jack-rule in Mr. Coates's store."

"If this one is the well hole," Char said, running his finger along the pulsing blue line, "then what is *this*?" He pointed to the long crack connected to it by a tiny horizontal squiggle.

Ven passed the stone around for everyone to see. Everyone examined it but Ida.

"I don't know, but the starburst-shaped flaw is in a small squiggle off that long line," he said, taking the stone back. "I don't really think we can go back up the well. Maybe we should just go deeper in and see what's going on."

The others exchanged a glance of apprehension.

"You sure about this?" Char asked nervously.

"What else can we do?" said Ven. "Even if we could get out of the well, Felonia's thugs would be waiting for us. I don't see that we have any choice."

They turned back toward the inner part of the tunnel, and stopped.

There, where the three men had been, were at least thirty more.

At the front of the group was a withered old man. In the glow of the Lightstone, they could see he was clothed in a ragged robe with sleeves that ended just above his elbows, a necklace made of large metal squares that had stones set in the middle of most of them, and a battered crown on his head. His eyes were black, but they sparkled with interest, and his thin lips spread into a broad smile, showing white teeth separated by gaps of darkness.

"Welcome," he said in a scratchy voice that sounded amused. "The name's Macedon, Ruler of the Downworlders, but most just knows me as the Rat King. These splendid gentlemen behind me are my court." The scruffy men behind him laughed ominously. "So to what do I owe the, er, pleasure of yer company, young'uns?"

The friends looked at one another.

"Uh, we took shelter in the well," said Ven. "We're sorry to disturb you—we didn't realize you were here."

"Ah." The Rat King nodded. "So King Vandemere didn't send you, then?"

"Oh! Well, yes, sort of," Ven admitted. Reluctant as he was to reveal too many details, he felt it best not to pretend or lie to someone who knew more about what he was doing than he did himself. "He gave me the Lightstone, if that's what you mean."

"But he didn' understand what it was, then." The Rat King sighed. "Too bad. I had heard a few years back he was an inquis-itive youth, out pokin' around to learn as much as he could about the kingdom he now rules. Too bad he didn't get more of a chance."

Ven's excitement was raging, setting his skin on fire. He stepped forward a little.

"You can tell me whatever you want him to know, and I will tell him," he offered. "That's my job, actually—or at least it was." His face grew hot as he saw the men behind the king look-ing at each other skeptically. "Please, Your Majesty—what can you tell me about the Lightstone?"

The Rat King smirked.

"Firstly, it's keepin' you safe right now," he said humorously, but with a dark undertone of seriousness. "There's many things what crawls around in these tunnels asides us, and they don't take kindly to being disturbed, especially by strangers. An' they're always hungry."

"Hoo boy," Char said quietly.

"Other'n that, it was an invitation, from one king to another. An' it wasn't sent to him—it was sent to his father."

"Yes, he did say that," Ven said.

The Rat King chuckled. "Well, since yer here, why don't you

come in? You're our guests now, so's it's proper to find you something ta eat." His dark eyes glittered. "And we'll show you the Wonder."

"The Wonder?" Clemency said aloud before she could help herself.

The Rat King nodded. "Yes, indeed, my girl. So if you wants to see it, come with us. Give me the Lightstone and I'll show ya the way." He put out his hand.

Ven stared at the king's stone. *Do I have a choice here?* he thought. The Downworlders were the only people in the world who might have the key to what the king wanted to know. At last he decided there was no other choice but to obey. He handed it to the Rat King.

The scraggly man waved them forward, then turned around in the tunnel and walked off, the court already gone in the shadows ahead of where the light reached.

The friends exchanged a glance, then hurried to catch up with them.

"If you don't mind my asking, why are you called the Downworlders, Your Majesty?" Ven asked as he walked.

"What if I *do* mind ya askin'?"

"Then I'll be quiet."

The king nodded. "Well, not much fun in *that*," he said. "I mean, ya came all this way and all. Not much point in havin' company if you're not gonna share stories. Here's the beginning of ours." He stopped at the end of the tunnel where another opening yawned, stepped out of the way, held up the Lightstone, and gestured for them to look beyond it.

Ven stepped forward and leaned through the tunnel opening. He gasped in surprise.

*Beyond the opening was a vast vertical tunnel, many times the size of the well shaft, leading down into darkness at the bottom, as far as the light reached. In fact, this tunnel was so huge that it looked like the square of a vast city, with many levels where other tunnels led off in all different directions. The largest of those tunnels matched the squiggles and lines within the Lightstone. The large vertical line was now glowing blue.*

*Directly in front of us, hovering over the seemingly bottomless tunnel, was a floating floor of sorts, strung with ropes that reached up to the earthen ceiling above us, where they ran through round gearlike machines. This floating floor was only one of many that were being hauled up and down all across the wide central shaft, ferrying raggedly dressed people back and forth to each of the tunnel openings. There were more people than I could easily count, scurrying from platform to platform, as if to get out of the range of the Lightstone.*

"The Downworlders aren't used to brightness below the ground," the Rat King said. "We like the dark." He put the Lightstone inside the ill-fitting crown, making his head glow eerily. Then he stepped onto the floating platform and took hold of a rope. "Are ye comin'?"

The children followed him gingerly onto the swinging platform.

"Grab hold," said the Rat King, pointing to the other ropes around the edge of the platform. "Down here, everybody works. No free ride for *nobody*, not even me." He began pulling on the rope, hand over hand, and the others followed his lead.

The floating platform began to descend into the huge dark tunnel.

"I s'pose by now ye've figured out why we're called Downworlders," Macedon said as they continued to haul on the ropes. "Our people live below the streets, below the grassy fields, in the deepest parts of the world—well, perhaps not as deep as yer folk, Nain, but out of the sight of the humanfolk of the island, upstanding and otherwise. None of us has ever seen the light o' day, 'cept from inside a tunnel."

"Why?" asked Clemency as she pulled.

The Rat King regarded her thoughtfully.

"Now, that's a good question, miss. Wish it had good answer. Long ago, we were outcasts among outcasts—our forefathers were citizens of the Gated City, but not part of its ways. We were considered unworthy even by the standards of the scum o' the earth, and that's about as low as ya can get. So we live here, away from everyone, keepin' to ourselves. We've been here so long that even the thieves have forgotten about us. Which is as it should be. And as we want it."

"Seems like a pretty lonely way to live," Char said, hoisting away.

"Naw," said the Rat King. "There's a lot more of us Downworlders than you can imagine—a lot more people lost from the sight of the world than anyone knows. We live beneath the cobblestones, under the walls, below the houses, even—and nobody realizes we's here, 'cept the occasional runaway from the Market, which is what we thought you all was. Just because we keeps to ourselves don't mean we don't have fun. It's a good life, fer what's it's worth. There's worse ways to live, believe me. Our tunnels go all over the island, so we sees a lot of what goes on upworld. Wouldn't want to trade places with anyone. You all can stop pullin' now."

He tossed his rope to several members of his court, who were standing on a platform several levels down from where they had been, and all the way across the central vertical tunnel. He reached out a gnarled hand and held out the Lightstone. He tapped the glowing, starburst-shaped flaw with his long yellow fingernail. "Almost there."

Ven stared at the Lightstone. The starburst was gleaming brilliantly, brighter than since they had been in the tunnels. He looked down the dark hallway before them, where a slight light of the same golden color could be seen farther in.

"Is this where you reign, Your Majesty? Like a—a castle?"

A round of laughter went up from the Rat King's court.

The Rat King smiled widely. "No, lad," he said. "That be the tunnel what leads to the Wonder."

Ven heard a sharp intake of breath behind him. He turned around to see Ida's eyes narrow in suspicion. His other friends were looking at each other in confusion. Ven nodded encouragingly to them all, amazed that they didn't seem to feel the same sense of excitement, of thrill that was coming, that he was feeling.

The Rat King stepped off the platform and started down the tunnel.

"Shield yer eyes," he said.

The companions followed him down the tunnel until it ended, suddenly and completely. In front of them was a heavy door. The golden light seeped like water under the bottom of the door.

"Make sure yer eyes are covered, now," cautioned the Rat King again.

Ven squinted as tight as he could, leaving his eyelids open only a crack. Then he put his hand over them, peering out through the space between his fingers. He heard the Rat King opening the door, and braced himself.

Like the steel fires of his father's factory, a blinding light, burning bright and golden, blasted them. The children shrank away from the radiance and the heat.

The Rat King laughed.

"Hurry in," he said. "Can't keep the door open too long."

Ven stepped into the room, followed immediately by Char. A moment later, the others came in as well. The Rat King shut the door.

They followed him into the endless brightness until they came to what was apparently the center of a relatively small chamber. Once closer in, the light seemed to fade, as if they had stepped beyond it.

In the center of the chamber was what looked like a floating glass globe the size of an apple, hovering without support in the air. Below it in the dirt floor there was a small hole, almost too small to see.

Within the globe was a pinprick of light burning so powerfully that it stung their eyes even to look at it. It leapt and danced, like candle flame, radiating heat and light of almost unbearable intensity. It seemed almost fluid, like brightly burning water.

"What is that?" Ven whispered, awed.

The Rat King smiled his crooked smile.

"Why, lad, yer lookin' at a piece of the sun."

## - 21 -

# The Wonder, and the Way Out

Then the Rat King told us the story of the Wonder, and how it had come to be here, in this dark place of tunnels and secrets, hidden away from the rest of world. His voice was hushed, like he was telling a holy story, which in fact he was. It was sort of like a poem, sort of like a song. I tried to keep careful notes in my head, kicking myself for not bringing my journal along with me, a mistake I will not make again.

At least his tale was short, so it wasn't impossible to memorize it.

We were too entranced to notice at first that our clothes were dry, our skin warm. But we were suddenly hungry.

And the Rat King seemed to know it.

ᴺow that you've seen it, come an' i'll show you what we do with it," King Macedon said. He hiked up the falling sleeves of his ill-fitting robe, straightened his battered crown, and stepped back into the circle of blinding radiance to the door again, followed quickly by the children.

"Go'n git our young guests somethin' to eat," the Rat King ordered one of the thin men who made up his court. The man eyed the children, then turned and disappeared into one of the side tunnels.

"That would be great, thanks, Your Majesty," Char said as he followed the king. "I've been hungry ever since I've been in the Market."

The king stopped in the middle of the dark tunnel.

"That's prob'ly 'cause yer spoilt," he said. There was no accusation in his voice. "I bet yer usta three squares a day. This is one of the places in the world that hunger lives, or at least spends a lot of hours. Most of us down here is hungry all the time, lad. In fact, most of the world is hungry all the time. Be grateful that for you it's only once in a while."

They returned to the wide central shaft and stepped back onto the swinging platform, which the Rat King skillfully guided down a level directly below them, then stopped.

"Everybody off," he said.

They followed the ragged man down another tunnel, to a door very much like the one in the room above. Ven noted that he had seen no other doors anywhere in the Downworlders' realm. It was like being inside a giant nest of ants, or a hive of mud wasps, all these tunnels twisting and turning in the earth under the streets of the Gated City.

The Rat King opened the door.

"You go in first," he said to Saeli, smiling his black-gapped smile in the glow of the Lightstone. Saeli blinked nervously and looked back at Ven, who nodded. She straightened her back and walked through the door, followed by the rest of them.

Even before he made it over the threshold, Ven knew that

whatever the room contained was very different from the rest of the Downworlder's realm, just by the smell. Out in the dark tunnels there was a constant odor of dampness and dirt, which was not unpleasant to Ven or Saeli, but clearly had taken its toll on the humans with them.

Beyond the door, that odor changed to a fresher scent. It was not clear, like a place that had been swept by the wind, but was strangely rich and green.

When Ven got through the doorway, he saw why.

Inside the room beyond the door, and below the chamber of the Wonder, was a small garden filled with drowsy light. The plants were mostly ferns and lichens, the sorts that grew in shade, with softly colored flowers scattered across the mossy ground, violets and bleeding hearts and night roses. They filled the room with a sweet, dreamy fragrance.

Ven shuddered when he saw a patch of pink-and-white Stuff-of-Dreams.

"What is this place, Your Majesty?" he asked the Rat King.

Macedon inhaled, his bony body taking in the sweet air.

"This be the fruit of the Wonder's labor, lad. Upworld, where you all live, in the bright world, there are many things the sun makes grow—vege'bles, fruit, grass an' trees, people—the Wonder's a magic thing, but it's not bright enough to replace your sun in our kingdom. But its power is used for nothin' but good here. There's just enough light ta have a little garden, a little special place where the darkness of our daily world goes away fer a while. It's too small a place to actually live, so we jus' bring folks here on special occasions, like when they're being born, or dyin', gettin' married, and especially when they're sick. Sometimes this place is all a sick person needs to get better again."

"I can believe that," Clemency said, looking around in amazement. "This is a magic place."

"That it is," the Rat King agreed. He bent over near a small bush where dark red berries were growing, snapped one off, and handed it to Ven. He held the Lightstone up.

"Ever seen one of them, Nain?"

Ven held his hand under the Lightstone, but he didn't recognize the fruit. He shook his head.

"That be a kiran berry," said the Rat King. "Most fruits, most berries especially, needs lots and lots o' light and water to grow. We don't have neither of them things here. But the kiran is different. It grows in bad soil, in harsh conditions, in little light and with almost no water—it's a favorite of the Nain for all those reasons, I'm told. And it makes good medicine, just like all the flowers that grow here as well."

"Even the Stuff-of-Dreams?" Clemency asked. "Isn't that poisonous?"

The Rat King chuckled. "Only when misused," he said. "Almost anything can be used to do good or bad; it all depends on what you want. 'Tis true of anything—and any*one*, no matter what they're born into."

Ven looked at Ida. She was staring at the ground.

"This is the place where we remembers that we was once part of the upworld," Macedon said, looking up at the soft light beaming down from the ceiling. "And the place we remember what is to come, when one day we will be part of the light again."

A tap came on the door. It opened, and the man whom the Rat King had sent for food appeared, a bag in his hand.

"Look's like yer supper's here," said Macedon. "Come along, young'ns."

*It was surprisingly hard to leave the little garden. It was a drowsy place, a place that felt completely safe, even within tunnels below the streets of a city of thieves. The everyday realm of the Downworlders was so bleak, so poor, that it was difficult to turn our backs on such a pretty place to go back out into endless tunnels of dark dirt. But the Rat King was holding the door, so we sighed and followed him.*

The man handed the Rat King the sack, then turned and went away into the dark.

Macedon rummaged in the sack. "Well, yer in luck," he said, pulling out a few mushrooms and some little potatoes. "We got a regular feast here, though I'm afeared that we got no meat ta share at this time. The rats are all feastin' away at the leavings from the Market, and don' come 'round much in the summer. We mostly get 'em in winter, when they burrow deeper for warmth."

"We'll try ta contain our disappointment," said Char under his breath.

The Rat King handed the mushrooms and raw potatoes to Ida and Clem. "Pass those around."

"I may regret asking this, Your Majesty," said Ven as the girls divvied up the meager food, "but what is going to happen to us now?"

"Keep walking. While you eat, I'll tell ya," said the Rat King. "Just remember ta be thankful for each bite while yer listenin'. Come this way."

He held up the Lightstone at the opening of another passageway, one that led off for as far as they could see in the glow.

Several dark shadows were there as well. The Rat King's court had returned.

They followed the shriveled little man and his court until there seemed to be nothing but endless tunnel both ahead of them and behind them. Ven was given one of the mushrooms, which he ate thankfully, while Char struggled to chew on a raw potato.

Finally, after what seemed like hours, they came to another branch in the tunnel. The Rat King and his men stopped. Macedon turned around.

"If ye follow this path here, to the right, all the way to the end, it'll bring ya out at the Great River, a mile or so north of the bridge," he said. "Mind yer manners there—some friends of ours live around there. They won't bother you if you don't bother them. You'll be out o' the Market and free ta go on yer way from there."

Ven's mouth dropped open in astonishment. He heard his friends behind him perk up in excitement.

"Really?" he exclaimed. "You're letting us go?"

The Rat King's brow furrowed in confusion.

"Why wouldn't we?" he asked. "Ye came by invitation—and we's good hosts. Even if you aren't the king himself. All we ask is that ye keep our secret, an' not be leadin' others back here. We like our privacy."

"You have my word," said Ven. "The only one I will tell is the king."

Macedon nodded. "Good." He pointed to the way out, and the men in the court moved out of the way.

"Get back safe, now," the Rat King cautioned. His black eyes sparkled in the fading glow of the Lightstone. "And don' ferget to tell the king this—that what belonged to his father is by right his now." He handed the stone to Ven.

*Then I remembered—the whole reason we had come into the Gated City in the first place. In all the running from Felonia's thugs, the searching for Saeli, and the heavy smell of spice and soot, I had lost sight of it. The thought struck me as hard as if a brick had dropped on my head from the sky. My eyes shot open until the skin of my forehead hurt.*

"Of course!" Ven exclaimed. "The Wonder! That's what the coded message was talking about: 'the brightest light in the darkest shadow.'"

In the glow of the stone he could see the white teeth in the Rat King's smile next to the larger, darker spaces in his mouth. The shriveled man shook his head as if he were amused.

"Alas, lad, I'm afraid you're like all the ones afore you. You've seen the Wonder—but you haven't seen the light. Ah, well." He pointed down the tunnel. "Be off, now. If you see anything movin' in the dark, stand still an' let it pass, if it's gonna. It can move a lot faster than you in the tunnels." He looked back at the glittering eyes of the other children. "Well, faster than *them*. You're Nain. You might have a shot at outrunnin' it."

Ven peered down the dark, dank tunnel. "We'll stay together, no matter what." His skin was prickling from the Rat King's words. *How could I have been wrong about the Wonder?* he thought. Then he remembered he should thank the Downworlders for rescuing them. He turned back.

"Thank you, Your Majes—"

The king and his court were gone. Ven's words echoed up the tunnel behind him.

"Come on, Polywog, get *moving*," Ida insisted.

It was strange to hear her voice. They were the first words she had said since entering the well.

"Right," Clemency agreed. "We don't want to be here one second more than we have to be." Saeli nodded behind her.

"I dunno," said Char. "We might want to take our time, so as not to disturb any dirt, or things that might be hidin' in that dirt."

"We'll be careful," Ven promised. He held up the Lightstone and started down into the darkness ahead of them.

They walked for so long that it seemed like there would never be an end to their journey. Several times they stopped, needing to sit down and rest, but hurried back to their feet and on their way as soon as they had caught their breath. The tunnel floor was a dark place that skittered with movement, and no one wanted to remain there any longer than necessary.

Finally, from ahead of them they felt a gust of wind. It was cool and heavy with moisture, as if it were about to rain.

"Feel that?" Clemency said excitedly. "We must be near the outside!"

The fresh air gave them hope and new energy. All five started to run, Char in the lead, followed by Ida, Clem, and Saeli, while Ven brought up the rear, still holding out the light.

The glow of a different kind of light was shining at the tunnel's edge up ahead. They could hear the sound of rushing water in the distance.

"It's the moon, and the river!" Clemency shouted. "Come on, Ven, we're almost there!"

"I'm right behind you," Ven called in return.

At its end, the tunnel shrank down to the size of a large rabbit hole. The children had to crawl out, one by one, even Saeli. As they did, they found themselves in the gravel along the banks of the Great River. Ven waited until everyone else had crawled out, then followed.

When he stood up, free of the tunnel, it was like stepping into a different world. The wind greeted him, rushing through his hair and making his clothes snap like the sails on the sea. The moon overhead was rising into a clear sky, shining silver light across the fields around them, pooling in the river, making it seem alive.

A tall, dark shadow loomed above them, moving like a giant in the dark.

Ven looked up.

They were standing near an enormous mill that spanned the Great River, its huge stone turning night and day, powered by the flow of the river, grinding grain into meal, and meal into flour. Beyond the mill to the north there was a town, where bright lights blazed and music could be heard in the distance over the sound of the water. *I wonder if that's one of the mill towns the constable said was such fun*, he thought. Then his gaze went higher.

Turning the huge grindstone was a towering machine, with four giant blades on which large sheets of canvas caught the wind.

A windmill.

Ven stared at the giant machine, then felt a chuckle well up inside him, like a bubbling spring. He laughed out loud, causing the others to turn and stare at him as if he were daft. Ven paid them no mind; he laughed and laughed until Char finally came over and shook him by the arm.

"You all right there, mate?" his friend asked nervously.

Ven nodded, finally out of laughter.

"Yes," he said as the wind blew through again, chasing the clouds along overhead. "Let's get home. We've quite a ways to go still."

They followed the river south, walking along the banks. Ven had pocketed the Lightstone, because the light of the full moon was almost as bright as day. Clemency came alongside Ven and nudged him, then looked at Ida. The Thief Queen's daughter had her arms wrapped tightly around herself, as if she were cold, her face set in a firmly indifferent expression.

"I've tried to talk to her, but she's not having any part of it,"

Clemency whispered so that both boys could hear. "Remember how she told us that she didn't know her own real name? Well, I told her at least she knows now that her mother thinks it's beautiful. She gave me a look so cold that I thought I was breathing icicles. It's time for me to shut up now. Maybe you could say something, Ven."

"Oh, sure, I'm someone she *really* wants advice from," Ven said, rolling his eyes. "I think anything I might say would only make things worse. Sometimes the best thing you can do for a friend is to *not* say something when there's nothing to say."

"What a horrible deal," Char agreed. "For once, I really feel sorry for her. Did you get any idea who that man—her father—might be?"

"I thought his voice sounded familiar," Ven said quietly. "I wondered if it might be Mr. Whiting."

Char and Clemency shuddered at the same time.

"That would be pretty disgusting," Clem said.

"And dangerous," Char added. "I guess it's prolly possible—they were talkin' about Northland. When I was working on the *Serelinda*, that's where Mr. Whiting got onboard the ship."

"Well, whoever her father and mother are, she just needs to know that to us, she's still Ida," said Ven. "Not that that is a good thing much of the time—but it's what she's comfortable being. So I think that's how we should treat her. But, as far as that goes, you at least have something *you* should say to her, Char."

He could see Char's face flush, even in the moonlight.

"Uh, yeah, I guess so," Char said reluctantly. He slowed his pace, waiting for Ida to draw closer, then walked closer to her.

"Ida, I—er—I need to say sorry for callin' you a liar," he said awkwardly. Ida didn't look at him, but wrapped her arms tighter and set her jaw. "I guess you really *have* been in the Market a bajillion times. I apologize."

Ida kept walking.

"An' I'm sorry if I hurt your feelings," Char continued. He looked pleadingly at Ven, who shrugged.

"You didn't," Ida said curtly. "I don't have feelings."

"Of course you do, Ida," said Ven. "Everyone has feelings."

For the first time since they came out of the tunnels, Ida turned and looked at him.

"That's such a stupid thing to say, Polywog. Surely you've met a few people in the last couple o' days who don't. But maybe now you know that just 'cause someone takes your stuff or isn't all that nice to you, that doesn't mean they're a liar. I may steal, but I never lie. I do have *some* standards."

Ven exhaled. "Yes, yes you do."

"So drop it."

"It's dropped."

The thin girl stared at him a moment longer.

"Don't you dare feel sorry for me, Polywog."

"I won't. I don't. I wouldn't dream of it."

"Good."

They walked the rest of the way to the bridge in silence.

The day was beginning to break by the time they finally saw it in the distance. The rushing current swelled around the stanchions, the large upright supports made of stones that held up the span, then rushed between them, sending white plumes of spray skyward around them. The sky above had turned from black to soft blue, though the sun had not yet risen, and the birds were beginning to sing.

As they reached the foot of the bridge, Ven stopped in amazement. He broke off from the group and walked down to the banks of the river, staring.

There, beside the bridge, was a series of odd-looking footprints, short, wide tracks with strangely shaped toes.

Beside them were several wadded-up pieces of waxed parchment, and cookie crumbs.

"Blow me down," he whispered.

"What's that?" Char asked, coming up behind him. "Looks like trash."

"Not trash," Ven said. "Trolls. Another example of superstition, myth, legend, horsefeathers, and nonsense proved true."

Char shrugged. "Or at least proved possible," he said. "Come on, mate. Step it up. Only a little ways now and we're home."

# - 22 -

# Another Royal Visit

WHEN AT LAST THEY CAME THROUGH THE DOOR OF THE INN, THE door painted with a golden griffin, Mrs. Snodgrass let out an embarrassingly loud whoop of delight and relief. Her eyes were red as if she had been crying, but her round face glowed with delight as she hurried across the inn's floor and swept them into an uncomfortable group embrace.

"It's been four days!" she said breathlessly. "I've been so worried about you children since Nick came home, saying Saeli had been *stolen*!" She hugged the little Gwadd girl especially tight. "I can't tell you how happy I am to see you all."

The smile of delight faded to a look of mock severity. "Especially because there is dust all over my inn." She looked pointedly at Clem, who blushed. "And weeds in my garden," she said, staring at Saeli, who turned red as well. "And dishes piling up in the sink," she said sharply to Char, who shrank away in terror. "And a whole host of odd jobs that need tendin' to," she said to Ven.

"What about me?" Ida demanded. "What are you gonna yell at me for not doin'?"

"Go get into trouble or something," Mrs. Snodgrass said,

wiping her hands briskly on her apron and heading back for the kitchen. "It's been far too quiet around here."

The children looked at each other and sighed, then set to their tasks, all except Ven, who went over to the tabby cat drowsing lazily in the sun on the stone floor. He pulled the bundle of leaves from his pocket and dropped it in front of Murphy.

"The treat you were promised," he said.

"Catnip." Murphy sighed in delight. "Oh, happy day. A wonderful treat, to be certain. Well done, Ven. Too bad you're human. You are almost worthy of being a cat."

"But I'm not human, Murphy," Ven said. "I'm Nain."

"Ven," Murphy said haughtily, "by cat standards, you're *human*. Actually, you fall into an even broader category than that. There's cats. And then there's everything else. Unfortunately, you still qualify as 'everything else.'"

"Well, actually, the one who thought of bringing it to you was Ida," Ven admitted. "So if you are keeping track of points or something, she's a lot closer to being a cat than I am."

The orange tabby stretched. "Alas, neither of you will ever get there," he said as he walked off to find a warm place to sleep. "You will just have to get used to being what you are, and living with the disappointment. Good night."

"Murphy—it's morning."

The cat opened one eye, then pointedly stretched one paw, allowing the claws to extend fully.

"Do you really want to press this point with me, Ven?" he asked. Then he rolled to his side and returned to his slumber.

From across the room Ven could see the Lirin Singer smile.

"Don't ever try to confuse a cat with the facts," McLean said, tuning his strange harp. "They know better. Welcome home, Ven. How was the Market?"

Ven came over and sat beside him. "Terrible," he said. "And amazing. And depressing. And magical."

McLean nodded. "As I expected. But I see you had things well in *hand*."

Ven opened his mouth to disagree, then looked down at his palm. The stain with the image of the Time Scissors was still there.

"Can you see it, McLean?" he asked quietly.

"See what?"

"The picture in my hand."

The Singer smiled. "Now, Ven, you know better than that. I can't see anything."

"Not with your eyes—but you know it's there, don't you?"

"If you're asking because you want to be certain that *you* are seeing it, then I can tell you that it's there," said the Singer. "But you have to remember, Ven, Singers swear to always tell the truth. So can I *see* it? No. I'm afraid not. But when you're done with your chores, I'd love to hear the story of your adventure."

Ven sighed in relief. "Good enough," he said. "Well, I'd best get to work."

Mrs. Snodgrass came out of the kitchen, a plate of sausages in her hands. "All of your chores can wait until you've had breakfast," she announced to the children. "And a nap."

Ven came over and, feeling brave, reached up to steal a sausage off the plate.

*After venturing into a market of thieves, having a friend stolen, our backs marked with pickpocketing circles, seeing Mr. Coates's shop ransacked, being imprisoned by the Queen of Thieves, escaping and being hunted by the entire Raven's Guild, jumping into a well, facing the Rat King and the rest of the Downworlders—after all of that, how could I not be brave enough to steal one of Trudy Snodgrass's sausages in front of her very eyes?*

*I'll tell you how.*

*The fearsome wife of Captain Snodgrass, terror of the seven seas, the woman sailors from every ship in Serendair fear more than sea monsters and storms, who is not even as tall as I am, stared me straight in the eye. And as she did, my hand started to shake, my knees knocked, and I moved my hand quickly back into my pocket and backed away as quickly as I could.*

*I guess I'm going to have to work on that being brave thing.*

"Sit down at the table, Ven Polypheme, and eat from your plate, or I'll box your ears into next week," the innkeeper said severely.

"Yes, ma'am," Ven replied. "And afterwards I'll skip the nap and will get as many odd jobs done as you want, Mrs. Snodgrass, if you wouldn't mind letting me take a short trip to the castle first."

*So I caught a ride in the wagon with Otis, who was heading home across the bridge after a long night's work. He let me sleep in the back, and even though he's convinced that the stories of the trolls are nonsense, he was good enough to wake me up long enough to lay out the new cookies Mrs. Snodgrass packed for them.*

*He dropped me off at the gate of Elysian just as the sun was four fingers from the horizon. I knew it would soon be time for* noon-meal, so I asked if the king would like to play a game of Hounds and Jackals, then sat down and dozed off again while the message was sent up the bajillion steps to the castle.

The guards woke me some time after that to say that word had come down for me to come directly up.

On the way past the rocky outcropping that formed the Guardian of the Mountain, I watched carefully to see if it would wink at me again. But when I was looking carefully at it, all it resembled was rocks. I couldn't even see the face. Maybe there's a lesson there, that the magic of the world that the king is looking for sometimes not only hides in plain sight, but oftentimes doesn't want to be seen at all if someone is looking for it directly.

When he was shown into the place where King Vandemere kept his puzzles off the Throne Room, a grand meal had been laid out for them both. The king sat at his table, across from where Ven's plate had been laid, buttering a poppy seed roll when Ven came into the room.

"No need for that," the king said as Ven attempted to bow, waving his butter knife at Ven. "Have a seat. Will you be joining us, Galliard?"

The Vizier drew himself up haughtily.

"No, thank you."

"So, Ven, I've been meaning to ask you something," the king said as Ven took his place.

"Yes, Your Majesty?"

The king chewed ungracefully, then swallowed.

"Which of the girls in the inn is the prettiest?"

Ven blinked. "Excuse me, Your Majesty?"

"The prettiest—which one of the girls where you live is prettiest?" The king popped another piece of the roll into his mouth. "In your opinion, of course."

"Hmmm," Ven said. "I've never really thought about it. I'm not much of a judge of human beauty, sire, being Nain and all."

"Well, who has the nicest hair? Surely you can make a judgment about that."

Ven's face went hot. "Uhm, well, Ciara has very nice curls, I suppose," he said awkwardly. Behind the king's back he could see Galliard's eyes roll. "But Bridgette has the most, er, unusual hair of all of them—it's red—and long." He lapsed into silence, feeling foolish.

The king nodded, buttering another piece of the roll. "And the prettiest smile? Who has that? I don't get to see many girls where I am, being king and all. It's nice to hear about them at least if I can't see them."

Ven swallowed. "I would say that Emma's smile is probably the nicest. She's very shy—Emma, I mean—and so when she smiles it's, well, extra special."

The Vizier bowed sharply. "Excuse me. I have work to do." He turned and left the room, closing the door abruptly.

King Vandemere watched him leave, then turned to Ven.

"Sorry about that," he said quickly. "I haven't gone suddenly insane, Ven—I just wanted to be certain Galliard believes that we are babbling about things that young men babble about. Otherwise he would insist on staying and hearing whatever you said. And I want to be able to do that alone."

Ven sighed, relieved. "Oh, good. I had thought for a moment

that I had been observing the wrong things for you as your eyes out in the world, Your Majesty."

"Tell me about the Thieves' Market," the king said.

*So I told him everything I could remember, from everything in the street festival of the Outer Market, to the Arms of Coates and the dogs, Madame Sharra, and the Raven's Guild. And I told him about the Downworlders. He was especially interested in hearing the details of this lost group of souls who lived out of sight of the world, in tunnels below the streets of the Gated City.*

*While I was talking he took out a box I had seen before, a box of many strangely shaped pieces of glass that he used to form a puzzle that would help him figure out the answer to something he didn't understand. He had fit together a brightly colored ring when I told him of the sights of the Outer Market, forming an inner picture made of dark purples, blues, and blacks and we spoke of the Raven's Guild, leaving a center of black with one missing middle piece as I told him about the Wonder.*

"There's something missing," King Vandemere said, running his fingers over the puzzle he was constructing. "'The brightest light in the darkest shadow is yours.' I still don't understand, even hearing the story."

A thought struck Ven. "The Rat King told us a story," he said, "the story of how the Wonder came to be in the realm of the Downworlders. Would it help if I told you that?"

"Absolutely," said the king.

"Even though you fired me as the Royal Reporter, I took

notes so I could tell it to you as the hammered truth. Like my father always said, 'Tell people the hammered truth, and it will ring like steel against an anvil.'"

"Exactly what I want," the king said, taking more pieces out of the box. "Tell it to me as much in the Rat King's words, and voice, as you can."

So Ven did.

# ~ 23 ~

# The Rat King's Tale

*I tried to get the rhythm of it, the way the Rat King's voice went from being rough and coarse into being almost poetic. It was as if he were telling an ancient tale he had heard and repeated many times, like the chants my brothers and sister sing in the factory, even though they are Nain who have never even seen the mountains, let alone lived in them.*

## The Thief Who Stole a Piece of the Sun

This here's *our* sun.

Don't stare. You should never stare straight at the sun—you'll burn yer eyes. Then you'll never see nothin' for the rest of yer life but something that looks like the sun. Just a red glow to remind you that some things are too great for a man's eyes to behold for long.

But that's what this is. A piece of living fire, shaved right from the rim of *your* sun by a hero whose name was never spoken, so it is no longer known. But we honor him anyway.

Let me tell it from the beginning.

There was never a time, Nain, when we weren't a people outside. Our beginnings were the same as now, we live inside the empty belly of the world, and always have. For us, life is one long day, not marked the way your many days are, by the rising and setting of the sun. In the very beginning we had a sort of red sun that glowed for us all around, but as time and we grew older, the light faded. Hungry then, we grew hungrier.

And we lived in endless darkness. We knew nothing of the sun.

There was a Thief. Though we are not thieves, he was one of our kind. During the warm, short nights he would go upworld for us, get our harvest, the food and drink we needed. He would take it from barns and fields, from castles, whatever he could find. It was never enough to drive away the hunger. But he tried.

On one night that was too short, coming home he was late, and the sun rose before he was able to return to the Downworld. Then he saw the roof of your world, looked up and beheld the warmth, the light. He saw the sun for the very first time. And he wanted it. He didn't return to our realm, but stayed, entranced, and watched as it moved across the blue roof you call the sky. He watched as the sun cast ropes of clouds to the sea in the evening, and wanted to climb those golden ropes, to see for himself the altar of the sun, maybe help himself to a bit of the buttery gold there.

The Thief remained upworld for days. He stalked the sun, each time it rose in the east and traveled toward its home in the west. He followed it until he came to the great cliffs of the west at the top of the Great River. But he could not reach the sun.

Weeping, he sat in the evening shadow of the great fortress of the old kings. And a king found him there.

The king who found the Thief sang to him the sun's song, gave the Thief a sharp hard sword, gave him a long dark cloak, gave to him the secret that the king could catch the sun and hold it. These were the greatest gifts anyone had ever given to one of our kind. This is why we return gifts to the king.

The song of the king told of how to catch the sun, how to make it wait long enough in its journey from east to west to climb there. The Thief would need a road to the sun, not a road of bricks and cobblestones, but a road of song, light enough to float above the clouds to the roof of the world, strong enough to hold him.

There was a Singer who worked for the king, just a boy, but gifted beyond his years, who could sing the road, keep the wide path from sea to sun so strong a cart could ride it. He sang the road and followed the Thief, all day, all the way to the high altar of the sun, but he was a boy. He was strong but not wise, and as he sang and followed, he looked. And his eyes were burned, as your eyes will be should you ever be brash enough to stare at the sun. He became blind, blinded by the road, by the altar, blinded so deep that even his children were blind. Oh, what glories he saw, but no more to see what everyone else sees, to have only memories of sight.

But the Thief, he was a thief. He didn't look *at* it, like he doesn't look *at* you, he looked *for* it, for where the gold of it is, so that the full shine of it went around him, not into his eyes. He also had the gift of the long dark cloak, and that saved him as well.

And when he arrived at the altar of the sun, such brightness, such richness, I do not even have words in my own tongue to tell. With the sharp hard sword he shaved some slivers of the sun, with the greatest of care, as if it were a precious gem, carefully, so that none might be missed. He wrapped the slivers in the long dark cloak. Stones and flowers from the sun's garden, fruits and feathers from the sun's orchards, grains from the sun's fields, a great bundle he stole, all gifts from the sun to bring to us, his people.

The road was strong as a rope of sun, strong as the song, and the boy was a boy. They ran. The Thief led the blind Singer down the wide road, but on the way the song failed. High still, they fell, from the sun into the sea.

Deep in earth the Thief had been, and on it, but not in water. The king saw them fall. Came himself to bring the Thief and the boy to land. All the treasures in the bundle fell too, some lost in the sea. But one sliver came to us. Came here to warm and light our home.

So that is why some Singers are blind—they are the children of the boy. And that is why the Wonder is here, burning in splendor, even though it is just the tiniest shard of the sun. And that is why we sent the most precious thing we had to your king's father, as we do to each king—because that king long ago was the first Upworlder, and the last, to see us as brothers, as worthy of having the light of the sun shine upon us, too.

And we remember that.

# - 24 -

# The Riddle Solved

TELL ME AGAIN," SAID THE KING, "WHAT MACEDON SAID ABOUT my father."

Ven thought hard. "He said, 'Don't forget to tell the king this—that what belonged to his father is by right his now.' But when I told him I thought the riddle referred to the Wonder, he told me I was wrong."

King Vandemere smiled broadly. He took a golden puzzle piece out of the box and set it in the middle of the dark center, within the purple, black, and blue inner ring, which sat inside the multicolored outer ring.

"I understand now," he said, pleased. "'The brightest light in the darkest shadow is yours.' They're not talking about the Wonder, Ven. They're talking about *themselves*." He smiled as Ven looked puzzled.

"The Downworlders may be poor, wretched people who live in terrible conditions, in the midst of a city of thieves, but they are loyal to the king—that's what they are saying. *They* are the brightest light inside the darkest shadow—a place of lawlessness and treachery where some of the most terrible deeds are done, the most evil plans hatched. They are letting me know that, unlike everyone else beyond those gates, they are loyal to me, as they were to my father. As they were to every king back to the one in the story. That's why the stone glowed golden for my father and blue for me when he was alive—he was the king, and I wasn't. But now that I am king, it glows golden for me. It's a sign that I have their loyalty now."

Ven's curiosity was running wild. "Of course. And there are others there, too, Your Majesty. Not everyone in that city took advantage of us, or tried to harm or rob us. Mr. Coates could not have been kinder to us, and if he hadn't lent us Finlay and Munx, we would never have found Saeli. I hope he's all right."

"I suspect he is," the king said. "Weaponsmakers are hard to kill. I hope I get to meet him someday."

"I hope so, too. There was a Singer in there as well, though I don't think he was blind, who helped us, too. And even the woman who pointed us to the Stolen Alleyway—she said that some of the people who lived there weren't thieves, but were just the kin of thieves whose great-grandparents and before had been sent away to the penal colony. It's hard to believe there can be good in a place that's mostly evil."

"Why?" the king asked. "There is evil within places that are mostly good. That's why I fired you, in case you didn't know. I realized as soon as I made you the Royal Reporter that I had set you up as a target for people who might want to get to *me*—and by firing you in public, the word is now out, so that should not be the case anymore. So you should be safe—and I now know that there is a band of loyalists beneath the streets of the Gated City whom I can call on to stand with me when the time comes. You could not have brought me better news, Ven."

Ven's blood suddenly ran cold.

"This is the second time you've suggested you might be in danger," he said nervously. "Do you think something is going to happen to you?"

The king exhaled. "Not necessarily to me, but there is power in a castle. Those that seek to do evil seek power. I don't know if there is something afoot, or if I am just being paranoid. But there is something in the pit of my stomach telling me that I have to be ready for the day when something bad does happen, something that will be my responsibility to defend against. You are helping me discover what might be coming by helping me find all the magic that is out in the world, hiding in plain sight. Just as I seek to preserve that magic, it is not surprising that it is a target for destruction as well. As I said, I suspect that out there in the world are forces that would like to see that happen. Who knows—perhaps they are even within the walls of my very own castle. It's hard to say. I can't read the heart or mind of every page, every servant who works here. There are very few people I can trust, especially since Graal, my chief Vizier, has been away for so long. He is the wisest of men, having served each high king of Serendair from the beginning of the time when there were high kings. I always trust his judgment, for as a Vizier, he can see inside many places that are invisible to others."

"What about Galliard?" Ven asked. "Isn't he also a Vizier?"

The king nodded. "Indeed, and he is a wise man as well. But Galliard is still training in the Vizieri arts, while Graal has been one for centuries. Graal is an Ancient Seren, a race older than any other on the face of the earth. He understands history, because he lived through it. And he understands the future, because he can see it. I miss his counsel. I hope he returns soon."

"I do, too," said Ven. "I'm curious to see him."

King Vandemere smiled. "He will enjoy meeting you. He has

a fondness for Nain." He picked up the puzzle pieces and began to put them away.

"Remember, Ven," he said as he closed the box, "that riddle about the brightest light in the darkest shadow applies to more than just the Downworlders. I would say it also might one day be about your friend Ida."

"*Ida?*" Ven said incredulously. "No offense, Your Majesty, but Ida doesn't seem the type to me to have allegiance to you, or anyone else. Ida's loyalty is to Ida."

"Really?" the king said. "Then why did she go back into a city where her hated mother is in charge, knowing the chances were that she would be caught again?"

Ven thought about the question. "Because Saeli was missing, and we needed her help."

"That sounds like the definition of loyalty to me," said the king. "Don't mistake friendliness with loyalty, Ven. Friendly and loyal are two different things. There are a lot of people who are one and not the other. From what you told me a few days ago, your own mother doesn't sound like a very friendly person—but she is a good one, yes?"

"Oh yes," Ven agreed.

"Then judge Ida by whether she is there for you in times of need, as she seems to be, not by whether she is pleasant to you. In the end, you can get many people to be pleasant to you pretty easily. A true friend, someone who will risk her life and her freedom for you, as your other friends would, is very hard to come by."

"Thank you," Ven said. "I'll remember that. So what do we do about Felonia?"

The king rubbed his chin.

"She will be trapped in the Market for a while, by her own

actions. By releasing the Screaming Ravens, she shut the city down, even the secret exits, for a few days at least. That gives us time to destroy all the current Market Day tokens and replace them with new ones. I would shut down Market Day as well, but for the sake of the few people in the Outer Market who depend upon it for their living, I think I'll keep it open. But Felonia's chest of stolen tokens will bring her nothing now."

"Good thought," said Ven. He reached into his pocket and pulled out his own token. "I was going to give you this as a memento of my adventure—Char and Clem lost theirs in the well, and Ida and Saeli had theirs taken away. So as far as I know, this is the only Market Day token to make it out of the Gated City through an exit other than the Main Gate."

The king laughed as he took the ribbon.

"Excellent," he said. "Thank you." The expression on his face turned solemn. "To that end, I am thinking it might not be a bad idea to send you away for a while, Ven—and all your friends who were with you in the Gated City. By the time Felonia can reach beyond the walls again, if you're gone from the inn, that would probably be a good thing for all involved—including the other people who live there."

"Where would you send me?" Ven asked, his skin itching like fire ants were biting him.

The king smiled again.

"Actually, I have a mission in mind past the Great River," he said. "The good news is—being Nain is what is needed to deal with the situation. I would be sending you to the foothills of the High Reaches, where the Nain live in Serendair. You might even meet some."

"What's the bad news?" Ven asked.

"It involves a dragon."

"Oh," Ven said. "Why is that bad?"

The king blinked. "The dragon seems to be fairly annoyed with the Nain."

"Oh," Ven said. "How annoyed?"

"Torching the countryside annoyed."

"Oh," Ven said. "Should be interesting."

The king laughed. "I will need a day or two to put things together," he said. "Talk to your friends, but only inside the inn. Get your Singer friend to help you keep the discussion off the wind. I will send for you when I'm ready. In the meantime, rest up and get some good food into you. You deserve it, after your time in the Market."

"Actually, Your Majesty, ever since meeting the Rat King, I haven't really been very hungry," Ven said. "I'm beginning to realize how lucky we are to have all that we do have."

"Then that may explain the second whisker," the king said.

*My hand went immediately to my chin. And he was right.*

*There, just at the place where my neck meets the underside of my jaw, I could feel another little hair, smaller than the first one. But it was a sure sign that my beard was coming in.*

*I couldn't have been happier. Among the Nain, a man's beard is the story of his life.*

*Looks like I might have an interesting story after all.*

# - 25 -

# The End—and the
# Beginning Again

THAT EVENING, VEN WENT TO TOWN WITH NICHOLAS FOR HIS last rounds. While Nick was busy collecting the messages, Ven went north, out to the abandoned pier, and sat quietly on the edge, waiting for a glimpse of multicolored scales or a red pearl cap.

While he waited the sun began to set. Great streams of light were breaking through the clouds, like golden ropes. The thinnest clouds had formed what looked like a glowing road into the west, in colors of pink and yellow and white, leading to a burning orange sun at the horizon.

When finally there was nothing more than a sliver of the sun left, Amariel's head popped out of the water just off the pier.

"Well, I see you've learned not to shout," the merrow said, flipping her tail and splashing Ven with droplets of salty foam. "What are you doing here?"

"I came to tell you about the Gated City," Ven said, sitting cross-legged on the pier. "You always say I owe you stories in return for all the ones you told me those nights I was floating on the wreckage. I don't have that many to tell, but as I learn some, I thought I'd start paying you back."

The merrow considered, then nodded.

"All right," she said. "Tell away."

So Ven began with their entry into the Outer Market, trying to put each part of the story into terms that a sea-dweller would understand. He noticed as he went on that more and more heads seemed to appear, bobbing in the water some distance away from shore. They never quite crested the surface, but Ven was fairly certain they were listening as well.

When his story ended, the heads disappeared.

The merrow floated backward, allowing her beautiful tail to flip out of the water.

"Well, it seems there really *is* a lot to see in the Dry World," she said casually, drawing patterns in the gentle waves as they crested under the pier. "I guess that explains, at least a little, why you always have more important things to do than come to explore the depths with me."

"Nothing I have to do is more important to *me*," Ven said quickly. "It's usually more important to someone else, someone who gets to tell me what to do. But I really do want to come with you someday."

"Hmmm," said Amariel. "I'll believe that when it happens." She started to drift away. "But next time you get sent on one of these great adventures, let me know. Maybe I will be in the mood that day to come with you and see what all the fuss is about."

Ven sat up like a bolt of lightning had hit him.

"Are you serious?" he asked excitedly. "Do you mean it? You would give me your cap and grow legs? And come with me?"

The merrow smiled.

"Perhaps," she said, preparing to dive. "Perhaps not. We'll see when the time comes."

"Yes," Ven called as she disappeared below the waves. "We'll see—I'll see you tomorrow! Or the next day."

He ran all the way back to the inn, astonishing Nicholas by beating him there.

# One Last Thing That Needed to Be Said

So as soon as I got everything packed for my journey I went to dinner. The inn was warm and full of laughter, with McLean's bright music making the room even more cheerful.

It felt good to be home.

For all that she had put us immediately to work, Mrs. Snodgrass fussed over us the whole night, making certain we had seconds at dinner and extra helpings of Felitza's scrumptious desserts. Felitza even told Char she was glad he was back, and saved him an apple fritter, his favorite. He's been acting giddy ever since. If he doesn't quiet down soon, I'm going to smother him with my pillow or, better yet, let the Spice Folk into our room while he is sleeping. They like to torture him even more than they like to torture me.

After this crazy adventure in the Gated City I have really come to understand why the king felt the need to fire me in front of his court. I know he was trying to protect me. Just because I can't be the Royal Reporter in the eyes of the world doesn't mean I can't be the king's eyes as he asked me to. I will take my lessons from what the king did himself when he was the equivalent of my age, and go about my business, a simple, unimportant kid and his friends who mean nothing to anyone in this place.

That way I may be able to see the hidden magic of the world more clearly, without anyone seeing me doing it.

One thing I learned from all this is that each person has the chance to be what life decides for him, or to make life what he decides it will be. Ida actually taught me this, though I definitely can't tell her that now. She could have been the Thief Queen's daughter with the beautiful name. Instead she chose to be Ida No, royal pain and general nuisance, all alone in the world except for her mates at the Crossroads Inn, a place for kids who have nowhere else to go.

I'm glad she made the choice she did.

One day, if she lets me, I will tell her so.

At dinner I asked my friends if they wanted to come overland with me, past the Great River, on another uncertain quest that involves discovering why a dragon is destroying the countryside. I expected to get stares at best, and pelted with food at worst. Instead, I got five excited companions who can't wait to go exploring with me. Even Ida said she'd come if she wasn't doing something better.

She then gave me a long list of what would qualify as "better," including having the mumps, hitting herself in the face with a hammer, and privy-cleaning duty.

I bet she comes anyway.

And as soon the king lets me know the supplies are ready, I will go see if Amariel wants to come, too.

But tonight, I have a letter to write.

✳

Dear ~~Mother~~ Mum,

It was wonderful to receive your letter. I want to assure you that I am following everything you have taught me in life as much as I possibly can. I am striving to always be polite, well-mannered, and clean, though in truth that last one does not always happen. But I do try. I will keep trying to behave in a way that would make you proud, even though you are not here to see it.

All is well with me. I am healthy and hope that you and everyone else back home in Vaarn are, too. I will be going on a journey soon that may allow me to meet actual Nain who live as Nain do. I will write and tell you all about it.

I have some chores to finish before I can go to bed, but I just want to say that I am very grateful for all the time, attention, and guidance you have given me all my life. I benefit from the things you have taught me every day.

They have made me who I am.

Along with my gratitude, and greetings to Father and my siblings, I send you

All my love,
Ven

P.S.—My beard has finally begun to grow in. I think you should be the first member of the family to know that.


P.P.S.—If you haven't put my teacup away yet, please do. I won't be home for a while. But I will come home one day, and when I do, I promise that night I will be on time for tea.

# ACKNOWLEDGMENTS

In addition to the luminaries whom I thanked in the first volume, and who still deserve thanks but not actual *space* in this book, I would like to acknowledge the following helpful people for their contributions to our ongoing archaeological dig:

First and foremost, Dr. Alexander Vandersnoot, Vaarn expedition leader, who has handled every aspect of the dig as well as updating our blog at www.venbooks.com;

Edward "Dip Dip" Hillenbrand, our expedition's litter bearer, for transporting all our equipment (and, of course, me);

The Flower Sisters, Ella Rose Violet Daisy Iris MacDoodle, and Liliana-Susana-Banana-Chochita-Burrita Valentine, Gwadd caterers extraordinaire, who have kept our archaeological dig team fed and happy through months of dirty, backbreaking work (see their ad in this month's edition of *The Flower Gourmet*);

Madame Hildegarde Frint, Mistress of Manners and Decorum, for keeping a civil and serene atmosphere among traditionally coarse field-workers. I would especially like to thank her for ransoming me back from the chief of the Womba Looma tribe, and hereby promise to never again spit mango juice at anyone during a sacred Tongue-Waggling ceremony. (It really *was* an accident, Hildy.)

Sir Austen Frappier, famed socialite, for adding cuteness and beauty to an otherwise bleak seaside setting;

Sergeant-Major Blanche McGivney, the Iron Goddess of Mercy, for her vise-like grip on discipline in the ranks and maintaining the dormitories;

"Amazon" Julien Thuan, zookeeper and animal handler of the Royal Menagerie of Sorbold, for his assistance with research regarding prehistoric dogs;

And a grudging acknowledgment of the extremely shoddy work of Hoy T. Toity and Gobble D. Gooke, our interpreters, who really need to practice their Kith diphthongs (lawsuit pending—thanks a *lot*).

—EH

Elizabeth Haydon is now working
to restore the third volume of
The Lost Journals of Ven Polypheme,
*The Dragon's Lair.*

Turn the page for a sneak peek for your eyes only.

Ven was dreaming of fire pirates chasing him through the hold of a dark ship when he felt his shoulder being shaken.

He opened his eyes. He could see nothing but inky blackness all around him.

The moon had set, taking any light with it. The stars that had been so bright the evening before had disappeared behind racing clouds. All he could feel was the breath of the wind, rustling the grass around his head.

It smelled like the burnt porridge in the bottom of Char's cooking pot.

"Get up," Tuck said quietly. "It's time to go."

Ven sat straight up and looked around. He could see the shapes of his friends beginning to move as they, too, shook off sleep. He knew they could see even less than he could, except possibly for Saeli.

"What's burning?" he asked nervously.

Tuck's voice came from behind where he sat. Ven had not seen him move.

"Fields," the Lirin forester said. "The grasslands to the north of here, I'd wager."

"Is it the dragon?"

Tuck came around in front of him and crouched down. "Maybe. If it is, this fire has caught and spread from a spark. But this itself is not from the beast. Can't miss the smell of dragon's breath."

"Wh-why?" Char stammered from the darkness next to Ven. "What does it smell like?"

The forester was helping Clemency to her feet. He turned and looked at Char for a moment, thinking.

"There's a dirt smell to it, like wet firecoals," he said at last. "But sharper, like acid or pitch had been poured into the smoke. Once you've smelled it, you never forget it. It haunts your dreams."

"Great," Ven muttered. "My dreams aren't haunted enough."

"Let's move out," Tuck said, hoisting his enormous pack onto his shoulder. "The night-hunting ravens sleep when the moon goes down. Those that hunt by day will be up with the sun. We have to travel fast."

Ven nodded and slung his own pack onto his back, as did the others. They followed Tuck's dark outline over the fields, stepping through the highgrass that billowed like waves on the sea.

After what seemed like an eternity of wading through endless scrub, they came to the thicket where their horses stood, the wagon hidden among the trees. Tuck tossed his pack into the back of the wagon and helped the children in, then climbed up onto the board and took the reins.

"Go back to sleep," he said over his shoulder.

"Yeah, *that's* gonna happen," Char said under his breath.

"May as well rest while you can," Tuck replied. Char jumped.

He had forgotten how sensitive the forester's ears were. "Not a good idea to deal with a dragon when you're tired."

"I, for one, don't think it will be hard to fall asleep at all," said Clem, shoving aside a sack of cornmeal and moving away from the water barrel, which had leaked a little and dampened the floor of the wagon. "I feel like I could sleep for days."

*Not me*, Ven thought. His scalp was on fire, his fingers tingling. It was all he could do to keep from peering over the edge of the wagon, but Tuck's warning was still ringing in his ears, drowning out his curiosity for the moment. *Stay down, children. It's best that anything passing by thinks you are cargo, nothing more.*

Surrounded by blackness, his mind was racing. Ven tried to think of home, of his family, of boring lessons in school, anything to get his thoughts to settle down and allow him to fall asleep again. Hard as he tried, nothing would stick in his brain except the thought that at any moment they might be face to face with an ancient beast able to grant them a wish or swallow them up without having to chew. Despite the danger, the possibility that they might actually be seeing something that most people had only heard about in tales was making his heart pound.

Even more thrilling was the knowledge that, should they avoid the dragon altogether, he might be meeting Nain for the first time, in the mountains, and maybe he would see how his own race really lived. That alone was enough to keep him from being able to sleep.

He thought of the letter he would write to his family, telling them that after four generations, a Polypheme had finally returned to the mountains and had met downworld Nain. While these Nain were not the ones from whom his family had descended, it would still be fascinating to see how they lived and to speak to them in the language Ven had only ever used with his family and a few of the Nain that worked in his father's factory in Vaarn. *I wonder if they will be able to understand me,* he thought. *No Nain I've ever talked to has ever been inside a mountain, either.*

His thoughts raced even more wildly in his head. *Maybe I can finally make up for disgracing the family by making a good impression on those of our own race.* With that thought came sudden panic. *What if the language I've learned has changed over the years? What if what I say means something totally different in their tongue? I could be insulting them and not even know it. With my luck, I will start a war between Nain cultures.* His mind was churning along with these crazy thoughts, but Ven was unable to stop them.

Inside his shirt pocket, the thin sleeve of Black Ivory vibrated slightly. Ven put his hand on top of it and was surprised that he could feel warmth, even through the fabric. There was a pleasant buzz on his skin, even through the smooth stone. Without thinking, he slid the tip of the dragon scale out of the protective sleeve and ran his finger over the edge.

The rim of the scale was so finely tattered that it felt as soft as flax, but I knew that if I pressed too hard it would slice through my skin to the bone. There was a hum that tickled my fingertip, a feeling of old magic that shot through me, all the way to the roots of my hair, to my toenails as well. Even the two whiskers on my chin vibrated.

In that magical buzz there was a sense of joy. That's really the only word I can think of to describe it. Just touching something so ancient, so magical, made me feel good all over.

*Even in the scary darkness, even running from those who sought us by night, and those that would return with the day's light, I was excited.*

*At least I was until I was grabbed by the throat.*

All of the breath choked out of Ven. His head spun woozily and he felt sick as he was hauled out of the wagon and up onto the board behind the horses.

Tuck's voice spoke quietly in his ear, its tone deadly.

"Put that bloody thing away, Ven. Do you *want* the dragon to find us?"

"N-no," Ven whispered.

Tuck's grip on his collar tightened. "Well, *I* can feel it when you pull it out of the Black Ivory—it vibrates so strongly that my teeth sting. So if *I* can feel it, don't you think a *dragon* can? Perhaps from miles away?"

"Sorry," Ven said. He pushed the scale back into its envelope, and the envelope back into his pocket. The vibration vanished, taking with it the joy that had been coursing through him a moment before.

Tuck shook his head in disgust and released his grip on Ven, who slid off the board and clattered back into the wagon. The eyes of the other children were wide, staring at him in the darkness. Ven's face flushed hot in embarrassment, so he turned around and settled back down between two sacks of carrots, pretending to sleep.

*Great,* he thought. *I've just annoyed the king's forester, frightened my friends, and possibly alerted the dragon to our presence. I wonder if carrying around this dragon scale is making me more stupid than usual.*

He sighed miserably. Not since he had been floating on the wreckage of his father's ship after the Fire Pirate attack had he felt so vulnerable. The edges of the night seemed to be endless, especially when the moon was down. It was a little like being lost at sea, without the safety of the Crossroads Inn to return to. *What have I done, bringing my friends out here, with no settlements around for miles?* he thought. *If something happens to Tuck, how will we ever get home?*

He raised himself up a little and glanced back over his shoulder. The wind was growing stronger, battering the wagon and blowing the children's hair and the manes of the horses wildly about. Behind him Saeli was huddled close to Clem, shivering. The Mouse Lodge steward opened her woolen cape and wrapped it around the small girl's shoulders.

Just as she did, Ven caught sight of a tiny flicker of light in the fields behind her.

He sat up and peered over the side of the wagon behind the girls. The tiny light had vanished, but suddenly several more winked in the moving sea of highgrass.

Ven spun and looked over the side of the wagon next to him. At first he saw nothing but blackness, but after a moment the little lights appeared within the meadow grass there as well; a few at first, then several more, and finally dozens of them, only to disappear as quickly as they had come.

He reached over the sacks of carrots and grabbed Char by the sleeve.

"Look out there," he said, trying to keep his voice low. "What *is* that?"

The cook's mate scooted closer to the edge and peered through the slats in the wagon.

"What's what?"

"Those flickering lights—can't you see them?"

"Blimey, I dunno," Char whispered. "Hey, Clem, come 'ere, quick!"

The house steward raised her head sleepily. "Huummph?"

"Come an' look at this," Char insisted.

An annoyed snorting sound came up from the depths of the wagon. "All *right*, just a minute." The sacks of carrots wiggled as Clem crawled over them, looking less than pleased. "What do you want *now*?"

"There's about a bajillion tiny flickering lights out there," Char whispered.

Clem looked over the side of the wagon and stared into the dark.

"Fireflies," she said. "Lightning bugs. You've never seen them before?"

"Never *heard* of 'em," Char replied as Ven shook his head. "*Lightning* bugs?"

Clemency sighed. "It certainly is obvious that you grew up on the sea, Char, and you in a city, Ven," she said impatiently. "Anyone who's ever been in the countryside knows about lightning bugs. You can see them all over the fields where I live, mostly in the summer."

A soft cough came from the board of the wagon.

"Those are not lightning bugs," Tuck said quietly. The children looked at each other. Again the king's forester had heard them over the rattling of the wagon, the clopping of the horses, and the howl of the wind, even though they had been whispering.

Ven raised himself up onto his knees. "What are they, then, Tuck?"

The forester clicked reassuringly to the horses, who had begun to nicker nervously.

"They're the points of tracer arrows," he said.

Ven looked out over the side of the wagon again. For as far as he could see around him in the highgrass were thousands of twinkling lights, glittering like the stars above the sea at night. They winked in and out, not moving, hovering in the scrub. He turned to Clem and Char, whose faces were as white as the moon had been.

"Tracer arrows?" Ven repeated.

The Lirin forester nodded, urging the horses forward, though the wagon had slowed.

"Arrows whose points have been dipped in a kind of concoction that glows in the dark. They only glow when they are just about to be fired, sparked by being drawn across a bow string. Their radiance lasts long\enough to leave a path of light for others to see, so that the target is easier to hit.

"And behind each one is an archer."

# READER'S GUIDE

## ✦ The Lost Journals of Ven Polypheme ✦
# THE THIEF QUEEN'S DAUGHTER

### ELIZABETH HAYDON

*Illustrations restored by* JASON CHAN

## FREE CURRICULUM

Available now at www.venpolypheme.com.

## ABOUT THIS GUIDE

The information, activities, and discussion questions that follow are intended to enhance your reading of *The Thief Queen's Daughter*. Please feel free to adapt these materials to suit your needs and interests.

## ABOUT THIS BOOK

*The Thief Queen's Daughter* is the second of the Lost Journals of Ven Polypheme, ancient notebooks recently discovered by archaeologists, in which a young Nain boy chronicled the magical sights, mysterious places, and mythical beasts he saw on his travels throughout the known and unknown world. Bits and pieces of the centuries-old notebook, that include Ven's first-person narrative and sketches, are reproduced in this volume, and after much research, those parts of the journal that did not survive have been added in third-person narrative so that the story is seamless.

Ven Polypheme had just turned fifty years old (approximately twelve in human years) on the day his adventures (and misadventures) began. The youngest in a family of ship-building Nain, a race of people more often seen in mountains and deep within the caverns of the Earth, he is insatiably curious, wishing he could travel away from his home and see the great sights of the world. The opportunity comes upon him unexpectedly and tragically, forcing him to live on his own in an adult world where mystery, adventure, and magic share space with prejudice, danger, and supernatural evil.

Ven's journey leads him through many mystical wonders of the world, introduces him to great friends and terrible foes, puts his wits and will to the test, and teaches him that the meaning of home is "where you decide to stay, where you decide to fight for what matters to you." His chronicling of his meetings with Fire Pirates, merrows, ship-eating sharks, Rover's boxes, Spice Folk, Revenants, and other ancient magic, form the pieces of a map from a time when there were places that magic might still be found.

In the second of these journals, Ven recounts the story of his journey within the mysterious Gated City, a former penal colony that exists, surrounded by high walls and guards, within the capital city of Kingston. When the king gives Ven a glowing artifact he wants to know more about, Ven and his friends are led into the fascinating Outer Market of this city of thieves, a colorful and magical bazaar, then later into the dark and dangerous Inner Market, where they encounter the Raven's Guild and the deadly Queen of Thieves. As they struggle to find a kidnapped friend and escape with their lives in a place where they can trust no one, Ven and his friends learn the answer to the riddle that the king had posed, "the brightest light in the darkest shadow is yours."

Thematic highlights: First and third juxtaposed points-of-view, racial differences, self-reliance, relationships between mothers and children, looking beyond stereotypes, hidden magic in the world. Recounted in a faux-nonfiction style.

## ABOUT THE AUTHOR

Elizabeth Haydon began working in the publishing field even before her graduation from college. For most of that time she has been editing and developing educational materials and programs for kindergarten through twelfth grade, family literacy, and adult basic education programs. Her materials are used in schools both nationally and internationally, and many of her books for Young Readers and New Readers have garnered the PLA/ALA Top Titles award. In 1994, an editorial friend asked her to make use of her background in medieval music, anthropology, herbalism, folklore, and language to create a new fantasy tale that eventually became the award-winning *Symphony of Ages* series. Beginning with *Rhapsody: Child of Blood*, these novels have made numerous "Best of the Year" as well as national bestseller lists. Elizabeth Haydon lives on the East Coast of the United States with her husband and three children.

## WRITING AND RESEARCH ACTIVITIES

### I. Myths and Legends

**A.** Macedon, the Rat King, tells Ven a story, which Ven relates to King Vandemere, about how the Wonder came to be within the Downworlders' dark kingdom, and why they honor the human king. Have you ever heard a story like that before? Myths, legends, and fables are tales that try to teach a lesson, explain how something came to be, or tell why something is the way it is. Aesop's fables are some of the oldest and most famous of these kinds of stories, such as "The Tortoise and the Hare" or "The Grasshopper and the Ants." Most fables have a moral at the end, or woven into the story. Research a fable from anywhere in the world, and find out what its moral is. Then try your hand at writing your own fable. Don't forget the moral!

**B.** When she is reading his fortune, Madame Sharra tells Ven that the scales of the deck were given by dragons in order to do something very noble, something that saved the world. What does noble mean? If you aren't sure, look it up. Have you ever heard a story about something that was done to save the world? What about something noble that was done for a smaller, but still noble, purpose? Sometimes the most noble acts are very small ones, like standing up for someone on the playground or making a sacrifice to help someone else. Write about what you might do or have done that is noble.

**C.** Mrs. Snodgrass gives Ven cookies to take to the bridge for the trolls. Otis the barkeeper snorts at this and says it's all nonsense and superstition. Do you have anything that you are superstitious about, like a lucky number or a ritual you always follow? Do you believe there really are trolls under the bridge? What exactly is a troll? Do a little research in books or on the Internet and find out—there are many different answers. Then draw what you think a troll should look like.

**D.** Many cultures have a different versions of the same story. One of the most common is the Cinderella story, which is told in dozens of different cultures around the world. Research one or more of these Cinderella-like stories from around the world and share it with someone who has researched a different one. How are they different from the Cinderella tale you know? In what ways are they the same?

| | |
|---|---|
| Greece: | Rhodope |
| Germany: | Aschenputtel |
| Scandinavia: | Askungen |
| China: | Yeh-hsien |
| Scotland: | Rashin Coatie |
| Vietnam: | Tam and Cam |
| Russia: | Baba Yaga and Vasilisa the Brave |
| Korea: | Pigling and Her Proud Sister |
| Norway: | Katie Woodencloak |
| Ireland: | Fair, Brown, and Trembling |
| Georgia: | Conkiajgharuna, the Little Rag Girl |
| Serbia: | Pepelyouga |
| Kashmir: | The Wicked Stepmother |

**E.** Ven's own name, by coincidence, is shared with several legendary characters. Who is Polypheme/Polyphemus? Who was Charles Magnus? If you look up its Greek roots, what does the word Polypheme mean? Use your imagination about your own name and write a legend with a character that has the same name. Or find an actual legend or story with a character that really does share your name.

**F.** When they are traveling through the Raven's Guild, Clemency comments that the Meadow Folk are named after poisonous plants that the Spice Folk consider to be evil. Why? What plants do you know of that could be taken care of by an evil fairy? Look them up and see if, in fact, they have any good properties as well as bad ones, the way Stuff-of-Dreams can be both a medicine and a poison.

## II. Gated Cities and Penal Colonies

**A.** Much of modern day Australia has its roots in a penal colony. In 1788 the First Fleet landed with about 780 convicts on prison ships in Botany Bay in New South Wales. Read about this historic period and learn how the sending of prisoners to another land began one of the world's most interesting cultures.

**B.** What is a penal colony and why would a government want to use one? Look up some examples and read about them. Then draw a vertical line down a sheet of paper and make two columns, one for good and one for bad results. List why you think the penal colony system was a good idea on the left, and a bad one on the right. Then decide overall whether you would have used a penal colony if you were a king long ago.

**C.** All through history, people have been putting walls around their cities, mostly to keep invaders out. Can you name some examples? Look up some historic walled cities and find some pictures, if you can. What do they have in common? Do you think the wall helped the lives of the people in the city, or hurt them? Do you think it was easier to maintain and defend a walled city, or one with other types of defenses?

**D.** In historic times castles often had walls that surrounded them. Another type of defense around a castle was a moat, a wide trench of water that made approaching the castle difficult. Which do you think worked better, a moat or an outer wall around a castle? King Vande-mere has neither—he built his castle on the top of a huge, rocky cliff that seems to have a Guardian watching out for him. Why is this a good way to defend the Castle Elysian?

**E.** The Castle Elysian is positioned in a place where the king can see the sea to the north and the wide fields all around him. Design your own castle, including what sort of geographic features it would have.

Look up castles in a book or on the Internet to see what sorts of features most of them have, like bulwarks and a portcullis. Remember, a castle was like a small city, so you will need to account for all the things the people inside it need to live. How will you supply food and water? Then name your castle and draw a picture of it.

## III. Limitations and Special Abilities

**A.** Saeli is much smaller than most other people. Have you ever been in a group where you were much smaller or much bigger than the people around you? How does Saeli compensate for her small height? In *The Thief Queen's Daughter* we see how her special abilities with plants and flowers make her both vulnerable and more capable than the other children. Give some examples of both.

**B.** Everyone has talents. In *The Thief Queen's Daughter* we see how each person's special abilities help keep the group safe. What is Ida's special ability, and how does it help? What about Ven—how does his natural Nain ability to dig help? Char has lived on ships all his life; do you get to see him do something that makes use of that experience? What about Nick's speed as a runner, or Clem's common sense as a house steward? What are your talents and how do they help you? How do you use them to help others? Look up a famous person who is known for one kind of talent and see if you can discover another one, such as an actor who is also a painter, or a politician who also sings.

**C.** McLean, the Lirin Singer in the Crossroads Inn, has eyes that do not work, and yet he seems to have special insights that are very valuable to Ven. What would your life be like if you were blind? How would your days and nights be different from the way they are now? What would you no longer be able to do? Try it. Clear anything dangerous or breakable out of a room you are familiar with. Get a good blindfold or dark eye mask and put it on. Listen to music and a TV show without using your eyes. Try to make your way around the room just by touch. Try to eat, using silverware, without being able to see. If you can sit outside while "blind," try that, too. What do you hear, smell, and feel that you might not have noticed when you could see?

**D.** Why is Amariel annoyed when Ven asks her if she knows anything about the human city? Are you ever excluded from events or things you might like to do because of the way you are—for instance, because you have to be older to participate, or be able to speak a different language? If you could grow a merrow's tail and be able to breathe under water, would you? What if you could not become human again?

## QUESTIONS FOR DISCUSSION

**1.** In the Outer Market of the Gated City, Ven and his friends ride a carousel and swings that are made up of mythical beasts—a blue-green sea serpent, a lion with wings, a silver dragon, a griffin, a black unicorn. If you had the chance to ride, which beast would you pick? Or would you stick to a real-world animal, like a horse or a camel? Why? If you were building a magical carousel, what animals would it include, and what would it be able to do, besides going around and around? What other mythical beasts have you heard of, or can you imagine?

**2.** In this book, we see birds being used as messengers and spies. Both the albatross and the ravens seem to be watching Ven. Madame Sharra tells Ven that the albatross is acting as the eyes for someone else. Who do you think that might be? Whose eyes are the ravens? Why are birds especially dangerous spies?

**3.** At the beginning of this book, Ven receives a letter from his mother. How does that make him feel? Describe Ven's relationship with his mother, based on what he says about her. How does Mrs. Snodgrass compare to her? Or the Thief Queen? What do you think he learns about his mother in this book?

**4.** Who do you think the man with the hooked nose is? Why do you think this?

**5.** When Ven sees the bed in the Thief Queen's chamber, why does he know how to open the secret passage? When he enters the tunnels of the Downworlders, what does he realize about the Lightstone that he has seen earlier? Have you ever learned from an experience in the past that helped you later?

**6.** If you could go into the Outer Market, what would you go to see first? If you had the money to buy anything there, what would you buy?

**7.** Do you think Mr. Coates is a good person or a thief or both? What do you think happened to him?

**8.** How does Char respond to teasing about his crush on Felitza?

**9.** If you had drawn the Time Scissors scale and were given the opportunity to undo something you had done in your past, would you? What would you undo?

**10.** What did you think of Char's purchase of his stolen childhood? Did he get what he paid for? Would Char and Ven agree on the answer to that question? What do you think he was experiencing? And do you think he will ever get the whole memory back?

**11.** If you were Ida, knowing what would happen when you came back into the Gated City, would you have risked it to help find Saeli? Why or why not?

**12.** When Ven and Char climb up the ladder to the Skywalk, they discover a whole new world above the streets on the rooftops of the Gated City. How did Ven feel watching the children of the market of thieves playing in the garden, in sight of the sea but unable to go down to it? Have you ever felt trapped, kept away from a place you would like to be, like when you're inside a classroom on a sunny day?

**13.** When the Thief Queen is nice to Saeli and offers her food, it puts Saeli in a terrible position. Have you ever been in a situation where someone is being kind to you but cruel to other people? What do you do when a popular kid or an adult likes you but is mean to one of your friends?

**14.** McLean suggests that if the children need help in the Gated City, they look for a Singer. Why? Would you trust someone in a market of thieves who practiced a profession that required a vow of truth? Is a thief Singer more thief or more Singer? What about the other people Ven chooses to trust in the city?

**15.** Now that Ven is back home at the Crossroads Inn, do you think he is safe from the Thief Queen? Why or why not?

## FREE CURRICULUM

Available now at www.venpolypheme.com.

A free curriculum with integrated subject areas will be available for download upon publication of the book. The series-specific teachers' materials are cross-curricular, with customizable exercises and lesson plans in varying degrees of difficulty for different grade levels. Subject areas covered include Language Arts, Math, Social Studies, Geography, Science, and Art, with mini-curricula in Nautical Studies, Mythology, Environmental Science, and Music. Also includes comprehension and discussion questions listed chapter by chapter.

# Starscape

Award-Winning
Science Fiction and Fantasy
for Ages 10 and up

STARSCAPE

www.tor-forge.com/starscape

37613